At Night's End

Book 1 of the Beryllian Alliance

Katherine Matzen

Silent Owl Press, LLC

To Fred, my wonderful husband. Thank you for your belief and support. Even when I didn't think I could finish anything.

Chapter 1

The Feast

Lateef D'Oro had to admit his Hatti hosts were impressive. Not only was the food incredible, but the engineering feat required to make the feast hall feel like a platform open to the vastness of space boggled his mind. He knew they were not near the skin of the huge city-ship, not after that long trip down the drop tube. *That was fun. Glad they have a regular elevator for squeamish guests.* Several seconds of free fall revved up the adrenaline, but it was better than any planet-side festival ride. The Kanesh clan-ship, the *Alalakh*, was in orbit around a colorful gas giant, and the planet seemed to travel across the walls and ceiling, almost close enough to reach out and touch.

Wish I was back at work. Can't believe Trevan invited me to this ceremony and then got so drunk he doesn't remember I'm here.

The willowy woman to his right leaned closer to speak to him. "Is this your first Hatti feast, Healer D'Oro?"

Lateef threw off his irritation and smiled at the Mingorian Empire's representative. He liked this old friend of his mother, even if she did tend to treat him like an adolescent instead of the Master Healer he was.

"This is my first, Lady Casella. I have no idea what most of the dishes were, but everything was excellent."

Trevan had invited him to the ceremony to elevate a new Thane for the Kanesh Clan. Opening diplomatic ties with the long-lost race had propelled Trevan from junior diplomat to Ambassador to the Hatti and Lateef was glad to have an opportunity to congratulate his friend. While Trevan was young for the job, potential new allies were rare, and the Beryllian Alliance tried to keep the first contact people in place. On the diplomat side, anyway. The Field

Agents, like Lateef's older sister, Rissa, never stayed in one place much longer than necessary to wage a proxy battle against the implacable Falgarans. Then the diplomats moved in.

Lateef took a sip of an oaky, white wine as he tried to tune out the noisy babble of voices from the hundreds of tables. At least seven civilizations in addition to the Hatti were represented at the guest table.

"I find it better not to ask too many questions at these state dinners. Especially when our hosts are so passionate about their cooking. How is your mother?"

"She's well. I'll extend your greetings when I return to Beryl."

Lady Casella snorted. "Unless you stop at your Healer Hall first. I know you better than that, Healer Lateef. Once you see a patient, all other thoughts flee until you have restored him to health."

Heat crawled up his neck, but he couldn't argue. Healing was such a passion his mother feared he would never find love or give her grandchildren. Not that he didn't have several siblings more than capable of that task.

"I did not mean to embarrass you, Lateef. I find your talent admirable. I truly hope there are no new Falgaran attacks to fill up the Healer Halls." She took a sip of her wine, staring at the giant, holographic planet on the ceiling.

Lateef changed the subject. "Have you been to other Hatti events?"

"Nothing as elaborate as this." A pale hand gestured at the large room. "It has been many years since our last contact with any of the Hatti clans. They had become little more than legend until the Kanesh returned to our area of space."

"Why is that?"

"The clans are wanderers, always on the hunt for the most perfect ingredient to add to the next meal."

"What do you know about them?" Lateef chose his words carefully, torn between the desire to learn more and hiding his ignorance. Trevan should have given him more information before the dinner, but he had been late, and Trevan busy, so they didn't have any time to talk before the ceremony started.

Casella laughed, resting one slender hand on his arm. "Not much, my dear youngling. Legend claims several clans came from this region of space before their abrupt diaspora hundreds of years ago. The *Alalakh* is the first ship to return." She looked around and leaned closer. "Rumor is the old Thane was approached by a mutual enemy, but I have no proof. Be careful, Healer. The sands are not always as firm underfoot as one desires, and I would not wish for you to come to grief."

Lateef kept his polite expression frozen on his face even as his stomach clenched. The bloody Falgarans had never been reported in this sector before. Had their ancient enemies contacted the Hatti before the Alliance could? Was the Thane's accident really a murder?

He took another sip of wine and tried to still his frantic thoughts. His sister would be pissed beyond belief to think their implacable enemy was this close to Terra. She wouldn't let her favorite planet fall to their voracious foe without a fight. "Does Trevan know?"

Casella's smile turned frosty. "I am certain his sources are as informed as mine." She straightened and held out her glass for a young Hatti server. Her smile didn't hide the lines of tension around her eyes. No one in the Alliance could be complacent about the Falgarans gaining new allies.

She leaned closer and dropped her voice. "Walk with great care until you are safely home, Healer."

Her abrupt turn back to her companion, left Lateef confused and unsettled. *Thought I was paranoid. If so, I'm not alone.*

Trevan slammed down another glass of a delicate wine and elbowed Lateef in the ribs. "I told you the food was good, didn't I?"

"Yes. You were right." Lateef hid his disgust at the unseemly behavior of the Alliance's newest ambassador.

"These people are weird, my friend." Trevan leaned in closer to Lateef after looking around to see if anyone in the crowded room paid attention to them. "Every Hatti clan chooses a set of Matriarchs based on their cooking abilities. Marriages are based on the same thing." He shook his head and took another gulp of wine. "Poor Thane is supposedly in charge but seems to me the Matriarchs run things. Thane doesn't even get a girlfriend. Bunch of freaks."

Lateef blinked against the blast of rancid alcohol breath in his face. "So, the guy they made Thane in the ceremony tonight is the leader, but he's not really in charge?" The ceremony had been poignantly simple, rushed because of the previous Thane's unexpected death.

"Yep." Trevan burped and slapped a hand over his mouth before giving an embarrassed chuckle. "Rumor said he wasn't quite ready to be the leader yet, but the Clan must have a Thane, and clan means everything. A Hatti without a clan is dead."

"Do you think the Falgarans were involved?"

Trevan snorted. "You have Falgarans on the brain, my friend." He drained his glass then wiped his mouth with the back of his hand. "Look, Lateef, the Falgarans don't have any reason to deal with these folks. Hatti are cooks, not fighters. The Falgarans are not responsible for every wrong in the universe."

Lateef hesitated at the furtive look that flashed across his friend's face, surprised at his outburst. "What about the psionic blocking shield the Hatti have? Wouldn't the Falgarans love to get that? They could nullify our best weapons and there's nothing we could do."

Trevan waved a hand. "You worry too much, my friend. The Falgarans don't care about us."

Lateef leaned back in his chair, sipping his own wine to gain some time to think as his companion turned his attention back to his plate. Could Trevan truly believe the Falgarans, a race hell-bent on exterminating his people, didn't care about the Beryllians?

He tried to open his senses to get a read on the emotions in the large banquet hall. Instead of the expected rush of random thoughts and feelings, his brain filled with static. He raised a hand to rub his temple to ease a nasty headache.

"Don't worry. You get used to the shield. Although it is turned up higher than normal right now." Trevan grinned at him, but the mirth rang hollow. "I've been on the *Alalakh* for weeks and find I don't miss anything. You get used to doing without the telepathy and teleportation." Trevan raised a hand for a waiter to refill his wine glass. "These people sure know how to throw a party."

Lateef pushed away his concerns and took a bite of savory pastry left on his plate. There was no point in worrying too much about catastrophes that might not happen. The chances the Hatti and Falgarans were in league and had set up so many members of the Beryllian Alliance were next to zero. He should relax and enjoy the feast.

A Hatti woman approached and bent to whisper in Trevan's ear.

He nodded and rose. "Sorry, Lateef, but I need to go do some ambassador stuff. I'll be back before you leave." He gestured at the alien woman. "Bilal will take care of you until then."

He was gone before Lateef could swallow his last bite of pastry, Bilal fast on his heels.

Weird. He checked his watch. *Three hours gone. This feast can't last much longer. Once I get home, they'll have to use a pry bar to get me out of Healer Hall again, no matter how often my boss tells me I need to get out.*

Music swirled through the room and Lateef groaned as another procession of food-heaped trays started around the tables. *My stomach'll pop if this isn't the last course.*

"Your ambassador wishes for you to come with me."

Lateef looked back to see Bilal standing over him.

Her foot tapped an impatient beat and her dark eyes gleamed. "You are to come quickly."

She whirled and strode away.

He hesitated, remembering the protocol officer's strict instructions to remain in the area unless escorted. The woman was odd. Maybe it was something about her eyes? They lacked the soul of the other Hatti he had met. Could he risk ignoring her request? *No, that's not the best decision.*

With a resigned sigh Lateef eased out of his chair and followed his guide from the banquet hall into the depths of the ship, ignoring the little voice telling him he was making a mistake. After traversing many deserted, identical corridors, Lateef broke the silence. "Tell me why you pulled me away from the state dinner?" His voice cracked with tension, and he cleared his throat.

Bilal spared him a glare, then moved faster.

Lateef glanced down the hallway, wondering if he could find his way back to the banquet hall through the maze of twists and turns his guide had taken. He hated first contact situations. *Though this isn't technically first contact. Trevan knows the Hatti, even if he forgot to share much knowledge with me.* All his friend had told him before the banquet started was the clans were obsessed with food, and zealously guarded their food preparation secrets.

Wish they would turn off the psi-blocking field. Lateef tried to shake off his worry as his guide slowed. The skin on his neck crawled as sweat trickled down his back.

The Hatti woman stopped abruptly and pointed to an unmarked door. "Your Ambassador is in this room. He demands that you make haste to join him."

Lateef stared at the door, his nerves twitching with tension. He tried again to reach out with his senses to get a feel for what was on the other side. His mind filled with static.

What do you expect to find? A bunch of Falgaran warriors? There's no reason to be so paranoid. Trevan told you he didn't think the Falgarans were in contact with the Hatti.

Lateef turned to question his guide, only to find he was alone. *Maybe Trevan arranged a private meet-up with the Clan's Ambassador?* Although the timing for such a meeting was odd.

He ignored the anxiety making his shoulders itch and placed a hand on the door handle, assuming any place off limits to guests would be locked during a public event.

With a deep breath, he pushed the door open, subconsciously recognizing the clatter of pans and sizzle of cooking food. Momentum carried him a step into the spotless kitchen before the loud crash of a dropped tray, followed by a horrified gasp froze him in the sudden silence. His mouth fell open as adrenaline flooded his system. He didn't need to sense emotions to know he had committed the worst *faux pas* possible. His crime was stamped onto the horrified faces of the Hatti kitchen crew.

"I humbly beg your pardon." Lateef quickly averted his eyes and backed out of the kitchen. A knife flashed by him and he slammed the door on furious epithets shouted at him. An alarm blared as he ran. *Can't believe they are so touchy about their food prep.*

He briefly considered returning to the kitchen to explain his mistake, but the memory of the thrown knife and the murderous look on the face of the Matriarch Amman destroyed any hope for forgiveness. Where was Trevan? Someone had set him up. Who would have sent him to a forbidden place?

Lateef ran down the featureless halls, desperate to find the hanger bay. A shout caused him to rethink his strategy. He turned a corner and saw the unmistakable cluster of life pod hatches. He breathed a silent prayer of thanks as he slapped the entry button. He only had to get away from the ship to be clear of the psionic blanketing field. Then he could teleport home.

Just as he ducked through the hatch, he thought he heard Trevan call. He turned to look and a bolt ripped through his side. Shock kept him numb as he staggered, knocking the door closed. He sealed the hatch and stumbled to the central chair in the compact lifepod, taking three tries to hit the actual button instead of one of the blurry duplicates his eyes insisted were real. The sudden thrust of acceleration reassured him, even as fresh pain bloomed in his side. He pushed one hand against his bloody wound and buckled the safety straps with the other, sagging in relief as the autodoc administered a pain-reliever. He remembered the danger of being tracked and instructed the autopilot to disable the homing beacon and evade pursuit. There weren't many places to hide in this solar system, but it would give him a small head start.

His eyes closed to counter the spinning of the universe around him. Liquid fire pulsed in waves from the wound as his thoughts grew more fragmented. There was something about his assailant he needed to remember, but the image swirled away every time he reached for it. He gave up the attempt to remember and concentrated on healing the hole in his side. Sweat drenched his body and he groaned. Spots floated across his closed eyelids, dancing to the labored thud of his heart as he lost the struggle to remain conscious.

The scent of gardenias pulled him from sleep. He blinked, trying to make sense of his surroundings. His side no longer felt like molten lead flowed through his veins, but the skin remained tender. *Should have healed by now. I've never had a wound that lasted more than a few minutes once I worked on it.* He glanced around the small space, vaguely surprised to find he was alone. *Who was that woman with the sad, brown eyes?* He'd never seen her before and yet he felt connected to her. *Has to be some side-effect of the drugs.* The life pods were designed to handle any carbon-based, oxygen breathing life forms, but sometimes the drugs could cause odd reactions. Although he couldn't recall ever hearing about such realistic hallucinations. He would have sworn he'd talked with the woman for hours and yet he was alone.

With a glance at the control screen to confirm all was well, Lateef reached out with his mind in an attempt to contact anyone, and gasped at the painful nothingness. He was a strong psychic. His primary talent was healing, but he should have been able to connect with someone now he was out of range of the Hatti shields. There was nothing but static and the throbbing of his erratic pulse.

Guess my healing ability is as hosed as my telepathy. He glanced at the screens, reassuring himself no Hatti or Falgaran ship waited to pounce. "I'll remember this next time my boss, Mellora nags me to leave work more often. The Healer Hall after a Falgaran attack is a whole lot safer than some diplomatic event."

His throat ached with the effort of speaking, but the sound of his own voice gave him comfort.

The autodoc in the chair hummed and injected a fresh dose of pain-killer into his thigh. Concern about Trevan blended into anger at his own helplessness as the drug took effect, shoving him into a deep sleep.

Guilt. The overwhelming emotion flooded through Lateef until he realized it belonged to the brown-eyed woman.

"This is my fault." Self-revulsion poured off her in a nearly-visible wave. "I was supposed to die, not my baby."

He jerked awake with a curse.

"Just a stupid dream. They'll stop once the drugs wear off." Lateef shook off the residual emotions, feeling better than he had in hours. But he couldn't shake the feeling that he needed to find the woman. Raw pain was obvious in her, but underneath that he saw a spirit that attracted him like a moth to fire. He sank into a light trance and tried a scan of his own body. The exercise was painfully awkward. His attention wavered all over the place. A psychic numbness spread from the wound. What was on that bolt? Could it have been poisoned?

Need to call home. Lateef sent his attention outward, again trying to reach his normal contact on Beryl. An alarm bleated. He snapped out the unsuccessful trance, covered in sweat.

Lateef studied the flashing light as he scratched the skin near the hole in his side.

"Finally made it to a habitable planet." He hoped his meager piloting skills extended to a safe landing since he still couldn't manage to teleport.

Something about the blue globe in the view screen tickled his memory. Recognition hit him. This was the planet the Hatti were returning to. Terra was also the world where his sister, Rissa, spent so much of her free time. He hadn't realized he was in Terra's solar system already. The current inhabitants were pre-space, and had some latent psychic abilities, but were so far away from the rest of civilization the Falgarans left them alone. *Maybe Rissa's here.* He ruthlessly squashed the surge of hope that flashed through his body, as he sent mental threads in search of his sister. The unexpected jabs of pain radiating from his wound wrecked his concentration, and his abilities seemed to fade in and out erratically.

"Damn it." He slammed his fist against the armrest. "It would be nice to have one thing go right. Hope I can remember how to land this thing." He studied the controls and then poked at a few buttons, praying his memories of the long-ago lessons were accurate. "All I have to do is get to the ground in one piece then I can find a way to track down Rissa's contacts."

Alarms blared as the view screen flared with the heat of reentry. Lateef pushed more buttons and the sound stopped. He heaved a sigh of relief until a high pitch whistle broke the silence. Curses flooded out of his mouth as he examined the control panel in front of him. With a whispered prayer he pushed a series of buttons then checked the restraints and held on as the life pod shook.

The temperature in the cabin rose and the scent of burning metal contaminated the air.

"Just hold together long enough to land and let me get out." The shriek of tortured metal plowing through air drowned his words out. Flames flashed past the viewport.

The ship began a slow roll before he could wrestle control away from the malfunctioning autopilot. "Please remember how to land. I'm not ready to die."

The ground grew larger, pines trees and giant rocks expanding to fill his view. Just as he was certain he would plow into the side of a mountain, the ship rapidly decelerated, hovering for a second.

Lateef heaved a sigh of relief and had just enough time to think he would be okay when the ship lost power and fell to the ground like an anchor in deep water.

Chapter 2

Leave Me Alone

Dani Hamilton's hands shook with a momentary pang of unexpected nervousness as she looked out of the large, bedroom window. Concern about evil roaming in the night was stupid. Evil had already destroyed her life, and yet she still lived. Scratching the ears of the dog beside her loosened the knot of anxiety that threatened to send her into another spiral of panic down to depression.

"You have got to settle down, you neurotic, little fluff-brain."

The agitated sheltie threw Dani a glance before staring once again into the darkness. A rumbling growl shook her small frame.

Aspen leaves shimmered in the thin wind, but nothing disturbed the moonlit mountainside. Carl, her late husband, had loved summer nights like this. They would sit on the porch with a glass of Malbec and discuss the grand party to reveal their new home to his politician father. She wrenched her thoughts away from that memory. The accident had taken her husband and her precious baby from her. Her strangled sob made the dog lean against her with a soft whine.

She drew in a deep breath, forcing the pain away, and ruffled the anxious sheltie's fur. "I don't know what's gotten into you lately, Abby."

The dog had been on edge for hours, barking at creatures only she could see or hear. At times like these she wished the dog used actual words. Her one-sided conversations were usually enough to banish her loneliness, but sometimes she longed to hear another voice.

"Maybe I should take you over to herd the Saunders' goats. That should wear you out enough to sleep for a week. Especially if you piss off the buck again."

Her elderly neighbors raised goats and sold the cheese, combined with herbs they bought from her. She knew they worried about her. If she took the dog over there, they would politely force her to explain the dark circles under her eyes and then try to find a way to help her sleep. She needed to stay alone.

Her father-in-law still searched for her. Carl had been destined to continue the family legacy until the accident changed everything. Dani refused to be a prisoner to someone else's dream. She feared her father-in-law wouldn't hesitate to hurt anyone in his path, so she kept everyone away. She couldn't handle the possibility of any more 'accidents.'

Dani pulled the curtains closed with a decisive snap and limped to her side of the king-size bed. "Come lay down, you mangy mutt. I need some sleep tonight. And that won't happen if you keep barking at the wind. We have a mushroom hunt tomorrow."

She picked up the bottle of pain pills and hesitated before taking one. The dog's neurotic behavior was not her only problem. Her injured leg ached, and she needed sleep. She shuddered and pulled the worn coverlet around her shoulders. The relentless dream hounding her was the same every single night since she'd escaped the hospital with the help of friends who understood her need to be free. The pain medication usually made the dream worse, but sometimes she had to take the risk.

Abby hopped up on the bed to lick her face, and Dani hugged the dog with a sigh. The dream had changed last night when a new character appeared. Model handsome with shoulder-length, midnight black hair that framed a clean-shaven, square jaw, he made her pulse race with forgotten desire. The face was young, but his eyes were ancient. Those warm, sea-blue depths held a mischievous twinkle, when he didn't appear to be delirious. A twinge of guilt writhed in her belly. Carl had never been mischievous. The son of an ambitious man, he had followed in his father's footsteps, which left no time for distractions, silly or otherwise.

Abby gave a final woof and curled up in her normal spot with a doggie sigh of contentment. Dani echoed the sigh. If there had been something dangerous in the dark, the high-strung dog never would have settled down.

"Let's see if you can keep the bad guys away tonight, okay?" She caressed the dog's head and murmured the almost-prayer as her body relaxed.

"Please help me!" Desperation began to break through the dream lethargy gripping her body. "Come find me! I need your help."

She looked beyond the dream man's pain-twisted face to see the familiar, shad-owy figure grinning at her. The gaunt shape seemed to grow more solid as it fed on her pain. The dark-haired stranger spoke, and the shadow abruptly fled.

"Go away!" Her heart thudded painfully in her chest and she broke out in a cold sweat as the entire world vanished into a bright light.

Dani bolted upright, screaming soundlessly as she clutched her pillow with a death grip. Guilt over killing Carl and Caitlin knotted her guts. Abby whined and licked Dani's tear-damp face. The dog looked out the window and rushed back to check on her again, repeating the process numerous times before Dani could manage to get her gut-wrenching sobs under control. She pulled herself out of bed, oblivious to her stiff muscles, to look out the window. Sheer iron willpower kept her upright as her body shook to the thud of her heart. She pushed the curtains aside and was startled to see a bright light moving across the pre-dawn sky. The spot slowed and appeared to settle higher up the mountain before it vanished.

Dani ignored the whispers for help in her mind. The intriguing masculine voice had to be her imagination even if she could remember the feel of his skin under her fingers. At least the shadow that delighted in her intense sorrow vanished, making it far easier than normal for her to shake off the remnants of the nightmare.

"Won't get back to sleep now. The light had to be a helicopter flown by a maniac in the dark. Might as well get some coffee and watch the sun rise."

By the time she was dressed and on her second cup of coffee, Dani was restless. She heard a voice in her mind begging her to hurry, but that made no sense. The dream man had just been a figment of her imagination. Heat flooded her at the memory of his strong personality. It was a good thing he wasn't real. She had to be alone.

She finally gave in to the anxiety and packed some food and water. She and Abby would go up the mountain to find the wild mushrooms she needed for the Folly Springs Founder's Day celebration breakfast. Anna White Bear had guilted her into catering again. On a whim she tossed in a first aid kit and briefly wished she had accepted the cellphone Sheriff Charlie White Bear tried to give her. She gave a wry chuckle and added an extra blanket. *Probably no reception up there anyway.* She looked at the pile of supplies tucked into her supply baskets. *What are you preparing for? You're only going to spend a couple of hours looking for mushrooms, not camp out for a week.*

Dani tried to unpack, but every time she touched an item her hands shook with a nameless dread. Finally, she stowed the gear in her ATV, waited for Abby to hop into the passenger seat and headed up the mountain. Knots coiled and uncoiled in her stomach as she urged the little vehicle to go faster as a sense of urgency gripped her.

"There's no reason to rush. The mushrooms won't run away if I'm later than I plan to be." She snorted, shaking her head to clear it. She had lived alone in these mountains for almost a year. When the faint reminders of the past became too strong, she slept under the stars. Anything to avoid that black pit of despair. In the middle of the worst dark episode, Sheriff Charlie White Bear had deposited a young ball of fur in her lap to remind her she still had responsibilities. The presence of the sheltie had helped to shorten each of the subsequent dark periods. She blinked back the tears stinging her eyes as memories of her sweet toddler crossed her mind. Several deep breaths stopped the tears. Breathing was the one facet of her life she had any control over. Well, that and refusing to allow her father-in-law to use her tragedy to advance his political career. Keep breathing and moving. Then she would control her own fate. Carl had been the last hope to carry on the family legacy, and she refused to take his place, no matter what pressure his father brought to bear. Especially since he insisted that she should have been the one to die in the crash.

Abby threw her a look, barked once and strained forward in the seat, her stare focused on the trail ahead. The pointed nose lifted high as she sniffed the cool air and the slowly wagging tail brushed against Dani's arm like an intermittent windshield wiper.

"What is it?" Dani stopped the ATV as she studied the ground ahead. This wasn't the path she'd intended to take. The silence of the mountain soothed her soul, so she left the engine off. The dog looked around and stared at Dani reassuringly before once again staring straight ahead.

"You in charge today?"

The dog's tail wagged faster.

"You're far too bossy for a dog, you know? I don't know why you think I'll do what you say."

Dani tried to recognize the trail and Abby bumped her arm. Could the dog have guided her in the opposite direction of where she had planned to go?

Abby took advantage of her distraction to sneak a long tongue against Dani's ear, shocking her out of her daze.

"Gross." Dani rubbed her ear against her shoulder to wipe the slobber off. "I'm not sure what's gotten into you, but it's too late to hit the creek now. The afternoon thunderstorm is already gathering. Can't believe I was distracted enough to take the wrong trail."

The dog's ears perked up and with a quick bark she bolted out of the ATV, racing off the trail.

Dani heard faint shouts for help and hurried toward the sound. She ignored the warning twinge in her back. Now was not the time to worry about her own persistent injuries. Someone was in trouble.

She rounded a large boulder overlooking a shallow gully and found her dog at the bottom, snuggled up against a stranger. Dani halted abruptly and hissed as her leg gave a warning spasm.

The stranger slumped against a log, his head hanging so all she could see was a mass of sweat-soaked, black hair. His outfit was a cross between medical scrubs and a military uniform made of a dark green fabric. Between that and the wholly inappropriate shoes, it was obvious he wasn't a lost hiker. His shoulders rose and fell with each breath, so she knew he was alive.

"Are you okay?" Concern overcame her reluctance to get involved. She couldn't leave an injured stranger alone.

The man didn't move, even when Abby licked his face.

Dani studied the terrain to find the easiest way down the steep slope. She could climb down, but there was no way she was getting back up with a wounded man the way her own injuries were throbbing. *Never should have run after that dog. I'll pay for that exercise for weeks.*

"I'm going to go get some rope. I'll be back in a minute."

Abby barked her approval. Dani slowly made her way back to her vehicle. *This is getting stranger and stranger. If the dog starts talking, I'll have to check myself in for a psych eval. Maybe it's just a bad reaction to the pain pills and I'm still asleep.* She climbed into the driver's seat and her left calf cramped violently.

Tears stung her eyes as she stretched her toes up and rubbed at the knotted muscle. She was awake and this was all real. As soon as the pain subsided, she carefully drove the little vehicle as close to the ravine as she could.

The huddled figure remained motionless as Abby bounded up the slope to greet her. Dani hooked a rope to the winch and grabbed a blanket and the first aid kit. She carefully made her way down the gully, holding tightly to the rope as loose shale shifted beneath her feet.

Once at the bottom, Dani squatted beside the figure, pushing the excited dog away.

"Are you okay?" She touched his shoulder.

He shuddered and slowly lifted his head. He took a deep breath and winced, clutching his side.

"Shit, that's blood." Dani dropped the first aid kit and leaned forward to examine his side. "What happened? I have to go get help. Will you be okay while I'm gone?"

Words tumbled from her mouth in a torrent. Her pulse pounded as flashes of a mangled car, broken glass, and puddles of blood filled her vision. Her babbling increased until a warm hand gripped her arm.

"There is no need for you to get help. I will be okay with the proper rest. I merely need a safe space to sleep and heal."

The look in his sea-blue eyes sent shivers down her spine. He seemed to see right through her, straight into her soul. She froze, waiting for the condemnation she knew would come. If he could see her soul, he would know she was evil and wouldn't want her help.

"I only need shelter for a few days." His speech was hesitant, as if he had to search to find the right word. He blinked, and she was released from his spell.

Abby nudged her arm aside, demanding attention, and she stroked the dog's silky head as she finally took a closer look at the mysterious stranger. Shoulder-length, wavy, black hair framed a clean-shaven face marred by dirt and bruises across the high cheekbones. A jagged cut stretched along his left temple. Her heart slammed in her chest.

"It's you. You were in my dreams. How can you be real? Who are you? How are you here?" Once again, her questions spilled in a torrent of words.

"I am Lateef D'Oro." His answer stopped her babbling.

Questions buzzed like hornets in her mind, too fast for her to ask any of them. His gaze caught hers and time slowed as she fell into those peaceful depths. Her breathing synchronized with his. *What is happening to me? How can I feel so safe with a stranger?*

Abby bumped her shoulder before plopping down onto her belly with her long nose across the man's out-stretched legs. *I've never seen her take to a stranger like this. She usually barks and hides behind me.*

"Dogs like me." The man answered her unspoken question. He laid his hand across Abby's back to gently stroke her fur.

"What happened to you?"

His gaze flickered as if he searched for a good story. "I was hiking, and I slipped." He didn't look at her.

"Right. You went hiking dressed like this?" Dani draped a blanket over his shoulders before digging into the first aid kit for gauze pads and tape to staunch the trickle of blood oozing through his shirt. She couldn't shake the bone-deep feeling that she had met this man before. But that had been a dream, hadn't it?

Red seeped into the man's cheeks, and she decided to leave the questions for later. Thunder grumbled, and she glanced at the quickly gathering clouds. The storm would hit soon. The need for action focused her attention.

"Do you think you climb up the slope with the rope? I can help a little, but my leg and back are…" She bit off the explanation, hating herself for making excuses. "If you can't, I'll go get help."

"I will be able to get to your vehicle."

Dani had several opportunities to doubt his optimism. But he was stubborn, and she helped him into her home as the first drops of the regular afternoon thunderstorm fell.

"Thank you for letting me stay with you until I am stronger."

Dani helped him sit on the edge of the bed in a never used guestroom.

"You need a doctor." Her thoughts moved at the speed of molasses in winter as she pulled his shoes and shirt off. "I should call an ambulance."

"I will be okay once I get some sleep. There is no need to go to any further effort on my account."

Dani stared at the angry bruises that marred his well-toned chest and back, trying to decide what to do. Carl's clothes would hang on the taller, thinner stranger, but at least they weren't coated in blood. He didn't seem strong enough to take a shower on his own. She left to gather clean clothes and a bowl of warm water.

As she gently washed the blood and dirt from Lateef's face and torso, she was surprised the numerous scratches now appeared days old. The only wound that looked fresh was the hole through his side, which was weeping small amounts of blood-tinged fluid. Now the cut on his forehead looked a week-old, far more healed than the first time she saw him in the gully.

'I am a fast healer.'

The words drifted through Dani's mind and questions about the nature of Lateef's injuries slipped away. The formless panic that had become a constant presence was gone along with the sense of surveillance by the shadow figure of her nightmares.

Maybe I do need a human companion? Whatever, I'll enjoy the peace while it lasts. We'll see what happens when he's gone. A flash of pain shot through her at the thought of him leaving. Stupid because she wanted to be alone.

She gathered up the stained clothes and went to grab some ibuprofen. Given the number of bruises, Lateef had to be sore. When she returned, she found her guest stretched out under the patchwork quilt with the dog snuggled up to his side.

Lateef accepted the drink and pills, wincing as he stretched.

Dani worried the damage was worse than she knew. The level of concern she felt for the man surprised her. Something about him tugged at her emotions. She should at least call Charlie in case whoever had hurt Lateef was still in the area.

"I was alone until you and Abby found me."

Once again, he answered her unspoken question.

"I only need to rest now."

She rubbed at her temples trying to wipe away the buzz in her brain. "Are you sure no one's after you? Charlie won't forgive me if you bring trouble and I didn't warn him."

"I will allow no harm to come to you and I vow I am not involved in anything illegal." He raised his left hand, fingers cupped together. He touched his forehead then his heart and turned his hand toward her and spread his fingers wide.

Dani didn't recognize the salute, but the gesture obviously held meaning for her unexpected guest. Finally able to think without the ever-present dread that had enveloped her since the accident, she decided to trust him.

"Get some rest. I'll be in the kitchen. Send Abby if you need me."

The dog lifted her head and Dani swore she saw a wink. She shook her head. *Whatever. This day could get stranger, but I can't imagine how.*

Chapter 3

The Bad Guy Speaks

I must leave you alone for a short time, my lovely human. We're not ready to let the Beryllians know about our Apirri. But I won't go far, never fear.

A break is probably for the best, anyway. My Apirri tells me you are getting too weak. She thinks time to regain some strength will make your dreams far more satisfying for me.

Rest, little one. Grow strong again so you can provide me with many more nights of fear. And bring my enemy to me.

Chapter 4

Checking In

Lateef limped toward the kitchen counter where Dani cooked an omelet. His mouth watered at the scent of frying bacon. "Smells good in here." The deep bruises scattered across his torso were yellowish-green instead of the angry purple and black they had been a mere two days earlier and would be gone in another day or so. He had been able to heal the worst of his own injuries, but the less life-threatening ones were still not cooperating. *Wonder if the drug that trashed my other abilities is involved? Yet another mystery for later.* Much like the mystery of why he felt such a close connection to this woman he'd never met until he crashed in her backyard.

Not quite true. You talked to her while you on the life pod. Of course, he'd also been half out of his mind with a fever but her mental touch had felt like they'd been together for years, instead of seconds. He'd never believed the stories of love at first sight, but maybe?

Dani glanced at him. He heard the incomplete thoughts in her brain, but they disappeared before he could understand. The unexpected psychic connection he shared with this alien woman confused him. He had no trouble blocking other people's thoughts and emotions, but Dani's seeped through his tightest shields like she was constantly nestled into the back of his brain. He hoped she didn't catch as many of his thoughts as he caught of hers.

"Can I do something?" He felt well enough to help with some of the household chores. Rissa would laugh if she could hear him now. She was convinced he'd gone into healing only to get out of washing dishes. In reality, he was rarely in his quarters for much beyond sleep. Most of his meals were nutritious protein shakes, especially in the aftermath of a Falgaran attack. Those happened far too often for his stomach's comfort.

"Just sit and eat." Dani gestured at the stool on the other side of the kitchen bar where a plate of strawberry muffins and a squeeze jar of honey waited beside a mug of coffee.

His stomach growled as he sat, startling a grin from her. She placed the omelet in front of him before retreating to the kitchen counter with her own mug of coffee.

"I don't bite. You can sit by me and eat some breakfast yourself." Irritation at her remoteness put a snap in his tone he instantly regretted. He'd been here several days already, and she still treated him like a wild animal she expected to attack at any second. Obviously, she didn't share his attraction.

"I'm not a big breakfast person. I usually have coffee."

"It isn't nice to make me eat alone." Lateef gave her his best puppy-dog look and a chuckle escaped her.

With a roll of her eyes she gave in and sat across the counter from him. She snagged a muffin to crumble more than eat.

"See." Lateef grinned at her. "It wasn't that hard."

"How do you feel today?" The question was an obvious attempt to change the subject.

"A lot better," he admitted with a smile in between bites of the loaded omelet. "This is good! If you keep feeding me like this, I might have to pretend to never recover. You'll never get rid of me."

"Maybe you'd prefer the dog food?" Her tone was wry. "I'm positive Abby wouldn't mind sharing."

The dog looked up from her bowl across the room. She lifted one lip and snarled briefly before burying her nose back in her kibble.

"I'm not so sure the lady agrees with you." His laughter made his bruised ribs ache but being happy felt good. No one in his family would recognize him. He couldn't remember the last time he had been so joyful. His life had been one crisis after another since his last promotion.

Dani rolled her eyes again with a sigh and studied the contents of her mug.

The urge to touch her had his hand on her arm before he could think. Her skin flushed and she stared at him.

Sparks flew along his nerve endings as his pulse accelerated.

Suddenly, she jumped, spilling her coffee as a wave of guilt flooded over her.

How can I be happy when my precious child is in the cold ground?

"You okay?" Lateef gently took her hand in his to study the reddened flesh where the hot coffee had spilled as he tried to understand the emotion-laden thought she had projected so strongly.

"I'm fine." She pulled away.

He watched her through hooded eyes as she wiped the table and returned to the sink to run cool water over her hand. A flood of her emotions battered at his mental shields like a hurricane. Self-recrimination consumed the woman to such a large extent he was amazed she was able to function. He also knew she was not yet ready to give up the guilt she carried in an apparent attempt at atonement.

He wanted to help her recover from the trauma that tied her emotions in knots. That guilt affected her physical health as well. That was the only reason he hadn't gone home yet. It couldn't be because of the joy and peace he felt in Dani's presence. As deep as his debt to her was, he had to leave before the Hatti could track him down. This planet was not yet ready for an angry alien invasion, and getting Dani caught in the middle would be poor payback for her help. He pushed some calm emotions in her direction and they both jumped when she dropped the fresh cup of coffee.

She stared at the shattered mug on the slate floor, eyebrows drawn together and a frown wrinkling her forehead.

Lateef guiltily hurried over to clean up the ceramic shards, astonished she had reacted so strongly to his efforts to calm her. Maybe she had more psychic abilities than most of the Terrans his sister had told him about.

Abby darted toward the front of the house, barking wildly as the sound of a truck engine shattered the quiet morning.

"Oh, crap." Dani's shoulders sagged as if she carried a heavy weight. "I have to get an order out today and that's my delivery driver."

"Can I help?" Lateef offered.

"I have everything made—I only have to throw it in a box," she said. "And print the shipping label and..."

"And you don't want anyone to know I'm here?" He finished the dropped sentence.

"It's hard to explain."

"You don't need to explain anything. I'll hide."

The grateful look she turned on him melted his heart. The front door flew open before he had taken more than a single step toward the back of the house and safety.

"Hey Dani," the uniformed, middle-aged woman began speaking as soon as she walked in, staring down at a device in her hands. "I knew you had a shipment to go out..." Her voice trailed off as she looked up and caught sight of Lateef frozen in mid-stride.

"I'm ss-sorry," she stammered. "I never dreamed you'd have company. I didn't mean to barge in and interrupt..." Blue eyes were huge in her lined face as she stared at the half-naked, bare-footed stranger.

"It's okay," Dani hastily reassured the older woman. She darted forward to grab her elbow and get her settled at the table with a muffin and cup of coffee. "Holly Thompson, this is Lateef D'Oro —he was out hiking and took a nasty tumble. Got banged up pretty bad and needed some recovery time and I have room so..." Her voice faded at the skeptical look the older woman gave her.

"You're letting a stranger stay with you?"

"It didn't... I didn't plan... It just kind of happened." Dani shrugged helplessly. How could she explain a situation she didn't understand herself?

"You sure you're okay?" Holly speared Lateef with a deeply suspicious look. "Do you need to get to town for something?"

"I'm not a hostage, Holly." Anger burned off some of her lingering confusion. "I am quite capable of taking care of myself."

"No one doubts you." Holly turned to Lateef.

"Do you need anything?" she asked. "I can give you a lift down to Boulder."

"My ride will be here soon." Lateef slowly returned to his plate at the table. "But I appreciate the offer." He grinned and scooped up another forkful of omelet.

"And you wouldn't want to leave the food any faster than you have to?" Holly asked drily.

Lateef spared her a sideways grin. "I have been to high feasts not nearly so good."

A frown passed over his face so quickly Dani wasn't certain she had seen correctly.

Holly returned his grin. "I keep trying to get her to open a restaurant or at least a special-order business, but she insists on selling soap. Got a food critic down in Denver crazy about her coffee cake, but she won't even talk to him."

Dani shook off the tendrils of panic encasing her heart. She couldn't afford publicity for her cooking—her former father-in-law would watch for such an obvious clue. "I have to get the shipment ready, Holly. If you can hang out and give Lateef some company for a few minutes, I'll finish up."

"No rush." Holly waved a hand dismissively as she buttered a muffin then took a swallow of her coffee. "I'm early since I planned on catching up with you. Lateef and I can chat for a bit instead."

The dog remained in the spacious kitchen, her head on Lateef's thigh, patiently watching for any opportunity to snag a bite of people food as Dani reluctantly left them alone.

Several days later Dani and Lateef stood on the front veranda, watching her neighbor's ancient, yellow VW van slowly trundle down the long, gravel driveway.

"I thought you didn't have very much company." Irritation colored his tone.

"Bob buys herbs from me," she said. "He wants to buy a lot more, too."

"Is that why he's been here every other day since Holly stopped by?"

Dani sighed. "I told you to hide. You were too slow."

"So, all this extra company is my fault?"

His voice roughened and one corner of his mouth quirked up in a way that struck her as adorable rather than cranky.

Dani looked at him, falling into those deep, sea-blue eyes once again. He was casting some kind of spell on her and she didn't know what to do about it. Or if she wanted to fight it. She had been alone for so long. *Maybe it's safe to accept human companionship?*

"You have good people around here who care for you."

His sexy voice broke the fascination and she realized she was leaning toward him. She shook her head and looked around guiltily.

"They shouldn't," she muttered under her breath. "I'm not worth it."

She darted back into the house before he could respond. Lateef had helped her with several batches of soap in her shop as well as tending to the garden. He seemed to know what she needed him to do before she could ask. In the back of her mind she knew the situation was bizarre. She had never trusted anyone like this before—not even her husband. And Carl's touch had never sent such electric tingles through her body. Carl had always made her feel more like an item necessary to advance his career than the object of his passion. Their first talks about starting a family had felt more like one of his contract negotiations than an expression of love. She should tell Lateef to leave, but every time she thought about it, her heart stuttered and something would come up and the thought would slide away.

****

"Heyo, Danielle!" The deep voice boomed from the front yard. She sighed and continued to fill her basket with purple Echinacea flowers. She wasn't in the mood for company, but Sheriff Charlie White Bear would never take no for an answer.

Abby took off with a vicious bark, so she knew it wouldn't be long before her solitude was blown. She was surprised the dog was with her today. The sheltie had been glued to Lateef's side since his unexpected arrival, but today she'd remained at home when he went on his afternoon walk. Her guest had been antsy the last couple of days and she was just as glad to have him out from underfoot, although a tiny part of her felt an unexpected pang of loneliness. *Okay, maybe not such a tiny part.*

"Hi, Charlie." She stretched as the tall, copper-skinned man ambled up. She placed her basket on the ground and carefully removed the purple garden gloves covered in pink lizards. Caitlin had picked them out and they were one of the very few reminders she allowed herself of her previous life. "How are you and what rumors have Bob and Holly been feeding you this time?"

He laughed heartily and removed his hat to wipe his brow. "That's why I love coming to visit you, Dani," he said. "You always make me laugh."

"Can you stay for coffee?" She placed the gloves and garden snips on top of the large pile of purple flowers. "I have fresh crumb cake."

"Lordy, girl," he grumbled. "I swear you are on a one-person crusade to change the gravity of this place. You're gonna make us weigh a ton apiece and that much weight's got to go some way toward creating a black hole."

She frowned and then nodded, giving him a sideways look. *Sometimes I don't get his humor.* "So, would you like a piece?"

"I hate to say no." He declined with obvious regret. "But I can't stay for very long."

"Then I'll wrap some up for you to take home. Anna can have some, too."

"I wouldn't count on that." The stage whisper carried on the still air as he carried the heavy basket into the kitchen to set on the well-worn, large wooden table as she washed her hands and pulled out the cake and a paper plate. Her motions were quick and practiced as she placed a large piece on the plate and wrapped it securely in plastic film before leaning against the counter to stare at him.

"So, what brings you out here?" Dani's question broke the comfortable silence.

He gave her his best 'trust me' grin. "Just wanted to check on you. Anna's been on my case to make sure you're eating right. I'll have to tell her you look good."

Dani's breath hissed out. She loved Anna like a mother, but the woman could be such a busybody buttinski. However, she owed Anna her life. Anna and Charlie had been the ones to get her through the aftermath of the accident. They were the only ones who knew the whole story about her past, and who she really was. They had seen her reaction to the pain and constant calls from the media demanding she tell the story of the accident over-and-over until she wanted to scream. Her life had changed for the better once they helped her disappear from her previous life.

"You know how she worries, Dani. Besides, we've been hearing a lot about your visitor..." His voice trailed off and he looked around as if expecting Lateef to magically appear.

"He went for a walk," she said.

"Pretty strange, that accident," he said. His brow wrinkled as if he struggled to capture a thought.

"Strange things happen this far up in the mountains." She shrugged. She no longer wondered about how Lateef had arrived at her doorstep. So many other things were more important.

Charlie nodded agreement and continued. "Also wanted to warn you about some intruders around town. Nothing's missing other than some tomatoes and other garden plants, and no one's been hurt. Unless you count Fran."

"What happened? Did she break a bone this time? I swear she buys my entire supply of bruise balm every time she goes on a bender."

"She's convinced the Iranians or Russians or bug-eyed monsters from outer space have landed and are stealing fresh produce for some nefarious purpose." He shook his head with a wry grin. "So, when she heard a noise outside, she grabbed her shotgun and ran out shooting."

"Oh, no." All sorts of horrible possibilities flashed across Dani's mind.

"She's fine," He quickly reassured her. "Forgot to put in shells and tripped over a raccoon digging through the trash, but her version of the story is much better."

"I bet."

"Anyway, the real story is there's a group of strange men who claim to be looking for a friend of theirs that got lost several days ago." He watched her intently. "The man they describe is tall with black hair and blue eyes."

Dani gasped. They had to be looking for Lateef. Her mind spun with half-a-dozen plans to keep him hidden.

"They haven't talked to anyone who knows about your guest yet," he said, "But you should let him know about his friends. And maybe think about coming to stay with us or the Saunders for a few days?"

"No thanks. Abby will tell me if anyone comes around."

"That pretend dog of yours won't stop anything." He gave a derisive snort. "Probably try to herd them if there's more than one, but she's too cowardly to do much except beg for food. The dog runs from squirrels! You'd get more fight from those rose bushes out back."

Dani reached down to pat the dog's head. "She's a lot braver than she looks. You picked her out for me, so she must have some redeeming qualities. I don't expect her to do anything but sound a warning. The rest is up to me."

"Danielle..."

"I will be fine." She cut him off decisively. "I won't be driven from my home by Ho... not by anyone. If they're looking for Lateef, then that's his problem."

"And if this Lateef doesn't want to be found?" The look he gave her made it clear he understood who she truly feared.

"Not my circus, not my monkeys. You and Anna finally taught me that. I'll let Lateef know. He can decide what to do from there."

She picked up the plate from the dark granite counter, handing the dish to him in a definite gesture of dismissal. "Tell Anna hello for me. And don't send Bob out here to check on me, please. I have a lot of work to do."

He sighed and accepted the cake. "I would like to meet this stranger sometime." He paused on the front veranda. "He sounds like a good man."

"He is," she agreed. "And I'm sure one day you will meet him. He's a lot like you."

Charlie walked down the three stairs and across the sparse grass towards his patrol car. "You take care, okay?" He opened the door. "And give me a call if anything unusual happens."

She gave him a wry look. "You're on my speed dial."

"You don't have speed dial, girl. You don't even have a cordless phone!"

Her smile widened, and she waved as he drove off. Her ambition seemed to go with him, so she sat in one of the wicker chairs on the front porch, staring into the distance long after the trail of dust raised by the car had fallen back to the ground.

The late afternoon sun gave the foliage an unearthly glow as it briefly emerged from behind a bank of dark rain clouds and the rumble of thunder sounded sporadically. The whole world was unsettled today. She sensed something waiting out there but wasn't sure what it could be.

Her life had definitely taken a strange turn recently. Lateef had found a crack in the wall she had erected around her heart and was working hard to make the barrier crumble completely. She was afraid if he stayed around much longer the wall would crash and he would learn how evil she was. But she was more afraid of what would happen to her when he did leave. Apathy was so much easier than caring. And she cared about the stranger far more than she ever thought she could care about anyone.

Chapter 5

Calling Home

Lateef settled his back against a tree at the edge of an alpine meadow, shifting his hips to get comfortable. *Hate when my legs are asleep after a deep trance, but this time I'll stay under until I get someone's attention.* He no longer felt the drag of whatever drug had destroyed his talents, and it was long past time for him to return home, but he wanted to know what he was getting into. He didn't want to be arrested and handed over to the Hatti if they had reported him. Not that he believed his family would let that happen.

He took a final look around, extending all his senses. All was still except the normal squirrels, crows and chipmunks. Leaves shivered in the wind and thunder boomed in the distance. He closed his eyes and grounded his energy, quickly dropping into a deep trance. He sent mental feelers out into space, searching for his normal contact on Beryl, but met only an empty void.

Swearing, he broke contact and roused from the trance. The serene mountain mocked him with its timeless peacefulness.

"I will reach someone." He breathed deeply and relaxed into an even deeper trance than he used when healing, ignoring the potential danger of going too far without an anchor. He could sense Dani with the Sheriff. Concern glowed in the older man's aura. Dani's was a golden hue, marred by a shadow roiling the surface. Something about the feel tickled his memory, but he couldn't place it. He hadn't been on this planet long enough to learn what was normal. A thin thread of danger trailed out of the mountains, but he pushed the unease away to concentrate on his goal. There would be time later to find out what disturbed the woman he needed to protect. He owed her protection. It had nothing to do with the way she made him feel.

He took in a deep breath and exhaled, sending his mind further in search of his normal contact, but hit an adamantine barrier. His heart raced, and he breathed slowly, forcing the errant organ to obey his will. There were always other options. He had to find another path.

A bright, flashing light caught his attention and he reached for the glow, shocked when he recognized his sister.

'Rissa.'

'Lateef! We thought you were dead. Where are you? What happened?'

Lateef clung to the mental contact, fighting the surge of joy that threatened to tear him out of the trance. *'I'm safe on Earth. I found…'* The connection wavered as he tried to explain what Dani meant to him.

'Stay with me, 'Teef. Do you need help? I can be there soon.'

'I'm okay, Sis. No need to panic.'

'I need more than that, baby brother. You've been gone for over a week. No one can find Trevan, either, and the Hatti throw a royal snit fit whenever anyone asks a question. What happened at that ceremony?'

'I'm not sure.' He sent his sister a quick summary of events, gratified to feel her loving support in return. *'I can't believe Trevan is involved. He must be a prisoner on the ship. We have to find him.'*

'We're looking. After you two disappeared from the feast, Casella came to Beryl and told us what she knew. What did you learn at the ceremony?'

'The Hatti could be new allies. I got a good feel from almost everyone I met, but since they have a psionic blocking field, I'm not positive I trust my impressions.'

'What happened?'

Lateef's stomach did a slow roll and he swallowed heavily. *'I was set up. Someone arranged for me to walk into the kitchens in the middle of feast prep.'*

A warm chuckle surrounded him in a bubble of love. *'Talk about an understatement. The Embassy has already received several complaints about your reprehensible behavior. Taura is ready to strangle Trevan.'*

'She's not mad at me?' Lateef hated the insecurity that slipped into his communication.

'Trevan is a senior diplomat, though he was not even close to ready for that post. I always thought…' Her presence faded.

'Rissa?' He sent a mental nudge when the silence lasted too long.

'I'm here. Are you hurt?'

'I'm recovering. Nothing major. Is everything okay at home?'

'No new attacks. Mellora has the Healer Hall under control. Mom is worried but thinks it's good the other healers are coping without you for a change.'

'Let her know I'm okay?' Lateef shoved the twinge of guilt out of his conscience. He was the good kid, the one who never made his parents worry.

'She'd know if you were in trouble, baby brother. Trust me. I've caused enough of her gray hairs, you don't have to worry. The only way you could beat me is to bring the Falgarans into open conflict on Earth, and I don't see that happening.'

'I hope you're right. The Hatti are on my tail, and I have to protect...'

Understanding and excitement at his unfinished thought flowed through the link seconds after he paused.

'Did...?' She cut off the thought abruptly. *'Hang out on Earth, Lateef. I'll come to you as soon as I can but keep an eye on her.'*

'Her?' Lateef tried to project surprise. Rissa was mistaken. He cared about Dani because she saved his life, not because he was falling for her.

'You can't hide from me, 'Teef. I can tell you've finally found your match. Keep her safe and try to stay out of trouble. We'll do whatever we need to work this all out.'

Lightning crashed nearby, shocking Lateef out of the contact. While he was still in a trance, he sent his senses out, searching for trouble near his current location. A knot of anger drew his attention and he concentrated on it. *Damn, it's a Hatti crew.* He roused completely and stretched out cramped muscles until he was limber enough to move. He deliberately didn't search for Dani. He couldn't fall in love and leave her. Rissa was blowing things out of proportion. He was just doing his job. He teleported to a rise near the wreckage of his life pod.

Several of the Hatti warriors milled in the area, searching the ground for tracks. A harsh cough sounded lower down the mountain. *What in the universe was that?*

Lateef cautiously moved downhill, crouching to remain out of sight. He had to find out what creature had made such a horrifying noise. *Can't think of any native animal big enough.*

A musky scent smacked him upside the nose and he pinched his nostrils to stifle a sneeze. Branches rustled, and he hugged the ground, thinking invisible thoughts as his heart threatened to pound out of his body.

When he wasn't eaten after a few minutes, and the musky scent faded, he slowly raised his head, eyes scanning the area. With quiet ease he moved back uphill until he topped a slight knoll. Looking over the edge, he had to rub his eyes to be certain he wasn't hallucinating. *That sucker's huge.* The creature lifted its feathered head, the nostrils on the snout opening wide as it inhaled gusts of air. It looked in his direction and his body froze, not even his heart dared to take a beat. Large eyes took in the creature's surroundings for an eternity before one powerful front paw raked along a tree, leaving four deep gashes in the wood.

Lateef gulped. *Has to be one of those bloodhounds Trevan warned me about. I thought he was pulling my leg. Jangxing.* The unfamiliar word floated to the surface of his memory as he studied the feathered mammal straight out of a horror-writer's nightmare. The face had a short snout and eyes that were huge for the size of the face. Feathers formed a mane and followed the spine in an explosion of brilliant colors that complimented the tawny fur covering the rest of the body. All four heavily-muscled legs ended in vicious claws.

The Jangxing took another deep sniff of the mountain air, ruffled its mane, and then dropped its head to sniff at the ground in a questing circle.

I've got to get out of here. He wasn't positive his heart would survive a separation, but that was the only way to keep Dani safe. The Jangxing couldn't be allowed to find her because of him. He extended a thin thread of psionic energy and touched the mind of the creature. It shook its massive head, sending stray feathers to the ground.

He exerted a bit more energy, convincing the animal to change direction. It let out another barky cough and lumbered back up the mountain, gaining speed as it stopped fighting Lateef's command.

He watched until the Hatti squad followed. Once the last soldier vanished into the thicket of pines he sagged with relief. *Should keep them off the remnants of my trail long enough for the storm to wash away any scent.* Lightning crashed and a thunderclap followed seconds later. Storms moved fast in these mountains. *Have to leave tonight. I can't take any chances. I'll find some way to let them know I've left the planet.* They'd have to follow him, so Dani would be safe.

He gulped. *She won't like this. I'll tell her after dinner. That way she'll eat at least one more meal.* The stabbing pain in his heart almost made him change his mind, but he had to do what was best for Dani, no matter how much he ached.

Dinner was over and the kitchen returned to its normal, spotless condition. The harvested flowers had been hung to dry in the shed out back before the deluge had started. Abby had been fed and there were no more chores to be done, although Lateef racked his brain, desperately trying to find any excuse to put off this painful conversation.

"Okay." Dani refilled both of their mugs with a cinnamon coffee blend as the rain fell outside in a steady patter. "Out with it."

He decided to blurt the painful truth out. "I have to leave." A loud crash of thunder shook the house. "I don't want to go." His look begged her to understand. "But... well, I was being chased when I crashed."

"By whom? The men Charlie told me about this afternoon?" she asked.

"Probably." He ran his fingers through his shaggy hair. She had relayed her conversation with the sheriff while preparing dinner. "They think I've mortally insulted them and won't listen to my apology. All I wanted to do was help, but you can't help some people—they resist every effort." He shot her a glance and a brief surge of frustrated anger flowed through his veins. *There's no reason for her to live in pain. I could completely fix her old injuries if she wasn't so stupidly stubborn.*

"Why are you being chased?" She obviously wanted to understand his situation.

"I..." He paused and then shrugged helplessly. "You'd think I'd have my story worked out by now, but I really don't know how to explain any of it. If you were anyone else, I'd create a story, but you deserve the truth, Dani, and I can't give it to you. Not in a way you'd believe, anyway."

She snorted skeptically. "What makes me so special?"

He grasped her hands possessively then met her gaze, staring at her until he felt as though he was being pulled out of his body.

"I'm not sure," he answered. He could feel the pulse in her wrist, a comforting thud against his fingertips. "But you are special. I'll do what I can to keep you safe and you won't prevent it." His grip on her hands tightened. "Leaving's the only way I can accomplish that, Danielle Hamilton. My enemies are in the area and if they suspect you've helped me, they won't leave you alone. I don't know how far they'd go to get information from an innocent by-stander—but if they suspect I care about..." his voice faded and he looked away for a moment before recapturing her gaze. "I can't be here when they come. Don't lie to them. Tell them I was here and answer any and all of their questions. They'll leave you alone if they believe you've been honest."

"What about you?"

"I have to go home." His soul screamed at the thought of leaving her all alone to potentially face his enemy. Her long hair hung loose around her shoulders, instead of in her normal ponytail, obscuring most of the scars scattered across her neck and shoulders. She looked so delicate, but he knew the fragile exterior hid a core of tempered steel. *She'll be safer without me, but I still feel like I'm abandoning her. I don't want to go.*

She met his gaze, staring straight to his soul then snatched her hands free.

"I told you I sucked at this," he muttered, catching the look of confused horror on her expressive face. *What had she seen in his gaze?* He shook his head, then shoved his hair behind his ears. Conflicting thoughts ripped through his brain. He had to tell her as much of the truth as she could take. He owed her, but would she hate him afterwards? *First contact sucks. Can't tell if finding out Terrans aren't alone in the universe will destroy her psyche or not. Can't risk that when I have to leave.*

"What are you trying to tell me? Just spit it out, please." Dani clenched her hands in her lap, watching him with a guarded expression.

He took a deep breath, refusing to take advantage of his abilities to read her thoughts. His explanation would be ambiguous for now. "I'm a master healer. I work on people too badly damaged for normal medicine and I'm good at what I do. I spend most of my time at the Healer Hall, but occasionally I get sent to fill in for a social affair when everyone else is too busy. I hate it—I despise crowds and having to be nice to people I know want to kill my friends and family, but that's the price of being the youngest child in a family of diplomats." He jerked to his feet and paced restlessly back and forth, talking to himself as much as to her.

"I know we're speaking the same language, Lateef, but I have no idea what you said."

He halted and turned to face her. "I'm sorry. I'm not very good at this kind of thing. My sister, Rissa, does first contact all the time, but most of the people I meet are unconscious..." His voice trailed off and he closed his eyes to get his scattered thoughts back in order. He took a deep breath and glanced at her. "I know how odd this all sounds."

A lifted eyebrow was her only response.

"I really do. I'd like to tell you my life history and take you home with me, but the less you know about me, the safer you'll be."

"Okay." Her voice quavered and she tried to disguise the fine trembling of her muscles by twisting her hands in her lap. "You're a good guy and have to leave. I'm glad you've recovered from your accident. Thanks for all the help around the house."

He quickly went to her and laid his hand against her cheek. "I am a good guy," he whispered, his voice husky with repressed emotion as he leaned closer. "And I don't want to leave—I have to. It's the only way to keep you safe. I owe you my life and I'll do what I can to repay you."

Lateef stopped scant inches from Dani's lips, allowing her to make the next move. With a small sigh she leaned forward to close the gap. Heat flashed over him as he kissed her. When she didn't pull away, he deepened the kiss. Her hands slid up his back to tangle in his hair and he groaned with need.

Guilt flooded the room in a tidal wave and he caught a brief image of a man and then two graves from Dani. Tears overflowed her eyes and she pulled away, her chest heaving with intense emotion. The chair toppled over as she threw herself across the room and ran out into the dripping night.

His breath caught in his chest as he let her go. Deep in his bones he knew he was doing the only thing he could do for her now. He couldn't risk putting her in danger by staying any longer. And if the Hatti caught up with him and he didn't survive... Well, maybe it was better he left before she knew exactly how much she meant to him. She already carried far more guilt than she should. He couldn't add to the burden.

Chapter 6

Unexpected Company

Dani downed her fourth cup of coffee as she checked new orders on her website. *Need to pour an extra batch of honey soap next week. Never expected that one to be so popular.*

She jotted a list of supplies to order and her mind drifted to the Founder's Day celebration Anna had talked her into catering. *Most of the early prep's already done so it won't take too long to finish up the last-minute stuff.* Lateef would have been a lot of help.

She snapped the computer lid shut, wincing at the click. He'd only been gone a couple of days and she couldn't believe how much she missed his company.

"You've been alone for over a year. How on Earth could having him here for a couple of weeks completely change that?"

Abby's low, menacing growl interrupted her. She looked at the dog then lifted her own head, eyes un-focusing as her senses were overwhelmed. A babble of unfamiliar voices drowned out the normal kitchen sounds, accompanied by a feeling of distaste and determination, with an undercurrent of hunger. Suddenly she knew company was on the way. *Must be the people Lateef warned me about.*

She stored the laptop, doubly glad she was nearly ready for the brunch. *They've been stealing fresh produce in the area, and Lateef said they were obsessed with food. Treats distract Abby, so that should work on these guys, I hope.* With the ease of long practice, she whipped up a crepe batter and placed it in the fridge to rest. Then she finished a batch of semi-cooked diced potatoes and zucchini with onions and garlic, pouring in scrambled eggs and cream when the veggies were soft. A fresh pot of coffee brewed as she put together a Framboise and fruit sauce. English muffins went in the oven to toast and some of the Saunders's apple, hyssop and plain goat cheese went on a plate to spread on the muffins in addition to the butter and a squeeze jar of local honey. Just as she finished, she caught motion in the yard through the large window and looked down at Abby, who stood guard at the door.

"Show time. You be good, you hear? I don't want you getting hurt."

Abby stared at her as if understanding her instructions and then sneezed. A knock at the door startled her and she let out a yip of fear before barking maniacally.

"Enough, Abby." Dani snapped. "Behave."

The sheltie gave her a hurt look and retreated across the room, grumbling under her breath as Dani crossed the slate tile floor to the back door. She paused with one hand on the knob and took a deep breath to steady her nerves. *Just keep the visitors off balance so they don't have a chance to ask any questions I don't want to answer. Easy as pie.* She pasted a curious smile on her face and pulled the door open.

"Yes, can I..." her voice trailed off and she stared in surprise at the two men who waited on her back porch. They stared down at her with completely black eyes and awkward grins on green-tinged faces. Poorly fitting, dark grey suits with white shirts and red ties covered muscular bodies. Well-worn black, thick-soled boots peeked out from under the baggy pants. Giggles burbled in her chest at the sight of the too-small baseball caps perched precariously on top of their largish, bald heads.

The expression of one of the men began to darken and she quickly feigned a coughing fit to give herself time to recover her equilibrium.

"Sorry. You'd think by now I'd know you can't breathe and swallow at the same time." She opened the door wider.

The clickety-clack of nails on the slate floor gave her barely enough warning to catch the dog darting toward the door. She caught the motion of the men reaching for something at their sides and spoke quickly.

"I'm okay, Abby-girl." She crouched down to hide the frantic dog from the strange men, remaining frozen until everyone relaxed, and then pushed the dog back toward her bed.

She stood back up and smiled at her visitors. "She's a bit nervous around strangers. She'll be okay now."

"We are…"

"You're right on time." Dani interrupted the taller of the two visitors. She held out a hand to invite them in. "Breakfast is done."

"But…"

A faint whiff of burning butter rose from the stove. "Oh, crap!" Dani ran back to the stove. "Almost forgot about this." She pulled the pan off the heat and flipped the crepe over. "Didn't burn it, though."

The men stared at her with identical bewildered expressions.

"Come in before the food gets cold."

They slowly moved across the room to the table, whispering to each other in an unfamiliar language as they walked.

"I'm Danielle Hamilton, and the over-protective dog over there is Abby." She placed mugs of coffee in front of each of them, pointed out the sugar and cream and went back to the stove to load the crepes with a cream cheese filling and placed one on each of two plates, topped with the warm fruit and some Crème Anglaise. She then added a serving of the scrambled egg mixture and placed a plate in front of each of them and came back with a basket of toasted English muffins and the goat cheese and butter.

"We are not here for food!" The taller of the two men protested, but his companion took in a deep breath and then closed his eyes, blissfully sniffing at the fragrant air.

Dani watched in bemusement as he leaned close to the plate and carefully smelled everything before picking up a fork to taste a small bite of the crepe. She jumped as he let out a low moan of pleasure and half-melted into his chair, his eyes rolling back into his head. His color flashed from the light green to a darker shade and back. He spoke a few unfamiliar words and his companion eyed him skeptically. Several more intense words passed before the belligerent man took his own bite—only to have the same reaction.

This is too weird. Dani watched as her visitors carefully sampled all the food. *They look like a pair of wine connoisseurs, except thankfully they aren't spitting out what they taste.*

A sound at the still open back door made her glance up to see two more identically dressed men staring back at her.

"Well don't stand there," she said. "Come on in and have a seat. There's plenty."

The two men were hesitant until the shorter of the men at the table said something in that lilting language. The newcomers appeared to disagree with whatever he said. With a glare at her they stalked over to the table while she filled mugs of coffee and put two more plates together, sliding them onto the table as a heated conversation between the strangers concluded. The first man gave her an adoring look, while the two newcomers were much more skeptical, until their first bite. Dani had to struggle to keep from laughing hysterically as they too, moaned and melted into their seats.

The shorter man rose to face her, a note of respect in his tone. "I am Taltos of the Kanesh Clan." He introduced himself with a nod of a slightly too-large head. "We are here to..."

"Let me get you some more." She grabbed his empty plate and headed back to the kitchen before he could say anything else. By the time she got back there were more plates to fill and more people at the back door and she stayed busy making sure they were all far too busy eating to talk, much less ask her any questions.

Abby remained in her doggie bed, watching silently. Every once in a while, she would let out a muffled woof, but she didn't move from her bed, even when it looked like some food might fall to the floor.

An hour later Dani was exhausted, and her ten guests sat slumped and stuffed at the cluttered kitchen table. Their large eyes were glazed and looked as if they had been drugged instead of fed.

Dani stood at the kitchen island with a fresh cup of coffee, watching the men from the corner of her eyes. *Looks like I made a good impression.* She stifled a yawn. *I could so use a nap round about now. I've never seen anyone so fixated on food.*

Slowly and with great effort, Taltos pushed away from the table and rose to his feet. His crew copied him and Dani again had to stifle a laugh, trying not to attract attention. *I feel like Snow White facing the Seven Dwarves. Although there are ten of them, and they are all taller than me and I'm very definitely not the fairest in the land and... maybe that isn't the best analogy. Maybe it's more like Alice in Wonderland.*

The group of identically dressed men gathered in front of her and she straightened, keeping the counter between her and them. She put the mug down with a loud click in the suddenly silent room.

"Have you seen..." the tallest man said when Taltos interrupted him.

He snapped a couple of sharp words in the unknown language and the other man flushed green and looked at the floor. Taltos nodded his head and turned to her and bowed. The rest of the group followed suit and she bowed back uncertainly.

"We wish to thank you most profusely for the hospitality and the incredible meal you have provided," he said. "I am ashamed to admit we did not come prepared with proper guest gifts, since we truly did not expect to encounter anything like this." He threw a longing glance back at the table. "In all my life I would never have expected to partake in such an incredible feast on such a..." He halted abruptly, looking back at her and then bowed again as his face flushed deep green. "We thank you," he repeated. "We shall return with proper guest gifts when the opportunity arises and in the meantime shall inform Thane Hantili a Master Chef resides in this home."

"Thank you," Dani said, hearing the capitalization of Master Chef, like a title of some sort. "But your appreciation's the only gift I'll ever need. It is a true pleasure to serve those who enjoy food as much as you all did. Thank you very much."

The visitors' low bows caught her by surprise. She waited until they rose again.

"We shall take our leave now. Until we meet again." Taltos came to stand before her, holding his right hand up vertically in front of him, palm toward her. He looked at her expectantly and she slowly raised her own hand to mirror his. He reached forward and touched his palm to hers. "I am Taltos. For the bread from your table, I thank you." He nodded once and moved aside and waited as the rest of the crowd introduced themselves before they all moved out of the kitchen.

"But we..." The same tall man tried to protest, but his companions grabbed him and hurried him away from the house. Dani watched them leave from the doorway with Abigail panting by her side.

"What was that all about?" She closed the door and slid to the floor, hugging her furry companion. "This has got to be the strangest morning ever. But they did like to eat." She shook her head in disbelief. "I've done dinner parties for fifty people where I've prepared less food. Glad I've got time to order more. Holly'll die of curiosity trying to figure out how I ate so much." She buried her nose in the dog's soft back. "What's going on here, Abby?" she whispered. But there was no answer.

Chapter 7

Unwanted Company

Kyle Manning climbed out of his dark gray sedan and adjusted his sunglasses as he looked around. The two-story log cabin was surrounded by a veranda which sported wicker furniture and a variety of clay planters holding an array of colorful plants and flowers. Dog toys were scattered across the porch and a rawhide bone dangled precariously off the top step.

Nice place. Awfully big for just one person, though. High pitched barks carried on the still air. He moved toward the front door, but paused as he realized the sound came from the left. He looked over and caught a glimpse of a small head peering at him from the side of the house.

The dog bolted for the back yard, the frenzied barking never slowing.

He warily followed and saw a slender woman cutting flowers in a large garden as the dog stood between her and him.

Dog's got guts, even if it would be barely a single bite for a hungry bear. He shook off the silly image. *Get your head back in the game, Manning. This woman could get you the fat check you need to get rid of the client from hell.* He walked closer, one eye on the furry guardian as he studied the woman. Baggy jeans and a well-worn tee shirt were covered by some kind of apron and she sat on a rolling bench with her right leg stretched out to the side. Long brown hair was in a ponytail that reached to her waist and threadlike scars were scattered across her throat and collarbone. *Looks like the aftermath of a nasty car crash to me.* His mood brightened.

"Are you Danielle Hamilton?" He spoke loudly to be heard over the dog.

"Who wants to know?" The woman made no effort to hide her unhappiness with the interruption, continuing to snip the stems with an intensity that made him squirm.

"I'm Kyle Manning." He pulled out his ID and stepped closer, totally unnerving the dog.

"Get over here, Abigail," The woman snapped as she glared at the dog. The dog gave a final bark and refused to look at the woman as she walked over to give her face a contrite lick.

"You have your act together now?"

The dog gave her another excited lick and wiggled in place.

"Good watch dog." Kyle eyed the creature warily, ready to grab his weapon if necessary.

"Sorry. We've had too many uninvited visitors lately so she's a bit stressed out."

"Too bad." He kept his expression bland. "What kind of visitors have you been having?"

Her stare could have frozen a mammoth in seconds. "Unwelcome ones." She held the glare a long second before returning to her task.

Kyle adjusted the sleeves of his dark, well-tailored suit coat, trying to decide how to continue. *I'm so tired of the backwoods hicks in this community. They all talk a lot and say absolutely nothing useful. Old geezer at the last house even made me buy some stinky cheese, but getting the lead on this woman was worth the stench.*

"I'm sorry to disturb your day, Mrs. Hamilton, but it's important."

She shot him a disbelieving look, then snipped a plant stem with a bit more force than necessary. "That's what people always say. For the most part, I fail to share their urgency."

Kyle tamped down a surge of anger. *I want to be done with this stupid chase for a woman who vanished months ago, but the money's too good to pass up. And I'm afraid the want-to-be-re-elected-senator is a bit crazier than I want to cross.* He crammed the thought further down in his mind. Didn't pay to question the guy who wrote the checks.

"I'm looking for a dark-haired man."

"Good for you. I've always heard there's a partner for everyone. You might do better with an online dating site instead of bothering strangers, though."

Heat flashed through him and his words fled for a second. "That's not what I mean."

A wicked smirk played on her lips as she continued to cut flowers and his anger drained away. This interview could actually be fun. *She can't be the target. He described a vicious, gold-digging shrew, not someone who does her own gardening and has a sense of humor.*

The dog tore across the yard and dropped a ball on his foot, leaving strings of drool on his new leather shoes. He shook his foot in an effort to dislodge the disgusting mess.

"Guess the dog likes me."

"That brainless mutt will play with anyone." Another batch of orange flowers landed in the basket. "If you ignore her, she'll eventually go away. But you can kick the ball and make her deliriously happy for hours. You don't even have to get your hands dirty."

Kyle stared at her, unsure if she was making some kind of underhanded statement about him, but the woman's expression was serene as she focused on her task. He pushed his sunglasses up on his head and then kicked the ball. The wide smile on his mouth was unconscious as the dog dashed along behind it. The game continued for several minutes. He was surprised to realize the tension in his neck was fading away. Playing fetch was oddly soothing.

Danielle piled the last blossom into her basket and stripped off purple gloves covered with a cartoonish creature and he knew it was time to continue his interview.

"So, have you seen him?" He threw the ball far, smiling as the dog dashed across the large yard, panting happily in pursuit.

The woman looked at him for a long moment and then bent to gather her basket.

"I've seen a lot of dark-haired men," she replied. "Let me put these away and I'll start some coffee."

The dog dropped the ball once again at Kyle's feet. He reached for it, but she was faster. She danced back a few steps and dropped the ball again. He took a step forward and she grabbed the ball and ran in a circle, then bounced back to drop the ball at his feet. He bent forward and the dog once again grabbed the toy.

"Don't know what you want, do you?" he said under his breath. "Typical female." The face of the senator's niece flashed across his mind's eye. She wasn't your typical anything. He found it hard to believe the cheerful young woman was related to his obnoxious client. Mandy was like a ray of sunshine on a stormy day. He shook his head, dislodging the pleasant memory and finally managed to snatch the ball to throw again.

"She doesn't know when to stop," Dani said. "Come on in and she'll get the idea."

He followed her past the raised garden into a large, spotless kitchen. She washed her hands at the double stainless-steel sink set beneath a bay window framing an incredible view of a valley between mountain peaks before handing him a bar of soap.

"This is different." Kyle sniffed at the soap, pleased by the spicy, earthy scent. There was something gritty in the bar, scratchy enough to make his hands feel clean, but not scrubbed raw.

"It's one of mine," Dani answered absently as she made coffee then pulled a coffee cake out of the fridge.

"You make soap?"

"How I pay the bills."

She handed out cake and coffee, the perfect hostess as she got him settled at the large table before sitting across from him.

Kyle eyed the cake dubiously, not sure he wanted to take a chance. He spent a lot of time interviewing very lonely women who tried to keep him around by feeding him to prolong his visit. Usually those treats were anything but, as the desire for company seemed to be inversely related to any semblance of an ability to bake. He picked up his fork and took a deep breath before braving a tentative bite.

"This is good," he said, inwardly wincing at the excessive enthusiasm in his tone.

Danielle ignored him, finding the contents of her mug more interesting than his company.

"Would you like another piece?" she asked as he chased the last crumbs across his plate.

"No." He sighed regretfully and pushed the plate away to resist temptation. "Thank you very much. That was exceptionally good."

She tucked a stray strand of hair behind her ear and his heart stuttered. *Not good, Manning. You're not in the market for a girlfriend. And you really don't want to be involved with the senator's family. That bastard's crazy.* He ignored the thread of interest and got down to business. "Mrs. Hamilton."

"Call me Dani," she interrupted quickly, blinking as an expression of pain flitted across her face. "Mrs. makes me feel ancient."

"Okay, Dani." He smiled warmly at her. *Don't buy that excuse for a second, but I can let it go. Won't matter at all if you're not the one I'm looking for.* "I didn't come here to interrupt your work."

"Glad to hear it. Why are you here?"

"My firm has been hired to find a dead-beat dad who was last seen in this area. His kid needs some... bone marrow." He threw in the first thing he could think of then took a sip of coffee.

"Really? Are you sure he doesn't need a kidney?" Her mouth twisted in sarcastic humor.

"Too much?" He shrugged. "People are usually willing to help when a kid is in danger, so I might have exaggerated a little bit."

She let out a sharp bark of laughter. "Little bit is an exaggeration. So, what are you really doing out here?" Dani rested her elbows on the table, her mug hiding part of her face.

"I am looking for this man. He owes child support and his ex is worried about him. He's been off his meds and that never ends well. He has shoulder-length black hair, an athletic build and is a bit taller than you." Kyle studied her as he spoke, catching the sudden agitation she tried to hide as she turned her mug around and around in long, thin fingers.

Her warm brown eyes stared into his soul and Kyle felt his heart lurch.

"What does that have to do with me?"

"Apparently you found someone a couple of weeks ago and allowed him stay with you?"

Dani muttered a swift epithet under her breath. "I found an injured hiker. He stayed in a spare room for a couple of days, but he didn't have a family, and wasn't crazy."

"Have you seen the bald men who claim to be searching for a friend?" Kyle asked.

"Don't know." She shrugged.

He watched the life drain out of her expressive eyes. "Some people believe they're aliens."

Dani snorted. "Where would your belief come from?"

"Those guys all look very similar—kind of greenish, bald with large, dark eyes, odd accents and a bizarre way of speaking?" Kyle described them, his voice dropping off as recognition slid across her face.

"A similar group stopped by here a few days ago," she said. "Very polite gentlemen. I fed them breakfast and they left. The thought they might be aliens never crossed my mind."

"Did they ask for anything?" Excitement bubbled in his blood. Maybe he was onto something big. He had latched onto the hiker as a ruse in his search for his client's daughter-in-law and the bald men were just an excuse, but maybe they were suspicious?

"They ate, thanked me for the meal and left. Haven't seen them since. Do you want some more coffee?" She refilled their cups, deftly derailing the conversation. "Have some more cake." She rose and brought the cake to the table.

"Thank you." Kyle accepted another piece, letting the silence stretch as he finished eating. "What about your injured hiker?"

"What about him?" She stared at her plate, picking apart the thin sliver of cake on her plate with her fork until there was nothing left but crumbs.

"Did anything about him strike you as unusual?"

Dani briefly met his gaze then retreated into her coffee mug. "Not really."

"Why was he out here?"

"He didn't say," Dani said. "And I didn't ask. We didn't talk very much. I run a business by myself and this is one of my busiest times of the year. I don't have a lot of time to deal with visitors."

"That's the whole story?"

"What else do you think there could be?" Her unexpected anger startled him. "I was out looking for some wild herbs, and I found a guy who was hurt. I played the Good Samaritan and gave him a place to stay until he recovered enough to be able to get home." Her fork fell to the table with a clatter, flinging a spray of crumbs onto the polished wood of the table. "And now I have some obnoxious investigator bugging me and several people who suddenly think I'm an incompetent idiot unable to take care of myself." She pushed her chair back from the table and grabbed the plates from the table, stalking over to the sink. "You should go now."

Kyle joined the distraught woman at the sink. *Wonder what nerve I just crushed?*

"I don't mean to be a problem." He lowered his voice, deciding to treat her like a fragile crime witness. *Can't spook her now or she might rabbit before I can get proof of her identity. She has to be hiding to be so freaked out.* He took the plates from Dani's clenched fingers and put them in the dishwasher. "I'm trying to do right by my client. The kids deserve to know where their dad is." *What's a little white lie among strangers?*

He ignored the twinge of his jaded conscience and gently led Dani back to the table. He refilled her mug.

Dani reflexively took a sip, seeming to gather courage from the warm beverage.

Kyle returned to his own chair, and they sat in silence, as she regained her composure. His gaze roamed the room as he waited, noticing the lack of any personal touches. No photos or knick-knacks cluttered any flat surface. Despite owning a soap business, there appeared to be very few items that couldn't be abandoned. *Damn, she really could be the one.*

"Why are you asking me about this?" She finally broke the silence.

"I'm talking to everyone in the area." Kyle heaved a dramatic sigh. "It's what I do." He put a note of resigned impatience in his tone and was relieved to see her relax.

"I haven't seen anything useful."

"Will you give me a call if something does come up?" Kyle pulled a card from his wallet and slid it across the table. "Doesn't matter when—even the middle of the night. And doesn't matter what. If there's an odd light or if someone knocks on your door and makes you nervous, give me a call."

Dani shook her head. "If someone knocks on my door in the middle of the night you won't be much help from Denver. It'll take you a couple of hours to get here."

"I'm staying here in town for a while."

Dani shook her head. "I don't think you need to worry," she said. "It's quiet around here."

"But I want you to know you have help if you need it." He placed a hand on hers on the table, and her eyes darted up to his. "You don't have to face problems all by yourself."

She stared into his eyes for a long moment, then gently drew her hand. "Thank you," she said. "I appreciate your concern, but I'll be okay."

"Thanks for the coffee and the cake." Kyle rose to his feet. "It was really good."

He could feel her gaze on the back of his head as he walked across the yard to his sedan. She remained on the front porch as he waved and drove off.

Kyle pulled his phone out of his pocket and speed-dialed his office. "Find me everything you can on a Danielle Hamilton, but keep it uber quiet," he said to his secretary.

"Do you think she's the client's daughter-in-law?"

"Probably not, but something about her is hinkey." He was going to hell for lying to his efficient admin, but he could not reconcile the difference in the senator's description with the delightful woman he had just left. *I won't put anyone in that man's path until I'm certain.* "She's in the middle of the weirdness up here, and I want to find out why."

"Kyle Manning, don't tell me you believe aliens are in the Rocky Mountains."

"Of course not." He snorted his disbelief as he turned onto the only paved road running through the stupid town stuck out in the middle of nowhere. Folly Springs was an appropriate name for the wide spot on a road. The natural spring water was the only worthwhile thing in town. "I don't believe in aliens. But Ms. Hamilton's hiding something. I'll keep an eye on her until we find out for sure who she is and what's going on. The aliens are a perfect excuse to stay close and keep her from rabbiting out of here."

Chapter 8

Rotten Patient

Lateef's mind drifted in thought as his body lay in a deep trance. He was back in his beloved Healer Hall as Mellora finished healing the last of his wounds. He hadn't wanted to leave Earth and Dani, but he was grateful to feel the last, resistant pain fade away. *Rissa's right again. Healing someone else is so much easier than myself. Not that I'd ever admit that to her.*

"You're a rotten patient." Mellora's acerbic mental tone cut into his consciousness. "You're supposed to be too deep to think."

"There wasn't much damage left. I'd have been okay in a few days without your help, but I appreciate it."

Her grudging acceptance of his thanks manifested as a warm green light brushing across his hand. The head of the Healer Hall would crawl through a tunnel of broken glass to heal anyone beside a Falgaran, but the woman was incapable of accepting a compliment. Or showing happiness, for that matter.

Mellora's response reverberated in his mind. "I am happy. I just don't need everyone around me to acknowledge it."

Lateef winced. He'd forgotten how tight his psychic bond with Mellora was. They frequently worked together on severely injured patients, talents fused so closely he often struggled to tell where he ended and she began. There was less chance of keeping a secret from his boss than from his favorite sister.

"No need for secrets between us, Lateef. What are you going to tell me about this woman you've fallen for?"

He squirmed in his mind, body too relaxed to respond. "She's just a human from Terra who helped me out. I haven't fallen for her."

"Can't lie to me, remember?"

Embarrassment flashed through him. "I'm not lying. I'm responsible for her safety since I led the Hatti to her."

"So, a sense of responsibility is what I'm reading?"

He strengthened his mental shields, refusing to answer.

"Okay, then. I'll let it slide, but you need to sort this out before you come back to work. Your mind is not all here. We've had a lull in the fighting, so this is a good time to talk her into joining you. Maybe then you'll bother to use your quarters and free up a bed here in the hall."

Irritation, shame, and confusion tied his tongue in knots.

"I don't want to rattle you, Lateef. Your love life's your issue, not mine. I really wish we had a sample of whatever drug was on that bolt you got hit with. The Hatti have an energy shield—they wouldn't need a psi-blocking drug as well. I don't want to have to treat a bunch of blocked Field Agents."

He agreed. The Field Agents, like Rissa, heavily relied on their psychic abilities. The ability to teleport and communicate instantly were the only advantages they had in their covert fight against the Falgaran Empire.

"But that's a problem for tomorrow." Her mental voice faded as her focus centered on his condition. "You're good to go. Spend another fifteen minutes or so in a trance to rest and I'll release you for duty."

Joy surged through his veins. Being on the injured list sucked. "Thanks, Mellora."

Her response was a wave of amused affection.

He tried to obey her instructions and rest, but he was drawn to Dani. Before he had a chance to resist, he was in her mind. It was early morning and she sat alone at her kitchen table, peering at a computer and drinking tea. Her exhaustion dragged at him, and her hunger made his stomach growl, but she refused to acknowledge either need.

The scent of spiced tomato sauce snapped him awake.

"Thought that'd get your attention." Rissa waved a slice of pizza under his nose. An impish grin dominated her face.

"Smells good." He sat up, resisting the urge to gobble the pizza in two bites. Instead he ate slowly, trying to be certain the voracious hunger was his, and not left over from Dani.

Rissa settled in a chair by his bed, her legs tucked under her. "I can't remember the last time the hall was this empty. Seems like there's always a dozen or more patients."

He stopped mid-bite and extended his senses. The main Healer Hall on Beryl was a series of large rooms with smaller treatment rooms around the perimeter of the fortified building. Colorful curtains covered the walls and doors. Each section was painted in shades of a common color, to help the healers find their location.

During a major attack, most triage was done at the battlefield or on gurneys scattered throughout the center of the open rooms. Cabinets of supplies were paired with each bed. Most of the treatment was accomplished with psychic abilities, but sometimes injuries were bad enough that they had to supply extra hydration or nutrients.

His normal station was decorated in shades of calming blue in one corner of the hall, far from the chaos of triage. He was one of two healers in the present generation capable of healing wounds well beyond the capability of most healers. His patients were the ones who barely survived transport back to Beryl and most of them walked out whole and healthy.

"Have you heard any news about the war?" He continued to munch, the ache in his stomach subsiding.

She shrugged. "Everything's quiet. No one's heard a word from Emperor Morfran, may his rotten heart burst out of his chest and strangle him."

His eyebrows raised in surprise at the anger in her tone. "You think losing Morfran would slow down the Falgarans? Isn't his son ready to take over?"

"I don't think it matters which psychotic bozo is in charge. The Falgarans can't be trusted. My handler hasn't passed on any useful information, but she likes to thoroughly vet her data. She doesn't seem to think I can be cautious."

"Maybe because you end up in the Healer Hall more than any other Field Agent?" He held up a hand at her angry glare. "It's the truth. I had admin check a few months ago."

She swore under her breath. "See if I bring you pizza again."

"It's because you get stuck in the hottest spots, Sis. No one else has your success rate at gaining allies, either."

"Tell that to Mom." She rubbed at her temples. "She thinks I'm reckless and wants to send me to work as a diplomat for a couple of years so I learn what happens after the ambassadors move in and talk instead of taking action." She brushed imaginary crumbs off her emerald-green formal dress that served as a uniform for the diplomatic corps. "Like I never go back to visit once my peeps join the Alliance. I've seen what happens once the Diplomats take over. Not a pretty sight. They have a bad habit of talking us agents down. Not to mention the fact I'd have to report to dear brother Johfrit. I think I'm safer where I am."

Lateef blinked. "You know that Johfrit doesn't actually hate you. He's just... stuffy."

"Wound tight as a rabid snake, is more like it. Johfrit's feelings about me are his problem, and by staying away from the diplomatic side of the job I can keep it from being my problem. Makes us both happy." She snagged a piece of the pizza.

"Why are you dressed like an ambassador? Mom didn't change your status, did she?"

She shook her head and grimaced. The elaborately looped braids in her dark red hair bounced with the movement. "Made me go for a fitting 'just in case'. I came by to visit you before taking the uniform back. I have to keep the hair style until after dinner. Apparently, we're going formal tonight, in case you didn't get the message. She expects you to show up, too."

"It looks good on you. Maybe you could stay out of trouble in a dress?"

"Keep it up, 'Teef, and I'll show you how much trouble I can put you in, no matter what I'm wearing."

He grinned at her. He missed their verbal sparring. Rissa was out in the field so often they rarely had a chance to visit. "You know there's always a place for you here in the hall, right? You have more than enough healing abilities to be a senior healer, and Mellora really is great to work with."

She shuddered. Green eyes opened wide as her face paled. "I like sunshine, fresh air and meeting new people on a regular basis. Conscious new people. I've seen how long you guys spend in this building. I'll take my chances as a Field Agent, thank you."

"Merely saying you have options."

"Since we're speaking of the ambassador division, how much do you know about Trevan?"

Her question caught him by surprise and he tried to read her emotions, but her mental shields were firmly in place and she would not meet his gaze. He started to make a quick comment and then reconsidered. "We were in basic training at the same time and got along okay. He's one of the few people I've stayed in touch with."

"Who makes the most effort?"

"He does. I rarely get back to my quarters, much less visit people."

Rissa leaned back in the chair, swinging her legs back and forth. She was short enough that her feet didn't quite reach the floor. "I don't want to believe Trevan could be a spy. He could've been doing what he thought was right, but he got you into a precarious situation with a new race and left you without any guidance."

Heat flushed his cheeks and he leaned forward. "So, you assume he's a traitor?"

"Chill, bro." She rested a hand on his knee, sending waves of calming emotions through their mental link. "I'm not accusing him of anything. I just wonder how he came to be in the right place to meet the Hatti when his last post was nowhere near them."

"We never talked about it." He scratched the back of his head, trying to pull a coherent thought out of the babble bouncing around in his brain. "I thought he was on assignment to the Mingoran Empire, and they've apparently made contact with the Hatti."

"I know he made first contact, but I can't believe he was made head Ambassador." Rissa frowned.

"Isn't that the way the system usually works? If a diplomat is the first contact, don't they stay on at the Embassy?"

"Not always." She shifted on the chair, telegraphing uneasiness. "Sometimes the diplomat is too inexperienced. For someone like Trevan there is usually a veteran observer as part of the entourage. I've never heard of a newbie diplomat being made Ambassador and given a post as the sole representative of the Alliance. Trevan doesn't even have an assistant. He refused one."

"I'm not sure why you don't trust him"

She smiled, but he could see the tension around her mouth and knew she lied.

"Don't let my mood bother you. I've been stuck on Beryl too long. Most of the field agents are back right now. The whole war has gone quiet and it's making me antsy. I know the Falgarans aren't going to suddenly become peaceniks, so I'm waiting for the next catastrophe to hit."

"We'll handle it, whatever happens. We always do." His confident answer made her reach over to ruffle his hair.

Mellora walked in, a protein shake in one hand. "What are you eating?"

"Real food, instead of that crap you try to push off on your patients." Rissa answered for him.

"These shakes are nutritionally balanced and guaranteed to provide everything a recovering patient needs." Mellora's back stiffened and her eyes narrowed.

"Except taste." Rissa stuck her tongue out and shuddered. "I should know—you've poured enough of them down my throat over the years."

Lateef agreed with her. He used the shakes during the busiest times in the hall, but they were adequate, not satisfying.

"Think of them as an incentive to stop needing our services on such a regular basis," Mellora said.

He accepted the glass and gulped the contents, catching Rissa's exaggerated expressions of disgust out of the corner of his eye. *Good thing I'm used to these things. They really do reek after all of Dani's cooking.*

"You're wanted in command, Miss D'Oro. Your partner's looking for you." Mellora pointed at Rissa. "Says you have a mission but isn't trying too hard to find you."

"Crap. That has to mean the mission is something awful and he doesn't want to tell me."

Lateef grinned. "Maybe you get a vacation. You said things are slow."

Rissa bounced forward to wrap him in a hug. "I like the way you think, baby brother." She kissed him on the forehead. "Give me a call when you're ready to get your girl. She's the one for you, punk. If you try to let her go out of some misguided sense of chivalry, I'm going to beat some sense into you. We can keep her safe from the Falgarans."

She was gone before Lateef could catch his breath.

"I'm with her," Mellora said. "I think you need to go back to that planet and talk this woman into coming home with you. You're going to be worthless until you do. Take care of your relationship before we get crazy busy again."

"I can take care of my own love life." Lateef rose and slammed the glass down on the table.

Mellora walked away, waving her hand at him in dismissal. "Whatever you say, tiger. Go take care of things before I have to step in. You know that won't go as expected."

Lateef wanted to break into a few choice curses of his own. Dani wasn't an object to be carted around. She had to want him as much as he wanted her, and deep down he was afraid to find out how she felt about him.

'Won't know until you ask.' Mellora's voice filled his mind.

"Get out of my head." He tried to convey anger instead of affection, but his boss knew him to well.

"Just go take care of her without starting a new war? Leave that kind of trouble-making to your sister."

Chapter 9

Please Eat

Charlie White Bear blinked big, brown eyes at Dani as he waved a plastic food container under her nose. "Anna threatened to make me sleep on the couch if I didn't get you to eat. It's your favorite and it's still warm."

Dani gave him sideways glance and continued stripping mint leaves from the stems and placing them into a large glass jar.

"She was serious, Danielle." He tucked his hat under one arm as he retied the ponytail holding his thick, black hair, untouched by gray, although he was in his late forties. "I don't like sleeping on the couch. I'm too tall – my feet hang off the edge and get cold."

She counted to ten before glaring at him.

He quickly picked up the dish and blinked at her as he held it out.

"I'm perfectly capable of taking care of myself," she said. "I've done so since my parents died."

"Then you can call Anna and convince her," Charlie said. "I tried, but she didn't believe me."

"Not my problem." Dani stuffed the last few leaves into the glass jar and poured in enough grain alcohol to cover the leaves. She tapped the jar on the counter to get the air bubbles out and then tightly screwed on a lid.

"Why are you doing that?" he asked.

"Making a tincture." She filled out a label with the contents and the date. "I use them in some of my soaps and lotions."

"Waste of good alcohol if you ask me." He grimaced and waited until she put the jar away in her workshop and then pushed his container at her again, trying to lead her to the table.

"Now you can eat. It's lunchtime, you've finished what you were doing, and you'll keep me out of trouble."

She growled with exasperation. "I'm not hungry, Charlie."

"You're never hungry." A grin of triumph lifted the corners of his mouth. He helped her into a wooden chair and went to get a fork. "This is Anna's famous chicken noodle casserole. I know you like it." He pulled the lid off the container and put the utensil in her hand. "It's very obvious you're not taking care of yourself and we all care far too much about you to allow the situation to continue." He plopped his large body down across from her and leaned on his crossed arms to glare down at her. "I'll sit here until you eat, or I'm going to sit on you and force you to eat. Those are your only two choices."

"I had breakfast." She tried to protest.

"When?" He snorted with disbelief. "Three days ago?"

Her face heated, and he shook his head in irritation.

"Danielle, you're obviously losing weight again. You look like you haven't seen the sun in three years, and the bags under your eyes are huge. You're not taking care of yourself and if you don't want Anna coming out here to drag you home with her, you will eat lunch and then take a nap."

She let out her breath in a large sigh before taking a reluctant bite of the casserole. Charlie watched silently until she'd made a fair amount of progress and then poured her a glass of orange juice, snagging coffee for himself.

"Thanks," he said as she chased the last noodle around the dish. "I appreciate this. I honestly dreaded not sleeping in my own bed tonight."

"You know that wouldn't happen."

He choked on his coffee. "You obviously don't know my Anna as well as you think you do. She was on the warpath. Consider yourself lucky I kept her from coming out here to force-feed you herself. She's only a couple of rumors away from dragging you up to our farm until everything settles back down."

Dani pushed the empty container away with a contented sigh, conscious the gnawing ache in her gut was gone. She'd been hungrier than she realized. She had also enjoyed the food much more than she had expected to.

"Wait. What rumors?" His words sank in and she demanded details. "Who's talking about me?"

The older man looked around, avoiding her eyes. "Where's the dog?" he asked.

"She's out chasing rabbits. What rumors?"

"Are you sure that's safe?" he asked.

"My dog is fine." Each word was distinct. "What rumors are you talking about?"

He shrugged uncomfortably. "That investigator."

"What about him?" she asked. "He's already been by here." A cold knot of anxiety settled in her gut.

"The guy keeps asking about you and your guest."

Dani leaned her head against the back of her chair and growled under her breath. "What is his problem?"

"He wants to find the guy he's looking for."

She looked at Charlie. "Lateef isn't that guy. Why won't he move on?"

"How do you know?"

"I talked to him. Lateef isn't from around here and hasn't run out on any family."

"I'm sure he wouldn't admit something like that to a stranger."

"I know he isn't that kind of person."

Charlie studied her face and heat flowed across her cheeks as guilt flooded her system. "There's nothing for you to worry about. I'm not infatuated with the man. And besides, he's gone for good. I have no way to get in touch with him."

He nodded, but his expression remained skeptical.

"Come on, Charlie. You know me. I'm never going to find love again. I can't take another heartbreak, and I certainly don't want to risk another crazy family."

His face softened. "Don't rule anything out, Danielle. Carl was an okay guy, but what you had with him wasn't the best you can have."

Anger stirred in her gut.

Charlie shifted in his chair. "Don't get me wrong. I'm not knocking Carl, but it was obvious he didn't care about you nearly as much as you cared about him."

She closed her eyes, fists clenched in her lap as she fought the desire to run from the awkward conversation. Charlie wasn't wrong. Carl hadn't been capable of caring too much about anyone other than himself, but he had loved her and Caitlyn.

"Besides, I think the investigator is more interested in you, and he's easy to contact. I have his phone number." Charlie's tone turned sly and a grin spread across his weathered face.

"He shouldn't be snooping around me." Her head snapped up and she glared at her friend. "You all need to leave me alone and stop trying to force me to do things I don't want to do."

"Danielle, we all care about you." He appeared stunned at her outburst. "I know you don't think anyone should, but we do. So deal, because you can't change us."

She snarled silently and took the empty food container to the sink to wash out. "Tell Anna thank you for me." She dried the bowl and handed him the clean dish. "I do appreciate the food, but I want to be left alone."

"Anna's not your problem."

"I know that," she snapped. "But she's not helping."

"She's doing the best she can."

"I know that too." Dani leaned against the counter, trying to calm her racing heart. "I love her dearly, but I can take care of myself. I have to. Tell her thank you for me and I'll visit soon. I have a new Shea butter soap for her to try, but right now I need some time alone."

His sympathetic look immediately raised all her hackles.

"I'm afraid that might not be so easy," he said. "There's a reporter from Denver in town looking for the mysterious 'Chef of the Mountains'."

Dani felt the heat drain from her head and white spots bloomed across her vision. "I can't go through that again."

"He doesn't know who you are." Charlie grabbed her arms as she swayed. "We broke the links to your past when we got you out of the hospital. I've talked to Bob, but you know he won't willingly mention you if there's a chance of publicity for his cheese. I'm tracking down Holly next. She needs to get that food reporter to back off."

"None of that will matter." The whiny edge of self-pity in her voice made her clamp her teeth shut. "The calls will start again, and someone'll find my real name. Then they'll make the connection to Carl and Howard and the accident will be in the news again. I don't want to have to leave this place, Charlie."

"Then don't answer the phone without knowing who it is." His forceful, no-nonsense tone broke through her rising panic. "I can get a service to screen your calls and we can get someone to stay with you. You don't have to do this alone."

Dani forced herself to slow her breathing.

"It's okay," she said, unsure exactly who she was trying to convince. "Even if he finds me, I'll be okay. I have to be. I'm strong enough to tell him to go away. I don't owe him anything."

Abby's sudden frantic barking was drowned out by the sound of a car coming down the driveway. Dani's knees weakened.

"Wait here." Charlie made sure she was able to stand on her own. "I'll take care of it."

He went to the front room and looked out the bay window. He shook his head. "Just that Manning guy. I'll go talk to him. You can get some rest."

"Yeah, right. That's not going to happen."

Charlie shot her a grin before walking out on the veranda, firmly shutting the door behind him.

Dani watched through the window as Charlie leaned against the doorframe with his arms crossed across his massive chest to glare at the unannounced visitor. Abby took one look at him and dashed back into the woods.

"Afternoon, Sheriff." Kyle walked up to the steps of the large porch carrying a pair of coffee cups from Ernie's coffeehouse.

"Afternoon." Charlie's single word answer held no warmth

Kyle hesitated briefly. "Is Ms. Hamilton in?" he asked.

"Yes."

Kyle waited a long moment and finally shrugged. "May I talk to her?"

"Why?"

Kyle gave a strangled laugh, shaking his head. "I could say it's because I'm conducting an investigation."

"But that isn't why you want to see her, is it?" Sheriff White Bear retorted. He uncrossed his arms and pushed his hat back on his head before resting one beefy hand on his belt, close to the butt of his gun.

"No." Kyle's answer was reluctant, and he was no longer able to meet the older man's eyes.

Charlie studied him for several seconds, apparently coming to a favorable decision. "Come on up." He moved aside to open the door. "Don't expect too warm a welcome. I told her about the reporter looking for her."

Kyle immediately bristled, nearly dropping the cups as his hand moved toward the gun on his hip. His voice deepened with menace as his narrowed gaze carefully studied the area around the house. "Why is a reporter looking for her?"

Charlie raised thick eyebrows. "Someone told him what a superb cook we have in town. Apparently now he's on a quest to find the source."

Several emotions flashed across the agent's face. "But this guy doesn't know who she is?" he asked.

The sheriff nodded.

"Then she should be okay. But I'll stick around to keep an eye on her."

"To keep an eye on whom?" Dani stepped into the doorway, no longer willing to be a spectator. "Why are you two standing out here? And where is Abby?"

As if her name had summoned her, the little dog tore out of the underbrush as if an entire herd of mountain lions was chasing her. She dashed up the steps and ran into the house, nearly bowling over the three humans. Both men immediately turned to find the threat, but the early afternoon remained still and quiet, except for the whimpering barks coming from the kitchen.

Dani finally broke the tense tableau by stepping out onto the veranda. "Weird," she said. She looked back into the house, but Abby was nowhere to be seen. "She's never done anything like that before. Must have found one of those imaginary monsters she's always barking at."

"Why don't we go take a look around, Sheriff?" Kyle suggested. He handed the coffee cups to Dani.

"What's this?" She automatically accepted the warm cups.

"Caramel macchiato." Kyle grinned. "I thought you could use a treat in return for feeding me the other day."

"I warned you about feeding strays," Charlie said, barely loud enough for her to hear.

She shot him an amused glance before thanking the agent. Kyle nodded and turned to the woods, one hand still on the butt of his gun, with Charlie close behind.

"Don't know what they think they're going to find out there." She took the cups back into the house and set them on the table. She went over to the dog bed to check on her frightened companion, surprised to see the dog had her narrow head buried under the cushion, trying to shove her entire body in the small space.

"What is wrong, Abby-girl?" Concern made her hands shake as she sank to the floor to hug the frightened animal. Abby resisted for a couple of seconds and then buried her nose under Dani's arm.

Dani held her, whispering encouragement until the tremors eased and the dog finally looked at her. "What did you get into?" She examined the dog, running her hands along the slender legs and through the long fur, looking for an injury of any sort. She found no cuts or porcupine quills or swollen areas that could be from any kind of bite. The dog didn't smell like she had found an irritated skunk and if she'd disturbed a hornet nest the persistent insects would still be chasing her.

"Maybe the guys will find something." She went to the pantry to pull out a treat. A couple of fake bacon strips and dog biscuits later, Dani was able to walk without tripping over the rattled dog and she went to stare out the front window. She considered going out to look for the men, but an unshakable certainty she would be better off staying in the house kept her behind the closed door.

A low, buzzing hum began and she shook her head to clear the sound. A malevolent presence caught her attention and she briefly tried to focus on the menace. Sweat popped out on her body as she recognized the shadow from her nightmares, but that was pushed aside by a new danger. Her mind pulled into a tight ball, concentrating on the frantic thud-whoosh of blood against her eardrums to hide from the disembodied threat. She leaned against the closed door, trying to be invisible. Her breath came in short gasps as she put her hands over her ears. *What's happening?*

'It's okay. Stay inside and you'll be safe.'

Lateef's strong presence enveloped her like a blanket, and she eased into his imagined embrace. Her eyes closed as she remembered how alive he made her feel. She missed him more than she wanted to admit. Dani took a deep breath. She was finally losing her mind.

'There's no need for you to remember this. Let the memory go and sleep, my dear Danielle. I'll keep watch.'

Dani felt her head bounce as if she had nodded off. She looked around guiltily, but she was alone in her living room, except for the dog. She remembered the coffee Kyle had brought.

"Might as well drink it before it gets cold. Be a shame to waste a good macchiato." She took a tentative sip before curling up into the cushions in the big window seat of her front bay window and watched the yard as she sipped the caramel-coffee drink.

As angry as she had been at Charlie and Kyle for disturbing her, she was glad they were here now. A vague memory of fear tickled the back of her brain but vanished as soon as she acknowledged it. She hoped the men found a raccoon, or feral dog pack, or anything to explain her sheltie's odd behavior, but she knew things couldn't be so simple. Abby now lay with her long nose across Dani's legs, staring out and whuffing occasionally as her eyes constantly scanned the quiet landscape.

"You're barking at the wind now." Dani ruffled her ears. Abby rolled her eyes up, gave her fingers a lick and then resumed her watch, ears twitching constantly.

Dani shrugged and leaned back against the wall. She knew she should be working but sitting still for a few moments was nice. Her head dropped forward. She jerked up, but the house was exactly the same. Birdsong filled the previous silence along with the occasional grunts of an angry squirrel. She thought about drinking more coffee, but it was too much effort. Exhaustion tugged at her limbs. She set the cup down and snuggled further down into the pillows.

Chapter 10

I Only Gave Her One Bite

The low rumble of a male voice pulled Danielle from a sound sleep. She recognized Kyle Manning's quiet baritone, but could only catch a few random words, not enough to understand the conversation. She shifted and roused as she realized she had been covered with a blanket from the couch and Abby's warm weight was no longer draped across her legs.

She slowly stretched and came wide awake as she saw the long shadows of a setting sun stretched across the front yard. Just as she swung her legs around, she remembered the coffee cup she had put on the floor, but the cup was no longer there. Stifling a yawn, she tossed the blanket over the back of the beige leather couch and headed toward the kitchen on silent, bare feet.

"Yes, sir, I do understand the situation. I'll send you a report as soon as I can confirm... No, sir. Things are a bit complicated right now."

Dani peeked around the corner, hoping to hear more of the conversation, but Kyle saw her, giving her a warm smile as he motioned for her to come in.

"I'll call you back later. I know what I need to do." He pushed the end button on his phone and grinned at her, but she saw the raw irritation flashing through his dark eyes.

"Turn the microwave on." He waved at the stainless-steel appliance.

She checked to find out her caramel drink was in there, ready to be warmed back up. She hit start, then leaned against the counter, watching the agent suspiciously. *Can't believe Charlie left me alone with this guy. He's usually more protective than that. Hope that doesn't mean they found something I need to worry about.* Abby rubbed against her legs to get some attention before bounding back to sit patiently at the PI's feet.

"Must have fed the dog," she said.

"It was only one bite of my scone." His tone was defensive as he glared at the hopeful animal. "Two hours ago."

"Abby has a long memory for suckers." Dani pulled the cup out of the microwave and sat across the table from her uninvited guest.

"And I have sucker written all over me?" His light tone matched the mischievous smirk.

"I don't see it." She took a cautious sip of the hot beverage. "But I don't live for food like some furry critters I know."

His warm laughter filled the kitchen. She was surprised to realize all of the anger and terror consuming her earlier in the day seemed to be gone and she felt at peace for the first time since the accident. *What happened to me during my nap?*

"Did you find what scared the mutt?" she asked.

"No." He shook his head as he slipped his phone into a pocket of the dark suit jacket slung across the back of his chair. "We found a clearing with a bunch of funky footprints and some big feathers all around, but no sign of mountain lions or bears or anything. The dog was fine when we came back. Nearly took my leg off when we walked in. Good thing Sheriff White Bear was with me."

"Figures." Dani shot her dog a dark look. "Probably saw a butterfly and imagined a monster dinosaur."

Kyle laughed at her. "I never knew monster dinosaurs were indigenous to the Rocky Mountains."

"I've never seen one, but Fluffybrain here has had several run-ins. Although, this afternoon was the scariest ever."

"Then I'm glad we didn't find it."

They shared a comfortable silence for several minutes as she drank her coffee.

She broke the quiet. "Not to seem ungrateful or anything, but why are you here?"

"I wanted to repay you for the cake the other day. I stopped at Ernie's and he mentioned you liked caramel, so I thought a macchiato would be nice." His expression was innocence personified, but she felt undercurrents of some emotion she couldn't quite identify coming from him.

She studied him skeptically. "And that's all? You and Charlie seemed to be in a bit of a standoff before rushing off to be heroes."

Kyle blushed slightly. "It's a guy thing."

"Like ignoring his advice to leave me alone?"

He shrugged noncommittally.

"Don't intend to take his advice, do you?"

He flashed a heart-breakingly sweet smile. "I'm afraid I can't leave you alone. At least not until we find out exactly what's going on around here."

"I make soap," she said. "That's about as exciting as things get."

"And your dog sees monster dinosaurs. That's pretty exciting."

Dani groaned and let her breath out in a long hiss. "Only if you're a dog. Otherwise all you see are bugs and squirrels with the occasional raccoon or maybe a fox or porcupine if you're unlucky. Somehow doesn't seem worth pulling a PI up from Denver."

"And yet, here I am. Maybe Abby can show me one of her monsters."

"That would be quite the shock." Dani sighed again. For someone who wanted to be alone she sure had an overabundance of men in her life suddenly. But only one made her heart beat faster. She shook off the unwelcome thought, determined to get rid of her present company and get her routine back on track.

"Thanks for the coffee and for watching things while I took a nap." She couldn't stop the flush of shame moving up her neck. She still couldn't believe she had slept all afternoon with a stranger in her kitchen. She must have really needed the rest. She'd have to talk to Charlie about leaving her unconscious with a stranger, though. That wasn't cool.

"The sheriff threatened to hang me up by my balls if I let you be disturbed." The blond agent said, as if she had spoken aloud. "Told me my job was to make sure you slept for as long as you could and feed you dinner. That's why I ordered pizza."

She had to smother a grin at the satisfied look on his handsome face.

"Abby said you like either the chicken Alfredo or the margarita pizza, so I got one of each. Should be here any minute now."

"Abby told you?"

His grin widened, and his eyes sparkled with wicked delight. "Took some work, but I finally convinced her to talk to me. I am a trained investigator after all."

"Did you have to threaten her with your gun?"

He waggled his eyebrows and shrugged. "Won't admit to anything," he said. "I'm like a magician. Can't reveal my secrets."

Sunlight beat against Dani's head as she carefully packed bunches of anise hyssop into a box. Sweat trickled down her back and she straightened, lifting the heavy braid off her neck as a slight breeze shifted the oppressive air. The first hints of fall cooled the night, but the days were still as warm as mid-summer.

Kyle slowly moved through the garden, a determined look of concentration on his face as he pulled weeds. A sudden wish that Lateef was still around instead crossed her mind.

"Better get that boy a hat before he fries."

Dani jumped as Bob Saunders ambled up. Abby darted over for an enthusiastic greeting.

"If he gets sun-burned he'll have to leave." The anger in her tone surprised her and she forced a smile for her neighbor. "I tell him to go home, but he won't. He's convinced he'll discover some secret if he hangs out here long enough."

"So why is he working for you? It's been a few days now."

"To give me a minute to myself." She swiped a stray lock of hair behind her ear, a scowl on her face. "I don't want him here. I need to get caught up on my business. I have a ton of soap to process for the Christmas rush. And I picked up a new client who needs a whole line of custom Valentine toiletries I have to design and get approved."

"Sure you don't need some more help?"

She shrugged. "If you know someone I don't have to train or supervise, maybe. Unskilled help... no. Takes too long to get them going."

The older man gave a disgruntled snort. "Thanks for the herbs." He picked up the box. "Got a cheese shop down in Denver interested in the anise hyssop line. Some food writer from the *Post* wandered into the shop and fell in love with it. Drove all the way up here just to talk to me and Mary about the business. Had a nice little write up about us in the Sunday paper last week."

Dani felt a line of cold move down her body. "You didn't mention me, did you?"

A faint flush flashed over Bob's weathered face and he refused to meet her eyes. "No, I told him everything was local, but didn't go into details. Sorry."

"No, that's perfect. Congratulations on the nice press. I really am happy for you. Tell Mary hi for me, won't you? I'll see you later." She knew she was babbling but couldn't stop the flood of words tumbling past her stiff lips.

"Do you know when you'll have some more hyssop for me?" Bob asked before she could bolt.

"A couple of weeks." Her breath caught in her lungs as she fought the urge to run and hide. "I'll let you know."

She forced her feet to follow him around the house and wait until the old van had trundled down the gravel driveway. Charlie was right. Bob wouldn't tell anyone about her. Not when he was trying to promote his own business. He was a good neighbor, but his own self-interest came well before any thought of helping someone else. That certain knowledge helped her keep the panic at bay until the van was nearly out of sight. Then she broke and ran into her workshop.

She didn't want to be forced from her home. But she couldn't bear the thought of being revealed by something as stupid as a mention in a newspaper article. Or the days of harassment by the media that would follow on the heels of her unmasking. While she was still in the hospital, constant calls from reporters asking personal questions had caused the staff to remove her phone so she could get some rest while she healed. *Carl's father can't connect me to a newspaper article about herbed goat cheese. I'm still safe.* She grabbed the lock and started to turn it, but the thought of Kyle freaking out if he found the door locked stopped her. She'd rather risk the unlikely appearance of a reporter than the certain over-reaction of the PI. She curled into a ball on the floor, back against the door and fought to push the irrational fear away. *Just keep breathing and everything will work out. It has to. I am strong enough to tell him no this time. He can't make me do anything. I won't be a victim.* She thought she heard a masculine chuckle, but that had to be her imagination.

Chapter 11

I Thought it Wasn't Safe for You

Lateef teleported to a spot in Dani's dark backyard, shifting the large box he carried as he walked toward the back door. He could see her through the window as she sat at the kitchen table, working on her computer although it was two in the morning. *No wonder she's tired. The woman doesn't sleep.*

He had tried to stay away and monitor her from a distance to ensure he didn't destroy the life she'd made for herself, but he couldn't concentrate. He hadn't been so uncomfortable in his own skin since before he learned how to block out foreign thoughts. And despite Rissa's teasing, the persistent PI wasn't responsible for his decision to come tonight.

I'm only here to deliver a thank you gift. Then I'll find someplace nearby to hole up and watch until the Hatti leave and I know Dani's safe. They can't spend much more time looking for me on Earth. Not sure why they don't believe the report from our Embassy that I've returned home.

He stared through the kitchen door window, working up the courage to knock when Abby lifted her head to woof at him. She gave him a quick doggy grin of approval and settled back to sleep on her bed. He knew the instant Dani became consciously aware of his presence. Her gaze met his and the rest of the universe ceased to exist. Worry for her safety faded as their souls connected.

Dani rose to her feet and crossed the kitchen toward him.

The journey seemed to take forever as doubts crept into his mind. Her expression was not friendly. Had he misread her feelings for him? His thoughts raced until she opened the door to stare at him. He could sense her pulse pounding and his heart rate sped to match. He swallowed hard, unable to produce a sound as he took in the sight of her. Only a few days had passed and yet her jeans hung on her narrow hips and the bags under her eyes looked like dark bruises.

"I thought it wasn't safe for you to be here."

He winced at the bite in her tone. "My presence is dangerous for you if I'm caught, but the Hatti aren't here now, so we should be safe."

"Why are you here? You made the fact you got what you needed from me pretty clear when you left."

"I have a surprise for you." He ignored the pain in his chest caused by her angry words. With a fake smile, he carried the box to the table. "And I've been watching over you like I promised. I won't let you pay the price for my mistakes. I owe you that much since I brought the danger to the area."

"What does that mean?" She frowned as she stared at him intently. "And what makes you think you owe me anything? You've already thanked me for the crash space."

He sat across the table from her with a sigh. "Dani…" He paused, searching for the right words. "I…" He sighed again. *This is so much harder looking into her eyes. The whole speech went so smoothly back in my quarters. And she wasn't nearly as pissed off in my imagination.* "Let's just say I'm not from around here and I've irritated some people who are determined to get me."

Her eyebrows lifted and she let out a quick bark of a laugh. "Sounds like an understatement. What does that have to do with me?"

"The Hatti want to know how I escaped and where I'm hiding now. They don't believe I went back home. Since you didn't tell them the first time they came through, they might be a trifle irritated when they find out I was here."

Her back stiffened and her eyes sparkled with strong emotion. "If you mean the bald guys, then they've been here and I told them nothing because they asked nothing. They just bowed and apologized for not having a guest gift, whatever that means. Not threatening behavior unless you have a completely different definition than I do."

Lateef fought the desire to shake some sense into her. He knew his tone was harsh, but he couldn't avoid revealing some of his pent-up anger. "Danielle, that's the point. You impressed them, so they will return and you don't know what could set them off. They're touchy about the strangest things. I was an invited guest at a formal function when they turned on me."

"Maybe they had good reason. You can be very irritating." Her jaw clenched, and she looked away from him for a moment, her shoulders rising with each rapid breath.

He pushed his annoyance at her irrational behavior down. He couldn't expect her to trust him even though he felt like he had known her his entire life. *Rissa's right, damn her. I am infatuated.* He had to be careful and give Dani space to realize she cared about him, or she would run again. *I can't lose her.*

She gathered her hair up and flipped it into a ponytail in a nervous gesture, looking everywhere but at him. "If they come back, I'll feed them again. It's not a big deal."

"And if they ask about me?" His voice sounded calm to his ears, not revealing any of the turmoil churning his gut.

"I'll tell them I found you in the woods, let you stay for a few days and you left. The bare simple truth, just like you told me."

A low growl escaped his chest, and he leaned forward to rest his elbows on the table. *She's so stubborn. Why won't she listen?* He had to force her to understand. "You don't realize how dangerous they are, no matter how harmless they look in those ridiculous suits and hats. The friend who invited me to the Hatti feast is missing. No one's caught a whisper of a rumor about his whereabouts. I fear he's injured or dead because of me. I hate to think what the Hatti would do to you if you thwart them. Unlike Trevan, you don't even have diplomatic protection."

"I don't care." She shook her head in denial. "I don't want to hear what you know about them. They've met almost everyone in town and there were no reports of injuries or threats or missing people. Whatever your problem with them is, it's between you guys."

He snarled a nasty word under his breath, shaking with anger before he could get his reaction under control. *Won't win a head-on battle. Time to rethink my strategy.* His scowl faded. Time for a distraction.

"I brought a gift to thank you for your help." His unexpected change of topics derailed the argument.

He watched her fear fade into delight as he pulled out a variety of seedlings, plus two larger plants from the box.

Dani's smile was contagious as she examined the offering. Not all of them were the well-known green or odd-ball reddish-purple she was familiar with.

Soon, the table held a veritable rainbow of leaf colors in all sizes and shapes, ranging from smooth and shiny to furry and velvety soft.

"They come from… several different places." He stumbled as he decided not to reveal the extra-planetary nature of the plants. She had to suspect his alien origins, but as long as he didn't confirm anything, they could pretend he was from Canada. The head botanist of the Alliance had chosen the plants for him, to ensure none would be noxious weeds on Terra. No one wanted a repeat of the kudzu fiasco. "Some have medicinal uses and some are culinary herbs." He pointed to a plant with large, purple-fuzz covered leaves. "This one's just pretty."

"Thank you," she said. Words seemed to desert her as she looked over the unexpected treasure.

Lateef's mood lightened as he described the light and temperature requirements and potential uses as she matched each plant to the printed instructions the head botanist had provided. Her enthusiasm was contagious. He hadn't expected her joy. *This is the first time I've ever seen her so relaxed.*

"This orange basil should work in a chicken dish. I hope it grows fast. I can't wait to experiment." She moved to the fuzzy purple plant. "I love this one. I have the perfect spot here in the dining room."

She grabbed a plate from the kitchen and set the pot on an empty end table. "It looks good there."

"It does. Where would you like the rest of them?"

"I have a sunny area in my workshop."

He returned the smaller plants to the box and followed her to the room which ran along the southern side of the house. A long, soapstone workbench took up most of the wall under a bank of windows that had a beautiful view during the day. Rolling racks lined the interior wall. He remembered from his earlier stay that the cabinets near the large sink were full of folded towels. Bottles of oils and other supplies filled shelves on another wall. Open shelves held packaged product ready for sale. Safety goggles and a white lab coat hung on pegs by the door. The room was neat and smelled fresh.

"You're very organized. This is a great workspace."

"I have to be. Some of the raw chemicals are dangerous. I don't want to unexpectedly find lye crystals scattered on the counter. Those suckers can cause some serious burns."

He grinned. "You don't have very many unexpected moments, do you?"

Her expression turned hard, and a wave of pain radiated from her that vanished as fast as he detected it.

He babbled to cover up his mistake. "I like that about you. You are the most grounded person I've ever met. Where do you want these?" *Idiot.* He berated himself. He knew she had lost her child unexpectedly. She pointed to the workbench. "This should get plenty of light. The windows are tinted so the sun shouldn't be too bright although maybe I will go ahead and buy some shades." A sense of unease filled the room as she stared at the reflective surface of the window as if searching for monsters in the night.

"Have you wanted curtains?" He caught her tension though he couldn't pinpoint the source. He sent out a tendril of thought, but only detected the normal creatures moving in the night.

She gave him a guarded smile as she spread out the array of plants. "Not really. I like looking up to find a deer staring in at me. I enjoy living up here more than I thought I would. Carl would have hated it even though the place was all his idea."

"This place suits you. I can't imagine you in a crowded city." He handed her the last plant, glad her unease had dissipated.

"Anna and Charlie have made me belong." She stared into the distance and her aura shifted, settling to a calm gold.

"I have to work tonight, but you don't have to leave. Do you mind hanging out for half an hour or so while I cut up a batch of soap? I can get you some coffee while you wait."

"I'm fine, thank you." Relief made his knees weak. She couldn't hate him if she wanted him to stay. As connected as he was with her, his inability to clearly read her feelings for him made him nuts. *Maybe that drug's still messing with my abilities? Have to ask Mellora, not that I'll admit anything.* "Abby and I'll chat."

She groaned. "Don't you try to tell me you can talk to the dog. Kyle already insisted Abby told him what kind of pizza I like."

A red haze filled his vision and his fists clenched.

"It didn't work," she said when he remained silent too long. "I know he called the place and asked what I'd ordered before."

The breath hissed out of his lungs and he recognized the unfamiliar emotion as jealousy. *Cut that out. You're a master healer, not a pimply faced teen.*

The dog padded over and stuck her nose in Lateef's crotch and he jumped. "That's enough, you." He scratched her ears, grateful for the distraction. "Do what you need to do and don't worry about us. We'll be okay and when you finish, we can celebrate with a treat."

She looked at him with raised eyebrows. "You buying?"

"I brought the surprise with me." He grinned.

"What is it?"

"Get your work done first, you slacker." He waved his hands in a shooing motion. "And hurry up—or I might not wait for you." He walked back to the kitchen, Abby at his heels.

He plopped into a chair and rested his chin on his hand, trying to decide how the visit was going. *Did I make up for walking out like I did? Is this Kyle guy a threat?* The emotions surging through his veins threw his serenity into chaos.

A soggy tennis ball landed in his lap and he looked up to see the dog's intense focus on him.

"Guess you're not interested in helping me sort out my feelings?"

She stood and leaned forward to bump his leg and then sat down, eyes darting between the yellow ball and his face.

He laughed. "I know what you want." He tossed the ball toward the back door, hoping Dani would be too busy to care about the thumps and nails scrabbling on the tile floor to come investigate. He knew she wouldn't appreciate a game of fetch in the house but didn't want to go outside so late at night.

Abby continued the game long enough his mind wandered. *Guess I ought to get the surprise I promised.* Rissa had given him a box of her favorite pastries before leaving for her last mission. He'd decided to leave them at home until he knew how Dani reacted to his visit.

He teleported back to his quarters on Beryl and took a few minutes to wash his hands and freshen up. He was reaching for the pastries when a wave of fear from Dani paralyzed him for a few precious seconds. *Why didn't I stay in closer contact?*

He teleported to the workshop doorway and cursed as the dog plowed into him, almost knocking him to the ground. Her piercing yips of terror hurt his ears. He regained his balance and looked up. Dani stood frozen, staring at the window. His gaze followed. A face from a nightmare stared at him through the glass, fangs extended as the giant nostrils expanded to take in his scent through the wall of windows. Feathers grew in a mane around the reptilian head and in a crest down the sinuous back to the long tail. Clawed feet held the sturdy body high off the ground. Huge yellow eyes glared at them through the glass.

The Hatti bloodhound was still on his trail, and he had led the monster to Dani. Time slowed as he sank into a trance and sent tendrils of psychic energy into the mind of the alien creature. He painted new memories of seeing him in the meadow where he had crashed as he erased any thought of Dani or this house. The Jangxing hissed, its eyes half-closed before turning to lumber back down the mountain. *Good thing most of its brainpower is used to process scents or we'd be screwed.*

Lateef kept his attention focused on the menace until he was certain his compulsion had replaced reality and the creature was leading its handlers away from them.

"What was that thing?" Dani's teeth chattered.

"I told you I had enemies." He crossed the room to wrap his arms around her, but he continued to concentrate on the Jangxing's departure, making sure it left.

She shuddered violently and leaned her head back against his shoulder, relaxing into his hold.

Once the Jangxing moved beyond the valley that held Dani's home, he pulled his attention back to his surroundings. *How can I explain this?*

Her shudders slowed.

"Let's go get you a hot drink." He relaxed his grip, and she stumbled.

"Dani?" He stared at the blood pooling on the bench as his mind gibbered in panic for a few seconds. He should have smelled that much blood. He pushed the emotions away, helping her to sit on the floor with her damaged hand elevated. Bright red blood pulsed with every heartbeat and he tightened his grip on a pressure point above her wrist. White bone gleamed through the slice across her wrist and hand.

He entered a healing trance. Dani's state of shock rattled his concentration. Usually, he had help in these situations, and someone else would reassure the patient as he worried about the mechanics of healing. He focused part of his attention on the damaged artery and coaxed the edges of the slit in the muscular tube to line up and re-seal. He blocked the pain impulses flowing to Dani's brain as he encouraged her.

'Stay with me, Dani. I can heal your wounds, but you have to help me.' He spoke mind to mind.

'Why doesn't it hurt?' Her mental voice was faint and she slumped to lie on the floor.

'I won't let it.'

The artery nicked by her knife was whole again. He released the pressure on her arm and checked to be certain. When no fresh blood pulsed into the wound, his attention turned to coaxing the finger to reattach, and all of the veins, nerves and muscle fibers to re-knit.

Her life faded despite his efforts. She hadn't lost that much blood, and yet her energy was fading. A shadowy figure shifted at the edge of his vision, but he wasn't sure if the shape was real or his imagination.

Dani's heartbeat stuttered and adrenaline flooded his system. All extraneous thoughts fled as he focused.

'Don't leave me, Dani!'

Chapter 12

It's Just a Dream

Dani watched Lateef work on her from her vantage point near the ceiling. It was like watching a movie about someone else until she saw Abby crouched on the floor beside her body. Guilt churned her gut. *Not like I have a choice. Glad Abby's not alone for this. Lateef'll take care of her.*

"I'm sorry." She tried to whisper, but no sound escaped her incorporeal lips. The room faded into a gray haze and she was content to float. *I'd forgotten how nice a lack of pain can be.* She hadn't realized just how much pain she'd been since the accident. The fog brightened, and a breeze gently propelled her forward. The hint of a child's laughter caught her attention.

"Caity." Joy surged through her at the thought of seeing her baby again. Pressure landed on her shoulder and she tensed. Carl's scent surrounded her—a spicy, musky fragrance she had created for him. The breeze reversed, and she fought the currents of air pushing her away from the sound of her daughter's happy babble.

"You don't belong here, Elle. Go home. It's not your time." Carl spun her around and shoved her.

"Caitlin." The scream ripped from her lips as the wind increased to a gale, forcing her further away from the light. "Caity." Her breath came in huge, heavy sobs as she was forced further from her beloved daughter. She lost all sense of direction as her body spun.

The wind halted, and she looked for the source of the bright light. A monotonous haze filled every direction. The only sound around was her own blood pounding in her ears.

"No." The sound, half protest, half defeated sob tore from her throat and she collapsed to her knees. Her body shook with the force of her crying, but the mist absorbed all sound.

An eternity passed, and her tears slowed. Exhaustion dragged at her limbs and she got to her feet to stare dully around her, wondering if this was all the afterlife had to offer. A faint noise caught her attention, and she realized someone called her name. Carl? As soon as the thought crossed her mind, she knew she was wrong. There was a warmth to this tone Carl never had. Her body wanted to follow the voice.

An overwhelming compulsion to look for the light re-energized her. Then an irrational fear clawed at her and she tried to move away from the sound. She shifted her insubstantial body a few feet, but the relentless voice sunk hooks into her soul. She recognized Lateef, and the panic subsided. A growl vibrated the mist as she stopped resisting Lateef's pull.

She looked around for the source of the menace, but her surroundings remained blank. Then she heard breathing. She whirled to face the sound. A blurry figure solidified. At first, the shape reminded her of the shadow from her nightmares, but then the darkness morphed into Carl, although something about the way the man stood nagged at her subconscious.

"It's okay, Elle."

"Carl." His familiar voice caressed her, and she forgot all the bad times. "I thought you died."

He tugged her into an embrace, controlling her movements. "Aren't you glad to see me? It's been forever."

She took a deep breath at his attempted domination. He didn't smell right. Instead of the spice, she caught a whiff of sulfur. The spell shattered. She shoved against his chest get some space. "Where's Caitlin? Isn't she here, too?"

"She's fine, honey." He pulled her back in, his hold on the edge of discomfort. Irritation filled his voice. "It's not always possible to do things on your schedule, Danielle."

"I didn't... You just sent me..." Words failed her. Even in death, Carl had to be in charge. *If this is Carl?* Confusion slowed her thoughts as she struggled to reconcile the contradictory actions of this man who looked like her late husband.

"Of course you didn't mean anything." He gripped her shoulders and crouched a bit to meet her gaze. "Quit trying to turn your guilt into a virtue, Danielle. None of us has the power of life and death. You aren't the center of the universe."

Dani hesitated at the naked emotion in his comment. Carl never revealed the anger she knew he kept bottled up behind the jovial façade he presented to the world.

"I don't believe I am. I need to see my baby again, Carl. She shouldn't have died."

"You're right, Elle. You should have been alone when the car failed. That was the plan."

Dani blinked, stepping back as she tried to process the change in the man she had once loved. His bright eyes held shadows and the set of his jaw seemed wrong. "I didn't force you to come to the trade show."

"You are mine, Danielle Weatherly." Fierce jealousy flashed in Carl's blue eyes. "And no one can ever change that." He once again tugged her into a tight embrace, his lips demanding a deep kiss from her. "You will always belong to me and don't you dare forget it."

She endured his affection, gathering her energy to accomplish her true aim. He broke contact and her knees wobbled as he pushed her away. His body turned gauzy and Dani clung to him. "Don't go. Please don't leave me, Carl. I need to see Caity." She sobbed as his form faded from her fingers. "I want my baby." His smirk mocked her in the seconds before he vanished.

A bone-chilling cold enveloped her in an icy blast. She huddled into herself, her arms aching to hold her lost child. She blinked the tears from her eyes and realized she stood in the corner of her workshop. Her body was stretched out on the floor in a large pool of blood. Lateef knelt beside her with his head bowed, both hands spread over a horrible gash across her hand and wrist. Color spread from his contact. She moved closer when she realized she could feel heat on her disconnected body where the color was on her real body. Before she could understand what was happening, a silver cord shot from her navel and pulled her into her physical body with an audible snap. She moaned in protest.

"Danielle." Lateef smiled in relief. "I thought I lost you."

She opened her eyes and Abby bounced up to lick her face. She held up her hands to push the excited dog away.

"Back off, Abby," Lateef commanded.

To Dani's great surprise, the dog obeyed his stern command.

Lateef turned his attention to Dani.

"Are you okay?" he asked.

"I'm not sure." The weakness in her voice surprised her. She tried to lift her head, but it was too heavy.

"You sliced open your hand." Lateef took on a professional air. "Cut the muscle and nicked an artery. Nearly lost a couple of fingers. I didn't know if I could heal the vessel in time. You lost a lot of blood before I knew you were hurt."

She blinked slowly, trying to process the information. She heard everything—and the words seemed English, but it didn't make sense.

He gave her a sad smile and ran a hand across her left hand and wrist, following the path the knife had taken. The skin was tender but didn't hurt as much as she expected from her past experiences with cuts.

"Let's get you to bed. You need to rest." He picked her up and walked up the stairs.

Her head swam with the motion, but his grip steadied her. Once by her bed, he had her stand beside him as he pulled the blankets down. She glanced at her arm, but the skin looked normal—only a faint red line tracing the knife's path.

"How is this possible?"

He silently tucked her in.

She gave him the space he obviously needed. His grief and guilt pushed against her skin like a smothering weight and she ignored the emotional cloud as long as she could. "Lateef?"

He sat on the edge of the bed, avoiding contact.

"What happened?" she asked.

He met her gaze, and she could see exhaustion in the depths of his blue eyes. "I was running from the Hatti." His tone was clinical though the subject was bizarre. "I'd gotten away when my life boat crashed. They have these creatures called Jangxing they use to track fugitives. That's what you saw in the window."

"That monster didn't come from Earth."

His throat worked as he swallowed then sat up straight and met her gaze. "No, it didn't. And the Hatti are not from Earth although they lived here in the ancient past." He stared at her. "I'm not from here, either."

Dani stilled with shock. Part of her accepted the premise, but that part was deep in her subconscious. The same part of her mind that allowed her to accept all the odd things without question.

"Danielle?" he prompted when she grew cold and silent. He touched her head, then swore.

Her eyes twitched, and the bed swayed like a boat in a storm.

"Let's slide you down." Lateef's voice was an anchor in the chaos. He pulled her legs, raising them up and dropping her head. He propped her feet up on a pile of pillows and ran from the room. We he returned he held a straw to her lips. "Drink this." He forced her to drink until the room steadied. "You lost a lot of blood. It'll take a few days until the fluid volume is replaced. I can speed the process up, but it will still take time."

"Where's the cut?" Curiosity returned as her head cleared.

"I'm a healer." The sheer matter-of-factness to his statement made him believable. "I healed it."

Dani stared at him then shook her head. She must be dreaming. Her breath caught in her chest as she remembered Carl.

"I died." It was more a statement than a question.

"Only for a minute."

The anguish in his voice drew her gaze to him.

He sat beside her again and took one of her chilled hands into his. "I didn't think there was any Hatti activity in the area and I got complacent. I needed to throw the Jangxing off your trail, but I should have made sure you were okay first."

"What would this Jang... this thing have done to us?" She asked.

"I don't think it would have come into the house, although they can be tenacious," he said. "But it would let the Hatti associate you with me. I gave the creature a false memory, so it will remember me, but not you or this place."

"What about you?" she asked. Maybe it would be safe for him to stay. His presence soothed her soul.

One side of his mouth quirked up. "I'll be fine."

"Where is home?" she asked.

He laid a hand on her forehead and a wave of exhaustion washed over her.

"Far away from here." His voice grew quieter, and her eyes drifted closed. "I hope I can take you there someday."

"I'd like that." She didn't know if she spoke aloud. She thought warm lips brushed across her cheek as she allowed the warm darkness to envelop her, hoping her nightmares were over.

Chapter 13

You Continue to Amaze

You continue to amaze me, little one. Just when I thought you had provided all the energy I could get from you, you recover. My Apirri swore you were about to cross death's threshold. And instead you brought me a new toy to play to with. I'll use the new human's feelings to increase your pain. It will be lovely.

I'm glad the Beryllian scum is as talented as his reputation claims. I almost had both of you, but I'm content to extend our time together.

I'll come for you soon. This brief period of hope will make the ending ever so much more satisfying.

Chapter 14

Just Another Excuse

Kyle relaxed in one of the wooden chairs on Dani's veranda, enjoying a mug of cinnamon coffee while he texted instructions to his admin. Cheerful music floated on the warm air and he shook his head, puzzled by the drastic change in Dani's mood. He needed to get home and line up some new clients, but he couldn't ignore the mystery in this quaint, mountain town.

Thanks to trying for too long to satisfy a now-ex girlfriend whose champagne tastes had demolished his beer budget, he badly needed the money the senator promised. But after getting to know Dani, he no longer wanted to let the arrogant jerk get his hands on her. He tried to tell himself he wasn't positive about her identity, but it was a lie. When he arrived this morning, there had been a photo of a beautiful young girl, about three-years-old who was a dead ringer for the kid his client claimed was his grand-daughter.

He was finding excuses harder to come up with when his admin asked when he was coming home. His client's poll numbers were slipping. The rumor that he had killed an inconvenient daughter-in-law didn't help.

Just another excuse. The answer came from his subconscious. *Got to quit falling for the pretty, yet potentially crazy ones.* That was how he ended up in a financial crunch to start with.

The low growl of an engine coming up the long drive ended his internal conversation. He turned his phone off to ensure he wouldn't attract the Sheriff's attention with any untoward notifications. He wouldn't be surprised to have the man snag his phone and check his messages if he got interested enough.

Charlie White Bear climbed the veranda steps, tilting his head in confusion. "What is that noise?"

"Black Light Effect's *Never Again*," Kyle said. "From their 'Greatest Hits' album."

"I recognize the group." Charlie glared at him. "I meant I've never heard music here before. Or anything, really—I didn't think Dani even owned a radio or television."

"She found an internet radio station," Kyle explained. "It's strange. I came over yesterday and she was acting tired and a bit off and then today… I dug through the trash looking for the pod."

The older man gave him a puzzled look. "The pod?"

"From the alien that replaced her? You know, like in that body snatcher movie?"

"I heard you." Dani stood in the front door. "I have not been taken over by aliens."

"How are you doing?" Charlie turned his attention to her. "Anna wants to come by in the next couple of days to get your advice on soap or bubble bath or something girly."

Dani's mouth twisted into a smile. "Girly stuff, huh? Tell her to come by Friday. I should have things under control by then. Unless, of course, the alien pod people do come by and then she'll have to take her chances."

Kyle stared at her, having trouble coming to grips with the sudden personality shift. Dani had always been friendly in a reserved sort of way, but now the constant shadow of sorrow was gone. He adored this confident woman, and had no desire to see this spirit crushed by her father-in-law.

She grinned at them. "I've seen my share of science fiction movies. I'm not totally ignorant of the culture." She shook her head when they continued to stare.

"Want some coffee, Charlie? I've got blueberry muffins to go with it. And if you two need to compare notes I could work on lunch. Got a bunch of fresh trout I have to use or freeze."

"No, thank you." Charlie's refusal was full of regret. "I can't stay—although I wouldn't mind a muffin to go."

Dani laughed. "I'll be right back."

"What did you do?" Charlie whispered as he turned on Kyle.

"What do you mean?" Kyle leaned away from the intense stare in the sheriff's eyes.

"Dani's alive again. I haven't seen this woman since before... well since the first time I met her and her family." A shadow of sorrow passed over his face.

"You knew her husband and child?" Kyle kept his tone casual, hoping to get more information from the normally secretive sheriff.

Charlie held up a hand, looking quickly to make sure Dani was not eavesdropping. "We don't talk about them around here."

Kyle nodded thoughtfully. He'd wondered how the senator's daughter-in-law had vanished from the hospital without a trace. Dedicated friends able to keep a secret could be the answer to the mystery. He decided to muddy the waters a bit. "I think someone else has been here when we're all gone."

"Why?" The sheriff turned on him, no longer the friend, but a grizzly roused early from hibernation.

Kyle wondered if he had miscalculated. "Nothing definite." He decided against mentioning the bloody rags he'd found in the trash. He'd saved one for DNA testing, but wasn't sure he wanted to know who had lost so much blood. *Can't be Dani's, or she'd be in the hospital. The idea of her harming someone else is ridiculous, and yet... Maybe I'd better leave sleeping bears to snore.* "I'll stay close and keep an eye on things, I promise."

Charlie studied him for a long moment. "You armed?"

Kyle snorted disdainfully. "Of course."

"Oh, for heaven's sake," Danielle grumbled as she stepped out onto the porch with a bag. "Will you two please quit sniffing around each other? I can take care of myself. As much as I appreciate the sentiment, I don't need a father or big brother to keep me safe."

Charlie straightened with a guilty look at her return.

"Here you go." She handed the bag to the sheriff.

He took it in his strong hands and gave her a puzzled glance at the weight.

"There's enough to share with your deputies and to give Anna one. Make sure she gets it, okay?"

She added the last line as a look of happy greed crossed his face.

"Thank you." He tipped his hat to her. "Everything okay out this way?"

"No problems." She rubbed absently at her left hand.

"Will you call if there is a problem?"

She turned a brilliant smile on him. "You'll be the first one I call if I run into something I can't handle."

"That's not what I meant, young lady."

"I know, but it's the best I can do."

He gave her a long look and then turned. "I'll tell Anna she can come out. And you let me know if you need anything."

"Will do," she said. "Thank you."

Dani leaned against the door frame as she watched him drive away. The dog whined from inside the screen door.

"You need to stay there, Abby," she said. "I don't want you to run into another monster dinosaur."

"Did you see it?" Kyle hoped to startle her into revealing something that would help him decide what to do. He had to find a way to please his nasty client enough to pay him without putting her into danger.

She merely glanced at him out of the corner of her eye. "Depends on which one you mean," she said. "The butterfly or the raccoon?"

"The one that was outside of your workroom." He stifled his satisfaction as she turned to look at him in surprise.

"What do you mean?"

"What did you see out there?" He was confident he was on to something. "You put up curtains and I saw some weird footprints on the ground near the house."

"I got tired of the afternoon sun in my eyes." She turned back to the door in an obvious gesture of dismissal.

"And you won't let the dog run free anymore." He slowly rose to his feet to walk closer. He was onto something, he could feel it.

"She doesn't always run wild. She likes to stay home sometimes."

He opened his mouth to push her, but she suddenly stiffened, looking to the west for several minutes and then darted inside without another word.

His gaze shifted between the empty horizon and the house, but he couldn't see anything to cause such a strange reaction. He followed her to the kitchen.

"You need to leave," she said as soon as he walked in. She pulled an amazing variety of food out of the fridge and pantry. "Trout for the main protein, and a fresh salad and maybe..." her voice trailed off as she rummaged around in the pantry.

"What are you doing?" Kyle demanded. He followed her so closely she bumped into him when she turned around, nearly dropping a bag of flour.

"Company's coming." She pushed him out of the way gently. "I don't have much time."

He tried to make her stop, but she side-stepped his attempt and headed for the pantry. "If you won't leave, then be useful. Wash and peel these, please." She handed him a stack of purple, red and white potatoes, guided him to the sink and handed him a peeler, rushing on to another task before he could get a question out.

He could see strands of panic in her eyes, so he decided to help. *At least I'll be here to take care of any problems. The worst thing that could happen is we have to either freeze a bunch of food or have a party. This is pretty strange.* He peeled the huge stack of potatoes, as she slammed around the kitchen.

"Okay, all done." Kyle dumped a bowl of peeled potatoes into the sink with a loud clang. "What's going on, Danielle?" She looked calm. *What did I miss?*

She gave him a bright smile. "Grab a bunch of different ripe tomatoes from the garden, please?"

He accepted a bowl and trudged out to the garden, hoping he could figure out which plants were tomatoes. Fortune smiled on him and he had no trouble recognizing the correct plants, but the fruit came in a variety of sizes, shapes and colors. Finally, he resorted to grabbing a few from each plant, figuring green was still growing and yellow or red was actually ripe. He stopped when the bowl was nearly full and heavy.

When he returned to the kitchen, she was tossing the last handful of chopped potatoes into a pan of melted butter.

"Thanks, keep an eye on the potatoes for me? Give them a stir every couple of seconds. I need to grab some herbs." She thrust the spoon into Kyle's hand and ran out the door, leaving him speechless.

Before he could get too worried, she returned and dumped the batch of leaves and stems into a colander and rinsed them before taking the spoon to check the progress of the potatoes. She sprinkled salt and some other seasonings into the pan. "Keep stirring every few minutes. I don't want them to burn."

Kyle watched as she fileted the fish, moving with a practiced grace and speed that freaked him out. "Remind me not to piss you off."

She froze in the process of chopping some green plant and stared at him with wrinkled brows.

"I've never seen anyone use a knife like that. Are you positive you're not some ninja assassin?"

Laughter bubbled out of her chest, lightening the mood of the house. "That has to be the most ridiculous thing I've ever been accused of. I have a lot of practice on vegetables."

"Just vegetables, huh?" He gulped audibly. "I saw what you did to the poor trout."

Dani shook her head, her hands never slowing as she started a second dish. She cut the tomatoes, tore up chunks of fresh mozzarella cheese and some green herb, then poured balsamic vinegar over the top.

Her movements slowed as everything seemed to be close to done and he tried to get some answers.

"What are we doing here, Dani?" He put a snap of command into his tone and she glared at him.

"I can't explain right now. Get some plates and silverware and put them on the table please." The wind shifted and she lifted her head to listen. Abby whuffled by the door. Dani turned back to Kyle and placed a hand on his shoulder to meet his gaze. "You need to leave," she pleaded. "I can't explain why, but you'll be safe if you go now."

"Danielle." His voice took on a husky timbre that caught him by surprise. "I want to protect you, not be protected by you."

"Not your job." Her expression started out angry, but soon softened to concern. "I don't need anything from you. Please go home and take my thanks for your help."

She darted around him to pull the last trout off the grill to place on a bed of fresh lettuce.

"I don't care if you want anything from me." Kyle followed her to the stove but kept a distance. *Won't get anywhere by antagonizing her.* "I need to know if there's something dangerous going on. If I need to leave, then so do you."

They glared at each other, frozen for several seconds, until Abby began barking ferociously at the back door.

Dani's face went stark white and she swayed. "It's too late. You'd never get far enough away." She took a deep breath and stared him in the eyes. "Please don't say anything. Just help serve lunch and don't volunteer any information. Don't tell any lies—not even a little white one. If they ask any questions, give the shortest answer you can, but make sure it's the truth, okay?"

He studied her face intently, looking for a clue, but came up empty. The fear in her expression made him decide to follow her instructions for now. He hoped he wouldn't have to drag her off to find a psychiatrist. *I'd worry more if I didn't feel like some evil spirit lurked out there. I hope she's not bonkers, because otherwise I'll have to worry about myself.* He made light of the bizarre feeling but couldn't shake the desire to constantly check over his shoulder.

He heard her quiet sigh of relief as he went to gather plates. *Hope she doesn't think I'm letting this go so easy.* Once the plates and silverware were stacked beside the napkins, he helped carry the fragrant platters of food to the table. His mouth watered and he managed to sneak a couple of bites when her back was turned. *I could definitely get used to eating like this. Probably have to get a bunch of larger suits, but I'd make the sacrifice.*

Once all the platters were on the table, she rearranged a few, wiping drops off the edges of some and adding sprigs of herbs to others until the table looked like some edible art project. He had never before appreciated how much work and thought went into a fancy meal. Of course, he hadn't eaten very many fancy meals before.

A loud knock came from the door and he jumped. Despite everything he hadn't expected anyone to show up. How had she known?

Dani brushed her hair back with trembling fingers, and ran her hands down her legs, smoothing imaginary wrinkles out of her pants. She threw him a warning look then walked to the door.

He took a step to follow, then decided to let her run the show. He walked to the far side of the table where he would have an unobstructed view of anyone in the kitchen and subtly checked his weapon was easily accessible.

She gave him a final glance and opened the door wide. "Perfect timing. Lunch is ready."

"Oh no." The exclamation of dismay came from the tallest of three man, all dressed in the same cheap, gray pinstripe suits with identical baseball caps perched on top of their slightly too-large heads. All three men held elaborately decorated wooden boxes in their arms, and Kyle could see other men in the yard beyond the porch.

Dani stared with open-mouthed shock at the boxes for several moments until the man on the right sniffed in appreciation.

"Come in." She motioned toward the table. "Lunch is ready for you."

"You don't understand, Master Chef." The strange man's brow's pinched together. "We have come to pay our debt, not to incur another."

Dani frowned. "You didn't owe me anything."

All of the men bowed. "Yes, we did," he said. "You provided us with a priceless gift the last time we were here. And now we are here to attempt to repay our debt."

She stammered before getting a coherent sentence out. "I only shared breakfast with you."

The man stepped forward, holding out his box as an offering. "You are wrong, Chef. It was so much more. Very few are so willing to share bread with strangers."

Dani continued to stare at him, until Abby dashed out into the yard to sniff at the other men.

"What do you want?" she asked.

"To thank you." He gave her a deep bow.

Kyle noticed her knees shaking and began to cross the room, but stopped when the stranger's movement, revealed an unfamiliar weapon holstered at his side. *Damn it, Dani. Why are you letting armed strangers in your house? Hasn't that over-protective sheriff taught you anything?*

His fingers clenched into fists as he struggled with the desire to kick the green-tinged visitors out. He'd have to trust Dani knew what she was doing. For now, anyway. There would be time later to lecture her about basic safety precautions. His arm bumped his own holstered weapon and he checked to ensure his jacket was securely buttoned and made a mental note to be aware of the need to keep the gun hidden from the potentially hostile visitors.

The strange man held out the box toward Dani, a serious look on his too-large face. The solid-black eyes emphasized everything that was not quite right about the features. "I am Taltos, *gal gestin* to Hantili, Thane of the Kanesh Clan and I thank you for your hospitality and for the generous gift of your food."

"You are most sincerely welcome. What's in the box?" Her words were slow and she leaned away from the man.

"The smallest token of our respect." He lifted the hinged lid and she gasped in surprise at the sight. "These are liquors from our homeland." He motioned with his head and the next two men moved forward to open their boxes. "These are wines from some of the many different worlds we have visited."

The two men moved past her into the house and placed their boxes on the counter then went to stand by the table.

Kyle itched to move closer so he could see what was in the boxes the other men revealed to her, but the fear on Dani's face when she'd asked him not to make a scene made an impression. He'd have to wait till the bizarre strangers were gone, but he would see what made Dani smile with such obvious delight.

As the last man walked in, Taltos set his box on the ground at her feet and pulled a necklace of black pearls from his pocket. He bowed before placing the necklace around her neck. "This is a gift from Thane Hantili, the leader of Clan Kanesh, and Captain of the *Alalakh*. His duties did not allow him to come, but he hopes one day you may meet in person."

Dani stared at the necklace before smiling at the strange man and Kyle's heart lurched with an emotion he didn't recognize at the warmth in her expression. *Get a grip man. You can't be threatened by a geek with so many unpronounceable names. What's an Alalakh anyway?*

Kyle grudgingly helped Dani ensure everyone had servings of the grilled trout, potatoes and tomato salad. He began to fear his jaw would be permanently clenched as all of the men thanked her personally in a way that felt very inappropriate to him. There was no reason for them to touch her so often, and the virtual drooling was uncalled for. Stripper bouncers probably had less to worry about than he did. *This is a bit over the top. The last time I saw so much ado about food was the sap trying to keep a failed marriage together. And even he didn't drool this much.*

He did have to admire the way Dani adroitly avoided any question until Taltos pointed to her purple and pink furry plant.

"May I ask where you found the plant?" he asked.

Aha! I wondered about that one and the others in her workshop, too. Guess she didn't really get them at the local hardware store. He made a mental note of yet another question to be answered after the bizarre strangers left.

Dani looked where he pointed and a puzzled look appeared on her face. "A friend gave it to me," she said.

Taltos looked sharply at Kyle, half-rising from his chair.

"Not him," she quickly added.

Kyle snorted in derision from the other end of the table, although his heart pounded. This Taltos guy didn't seem to have much of a sense of humor. "I'll say." He gulped visibly as every eye in the room focused intently on him. "I wouldn't think of bringing a plant to a gardener." He raised one hand defensively. "I haven't even brought her flowers. I couldn't find anything nicer than what's already in the yard."

She raised one eyebrow at him. "Is that your story?"

"Damn straight," he said with a nod. "It *is* my story and I'm sticking to it."

He gave her a look of smug pretension and she burst out laughing. She laid one hand on Taltos' shoulder for balance and he froze with an unreadable look in his too dark eyes before he smiled back.

"Thank you for the compliment, I think." Dani finally got her laughter under control. She shot Taltos a conspiratorial smile.

Kyle relaxed as the atmosphere lightened, but he wasn't certain the danger had passed. Whatever the danger was. He had to learn who these armed strangers were and why Dani was trying to placate them. What was she hiding, and why? And where did his client fit in?

Once the uninvited men were finally satiated, he helped her gather up the platters and took them over to the kitchen counter, exchanging them for a tray with coffee mugs and sugar and cream. He took a carafe of cinnamon coffee to pass out as she put together several berry shortcakes with fresh whipped cream.

"How many people in your group didn't get to come today?" she asked as she passed out the dessert.

"Why?" Suspicion filled Taltos' dark eyes.

"So I know how many plates to send back with you."

"That is not necessary." There seemed to be a bit of panic in the green-tinged face.

"Maybe not necessary," she agreed. "But it is the right thing to do. And I owe something more than thanks to Thane Hantili for his beautiful gift." She rubbed the pearls as she spoke.

"Then only one plate," Taltos readily agreed. She glared at him with her head tilted to one side.

"Don't tell me if it's some kind of deep, dark secret," she said. "I'll send all the leftovers with you."

She went back to the kitchen and pulled out a plastic divided plate with a lid and quickly arranged a liberal serving of everything, tucking sprigs of fresh herb leaves as a garnish. Kyle helped her transfer the rest of the feast from the platters into other storage containers, handing them to her to label each one with the contents.

"Truly, this is not necessary." Taltos joined them in the kitchen, shifting from foot to foot, his face flushed a dark green in obvious distress.

"Look." Dani continued to work as she spoke. "I live alone with only the occasional guest. There's no way I could eat this much food before it goes bad. If you need to, consider you're doing me a favor. Otherwise I'd have to throw a bunch away."

A gasp from the table caused Kyle to whirl, hand automatically reaching for his weapon. All of the men at the table wore identical expressions of horror.

"I wouldn't really throw food away." Dani held up her hands as if to ward off a physical blow. "But I do like to share with someone who'll enjoy it."

"Very well." Taltos reluctantly nodded his head. "We shall accept your gift, although once again we are in your debt."

The guests relaxed, settling back to finish the last of the coffee and desserts. Kyle slowly pulled his hand away from his waist, hoping no one had noticed his reflex. He was confident about his self-defense ability, but here he was out-numbered.

"Thank you." Dani appeared confused but determined to send the men off as quickly as possible. "Kyle, would you go to the wine cellar and get a couple of bottles of the Rocky Mountain Mead? They should be close to the stairs on the right."

Kyle nodded at her gesture to the basement stairs. He'd never been in that part of the house. *Probably only a few bottles down there. I've never seen her drink. Although given her reputation as a caterer, she should know a lot about wine. A* green glow illuminated the light switch on the wall at the bottom of the stairs, and he flipped the switch on to see a smallish room full of dusty boxes. At the far end was an elegant wooden door that screamed fancy wine cellar. He pushed the door open and paused in amazement at the inadequacy of calling this area a wine cellar. Cool air flowed past him and he gaped at the size of the area. Slate tiles covered the floor. The walls were lined with wooden racks filled with bottles of wine. Two nooks bulged out of the straight hallway and he could see a table and chairs in each. Bottles of whiskey adorned the walls of the nearest nook, and he recognized his client's favorite brand.

Focus. He quickly skimmed the labels of the nearby bottles, looking for the mead. *Don't want to leave Dani alone too long. There must be some kind of reason to the organization of all these bottles. What's wrong with red vs. white? Give me a can of beer any day.* He found bottles of a 2009 Cabernet Sauvignon and winced. Not the most expensive wine out there, but one he knew could easily be a hundred dollars a pop. And there were at least twelve bottles gathering dust in this basement.

This Carl seems just like his father. Hope he wasn't as awful to Dani as the senator appears to be.

Finally, he made his way to the right side of the cool room and found a section dedicated to all kinds of honey wine. "Damn, woman. Why couldn't you settle for a beer?" He peered at the labels on several bottles, trying to make sense of them. "Aha." One of the labels had Colorado honey wine right under the non-descriptive name.

He grabbed a bottle in each hand and headed back for the insanity upstairs. As much as he regretted leaving Dani alone with all those strange men, he had appreciated the brief time alone to try to wrap his head around events. He hadn't seriously thought aliens were in town, but these men were definitely not local. The feeling of barely contained violence in their posture made his skin crawl, and yet Dani seemed to think they were less dangerous than friendly dogs.

He, on the other hand, hadn't been sure he'd survive the question about the stupid furry plant. *Yet another mystery my client has dropped me into. Hope he stays away long enough for me to figure everything out. There's no way I'm turning her over to him.*

Kyle made noise as he re-entered the kitchen. *Don't want anyone getting surprised and killing me.*

His entrance was greeted with a tense silence until Dani turned and smiled. "Thank you, Kyle."

She held out a hand and glanced at the label. "Perfect. I'm glad you didn't have too much trouble."

She extended the bottles toward the head alien.

"This is a wine made with honey from a local winery. I want to give this bottle to you, Taltos, to thank you for your kindness and ask you give the other bottle to your Thane."

"Never before have I received such a welcome." Taltos muttered under his breath as he searched her face for the answer to some question he wouldn't ask. "Not even..." His voice trailed off as he shook himself out of his reverie. "I thank you, Master Chef Hamilton. Your gift is much appreciated."

The strange men lined up and did some kind of ritual where they held up their right hand, muttered something about food from the table while touching Dani's hand, then bowed on their way out the door. Kyle watched the process from the dining room, amazed she appeared so comfortable with the bizarre ceremony.

He gathered up a couple of dishes from the table as the last visitor walked out of the house. Abby padded at his side as he watched through the window over the sink, glad to see the last hint of gray suit disappearing through the trees.

"What was that all about? Who were those men?" Kyle demanded after they were finally alone. "How did they get here? I didn't see any cars. Did they walk carrying those boxes?" He gestured to the stack of decorated boxes the visitors had brought.

Dani ignored him as she methodically loaded the dishwasher. When her silence stretched on for too long he pushed his temper down and cleared the table. If she was going to be this way, he would bide his time and get a look at the contents of those boxes. Maybe then he'd get a clue.

She continued to ignore him, moving around him like he was another piece of furniture. When she gathered up the trash he resisted the urge to do the task. Abby followed her out into the yard.

He dashed for the boxes as soon as the back door closed. Lifting one lid, he was surprised to see several bottles filled with colored liquids. He pulled the cork out of one and sniffed. The scent of licorice filled the room. A quick glance confirmed he was still alone. He stuffed the cork back and looked at another box filled with filigree metal boxes. He thought he could see some kind of bag inside the metal but wasn't sure. No time to study too much. Curiosity gnawed at him as he looked at a third box. What could Dani be involved in? Drugs? Why else would someone bring her such obviously expensive stuff? Rows of jewelry stared back at him. One necklace with a charm of an animal shaped like a feathered lion caught his attention and he held it up. The craftsmanship was exceptional. *The damn thing looks alive.* Clever hinging allowed the charm to move with the illusion of reality, and the color seemed to be a part of the metal rather than painted on. He didn't recognize the material the fine chain was made of.

The sound of the backdoor opening made him jump and shove the necklace in his pocket as he closed the lid. *I'll send it to the office to be analyzed. Should be able to catch the UPS driver without too much trouble. Then we'll see what these guys are up to.*

Dani ignored him and began to wash pans in the sink.

Kyle growled under his breath. He was running out of time. The senator was anxious and his assistant concerned him. She seemed to be falling under the suave politician's spell. He wasn't positive he could trust her not to let the client know exactly where he was much longer. Maybe this mystery could be a distraction while he found a way to get the bastard off the trail he'd put the man on.

He strode across the kitchen to tower over his hostess. "Are you ready to tell me what that was all about?"

She didn't acknowledge his presence, continuing to scrub a spot on a pan.

"Danielle!" He grabbed her arm when she ignored him.

She stiffened and stared pointedly at his hand wrapped around her arm. Slowly she raised glittering eyes to glare at him. He released her and took a couple of involuntary steps back.

"I do not owe you anything." She dropped the pan into the soapy water and turned to face him. Water dripped from her hands, but she seemed oblivious. "I did not ask for your help and I have not invited you to stay here nor have I ever hinted I want your help."

He tried to interrupt, but she continued right over him.

"I don't care if you're a PI or some hot-shot reporter or the Lord High Muckety-Muck from some secret society. I answered your questions fully and to the best of my knowledge when you first showed up, and you still won't leave. Not my fault you don't believe those answers."

"You never told me about the aliens." He allowed some anger of his own show.

"What aliens?"

"The ones who just left!" His fingers itched with the desire to shake some sense into the obstinate woman.

"I told you about their first visit when you showed up, uninvited in my back yard. What proof do you have they're aliens?" Her face was flushed and her body trembled.

"Oh, come on. You can't tell me you fed lunch to a bunch of humans." He took another step back, feeling his temper rise too fast. How did this woman get so deeply under his skin?

Her icy glare felt like a kick to his gut.

"Those men ate my food and repaid my hospitality with an overabundance of gratitude and pleasure. They left when they were done and asked no questions and made no demands, unlike some people I know." She faltered, and her tone calmed fractionally. "I don't know where they come from, and I don't care. But I will not listen to anyone speak about them in a less than respectful manner." She glared at him in the sudden silence.

He found himself unable to meet her eyes as shame washed through his body.

"You need to go, Kyle. Thank you for your help this afternoon."

"But I need to protect you." The request sent anxiety in a quick wave, replacing the unexpected shame. He couldn't leave right now.

"From what?" Her fury grew with each word until she seemed to tower over him. "Bald men bearing gifts? I don't need you waltzing in here trying to worm your way into my life."

"I'm not..."

"Yes, you are." She cut him off. "I'll accept interference from Charlie and Anna because I owe them a debt I'll never be able to repay. But I have no obligation to you."

His anxiety fled. This was his chance to impress her. Something deep in his soul shifted and his desire became need. "But I have to take care of you, Danielle. You've touched my heart..."

"Stop right there." She held up her hands as if he was about to strike her. "I don't want to hear... I... I love my husband."

"But Carl's gone." Kyle spoke calmly. He had to remain here with her. Deep in his subconscious he wondered at the words coming out of his mouth. He felt like an observer trapped in his own body. He did feel an obligation to protect her from the senator, since he'd pointed the bastard to her trail, but that didn't mean he loved her, did it? A shadow passed over his eyes and the doubts vanished. He needed Dani and he had to protect her from the dangerous world no matter what she thought. "I'm sure Carl wouldn't want you to be alone for the rest of your life."

"SHUT UP!" Her entire body shook and her eyes blazed. "Do not say another word, Kyle Manning. You do not get to tell me what Carl would or would not want. You didn't know him and you don't know me. Now leave."

She flung out an arm to point at the door, refusing to look at him. He opened his mouth to protest and she shook her finger at the door. "GO!"

The dog growled, rushing at his legs and nipping at his ankles until he took a step toward the door.

"You need me, Dani. I'm only here to protect you." Tears stung his eyes at her rejection. Why couldn't she understand?

Her shoulders slumped and she stared at the floor, her long hair hiding her face.

Hope flared and he prepared to gather her up in a big hug, ignoring the dog still snapping at his heels.

"No, Kyle. I don't need you. I don't want you, either. Go back to Denver and forget you ever came here. That's what I need."

Her quiet words hit him like a bullet to the chest and he staggered as the breath whooshed out of his lungs. *This can't be happening. She can't reject me like this.* Anger burbled in the depths of his soul, and his hands clenched into fists. He stalked toward her, but tripped over the dog.

The red haze obscuring his sight cleared and he saw the fear on Dani's pale face. Suddenly he was back in control of his actions. "Oh my god. I'm so sorry. I don't know what came over me. I didn't..." His tongue stumbled over the flood of words.

She merely stared at him, eyes wide and hands raised to ward off the anticipated blow.

Kyle ran, pursued by the faint sounds of her sobs. He'd go back to his hotel, get stupid drunk and take a cold shower. Then maybe he could figure out the whole ridiculous mess and figure out why his emotions were crazed as a pubescent teen's. And maybe figure out how he could possibly have considered beating the woman who had been so kind to him.

Chapter 15

Why Are You Here?

Dani wrapped her freshly-filled soap mold with a towel and bumped into Lateef for the third time that night. She closed her eyes and grumbled under her breath before glaring at him.

"Why are you here, Lateef? Why did you come here in the first place and why do you keep coming back if things here are supposed to be so dangerous for you? I thought you went home days ago." She absently ran the strand of black pearls through her fingers as she spoke.

Lateef stared at the pearls, a plethora of emotions swimming through his dark eyes. "It's hard to explain."

Dani gave an irritated growl and put the last of her soap-making materials away. She checked on the plants she had growing in the window. *I will not look outside. There's no monster waiting.* She was adamant, although her fingers itched to twitch the curtains aside.

"How are they doing?" Lateef joined her at the window.

"Might actually have enough leaves to try pretty soon." She ran her fingers over the seedlings, enjoying at the released scents. "I'm eager to try the orange basil in a salad."

"Sounds good." He stared at the plants. "You seem more interested in food prep than your soaps lately. Any reason in particular?"

She turned to face him, leaning against the counter. *This passive-aggressive crap is old.* "Is there a reason you can't ask a straight question? What do you really want to know?"

A brief flash of irritation moved through his blue eyes.

She smiled to herself, not in the mood to make anything easy on anyone—especially not her disturbing guest. Even if his presence lightened her existence.

His grin was too bright and reassuring. "I am always straight-forward, unless circumstances demand otherwise. Sometimes I have to come at a subject sideways to make my patients comfortable."

Anger stiffened her spine. "So, you think I'm just one of your patients?"

"No." His rapid response drained some of her irrational anger. He ran a hand through his hair as he began to pace. "That came out all wrong."

"Ask me what you want to know, Lateef. I'm not in the mood for games, especially not since Kyle went..." She swore under her breath and turned away, unwilling to tell him about her current problems.

"What did Kyle Manning do to get banned from your house?" Anger flashed in his warm eyes, though the emotion was muted, as if he already knew the answer.

"He overstepped his bounds." Talk about the understatement of the year. Kyle had banged on her door off and on for three days until Anna read him the riot act. Dani's face burned with shame at her inability to handle such a simple issue. She should have been able to take care of the bastard herself.

"In what way?" Lateef pushed too hard. She exploded.

"I thought you knew everything. That you were 'watching' me all the time." Dani couldn't stop the rush of angry words.

"I said I would keep you safe from the Hatti, not your boyfriend."

Dani's head flew back and she blinked rapidly. The air in her lungs grew heavy and her vision narrowed to a tunnel of light filled with black spots. Anger slowly replaced the shock.

Abby charged into the room, dashing between the two of them repeatedly before pressing against Dani's legs with a confused whine. Lateef sank back against the worktable, his face to the ground.

"I am sorry, Danielle. I don't have any right to speak to you that way." He raked his fingers through his hair. "I've never met anyone who makes me so stupid." He buried his face in his hands for a long moment.

Dani's uncharacteristic anger slowly faded, replaced by snippets of memories of the shadowy figure that haunted her dreams. She forced the mental image away as her pulse slowed. She refused to let that figure control her thoughts. Lateef wasn't Kyle. She wasn't sure Kyle was Kyle at this point. His sudden obsession with her was bizarre. He'd gone from irritating to psychotic in a few minutes. She hoped Anna's lecture was enough to keep him away.

"Let's go have some coffee, and you can try to explain. Life makes more sense with caffeine." She turned her back on the hopeful flash in his eyes, leaving him to follow behind her.

She waited until a pot of coffee had brewed and cinnamon coffeecake had been sliced and they were settled at the large wooden table before starting the conversation again. Her body was numb, as if all of her emotions had drained out. Now was the time for the truth, no matter how painful. From her as well as Lateef. He'd have to go forever if they couldn't be honest with each other, no matter how her heart felt.

"So, who are you?" she asked.

"Lateef D'Oro," he answered lightly. "This coffeecake's really good!"

"We are way beyond the point where flattery will do you any good. So, spill it. Who—or should I say what are you and why are you here?"

His grin wilted at her impatient look. "I am Lateef." He hunched his shoulders defensively.

"I believe you," she said. "That's not what I'm asking about."

"Then what do you want to know?"

She glared at him, tears in her eyes. "I'm so tired of games. I need some straight answers. I don't want to hear about how you're trying to protect me or it's too dangerous or you care too much." She stumbled to a halt at the last sentence. His gaze intensified and she felt trapped, aware she had said far too much.

"I do care, Danielle Hamilton." His voice was husky and his expression far more serious than she had ever before seen on him. "I care a great deal about you. That's why I'm here and why I keep coming back. And I promise I care enough to leave and never return if you want me to."

Dani was surprised at the sizzle of pain zapping through her heart at the thought of never seeing him again. Up until now she hadn't thought his absence would matter—that she wanted him to go away. She'd been hiding from reality. He made her feel whole again, but she was afraid to let him know. She chose her next words carefully.

"Why would you have to leave?"

"It's complicated," he hedged.

She laughed aloud, startling Abby awake. The dog lifted her head and stared for a long moment and then heaved herself out of her bed and came over to lay her head in Lateef's lap.

"Traitor," Dani muttered.

Lateef stroked the silky fur and sipped his coffee.

"I'm not from your planet."

She rolled her eyes at him. "I believe you mentioned that last time you were here. I don't know if I should believe you or not." Parts of the night she had died were still a bit fuzzy, but the memory of his revelation of alien origins was sharp enough she'd doubted its reality. "On one hand I'm pretty sure you're like no one else I've ever seen, so the whole ET idea's believable, but no one has ever proven we're not alone in the universe."

"What kind of proof do you need?" Irritation flitted across his expressive face. "Spaceship landings on live TV?"

"Maybe," she retorted. "And a few, verified by reliable sources stories wouldn't hurt either."

"Who would you consider a reliable source?"

She caught the trace of sarcasm in his tone. She opened her mouth to reply but couldn't think of a single example. "I'm not sure." Her admission came unwillingly, each word separate and distinct. "It's been a while since I've trusted anyone."

"Do you trust me?" he asked.

She hid behind her coffee mug, seriously considering the question. He waited until she finally met his gaze directly.

"Yes," she said. "I do trust you, although I can't come up with any reason why I should."

He smiled. Lateef always smiled, but this time he glowed as if the sun had returned after a hurricane and all was right with the universe. His joy was contagious and Dani found her own lips curving up as her heart skipped a few beats.

"I knew you were special," he murmured, more to himself than to her. He took a deep breath and then took another sip of coffee.

"You're stalling," she accused him.

He nodded. "I know. I'm afraid."

"Of what?"

"That you won't be able to deal with what I need to tell you."

"Lateef." She paused, searching for the right words. "Unless you're some kind of psychopathic serial killer who tortures small children for entertainment, you won't convince me to hate you."

"It's nothing like that." His overly hasty denial almost broke the somber mood.

"Then what's the problem?"

"I'm... Are you positive you really want the whole truth?" he blurted. "I can create a story you can live with and then leave and you can go back to your life and things can stay the way they are for you."

She looked at him, somehow knowing this decision would change the course of the rest of her life. The universe paused, waiting for her response.

"I don't want to go back to the way I was." The admission came slowly. "I want to hate you for making me feel again, but I can't. The night I died, I saw Carl." She paused, fighting to speak around the lump in her throat. "I don't know if he was real." She interrupted him as he opened his mouth. "It doesn't matter either way. Even if he was only my imagination, he made me realize I can't hide out here waiting to die." She stared down at her lap where her hands were tightly entwined.

"Immediately after running Kyle off my land, Anna tore into me. She pointed out I've been hiding from everything, so I haven't had to actually deal with my loss. I haven't wanted to." Hot, slow tears dripped onto her clenched hands. "I'm not sure I can stand to lose anyone else I care about."

"That's not living."

"I know." She suppressed the flare of irritation at his therapeutic tone. "I'm aware I'm hiding and I can't ever forget why. But I can't bear the thought of being hurt again. Losing my Caity tore me apart. It should have been me, and that hurt so much more than any of my injuries." She closed her eyes and took a deep breath. This was so difficult to talk about and yet, the more she spoke, the better she felt. She could feel the bands of depression loosening—a totally different response than she had received from her formal therapy at the hospital.

"The easiest solution was to refuse to care about anyone or anything. If no one truly mattered, then I couldn't be devastated when they left." She met his concerned blue eyes. "You're not like anyone I've ever known before. I know next to nothing about you and yet I feel like I've known you forever. I can tell when you're close and I'm lonely when you're gone. It's like a part of me is missing when you're not nearby. I thought I loved Carl until... but what I feel about you? It's so much more. It's overwhelming and I'm not sure I like it."

Lateef slumped at her explanation. He took a deep breath and gave her a huge smile. "That's the way I feel about you. I was afraid... well, I thought I might be imagining things. I can't stay away from you, Dani. When I'm gone, I feel like I lost an internal organ or something."

Dani returned his stare for a few seconds before something shifted in her mind. The shadow dogging her every movement blew away like a leaf on a gale. Light bloomed, and hope flowed through her veins for the first time since she woke in the hospital. The loss of her baby still hurt, but it was a distant ache, rather than the overwhelming pain she was used to.

Laughter bubbled out of her chest. "An internal organ?"

"You'd prefer being a limb?" He feigned indignation. "I can live without a leg. Surviving without a liver is a different story."

"I pour my heart out to you and you tell me I'm like your liver?" she asked. "Do you know what the liver does?"

It was his turn to glare. "How often do I have to remind you I'm a healer?"

"It might help if you defined healer. I'm familiar with faith healers and quacks and..."

He was at her side before she was aware he had moved. "I think you remember what I am." He took her hands and gently pulled her to her feet, all signs of playfulness gone. "Unless you refuse to be honest with yourself, you remember the night in the workshop and you know what I'm capable of."

She stared up into his eyes, breathless with the intense emotion hiding behind his calm exterior. "I remember," she managed to whisper. "I don't understand, but I remember."

He pulled her tightly into his chest and kept her gaze. "I'm not from Earth," he said.

"I know."

He beamed. "And you're okay with that?"

"Maybe." She shrugged, suddenly serious again. "But right now, I don't care. And last week I didn't care, and I can't see caring much next week, or even next year, as long as you don't leave me alone."

"I don't think I could leave you," he whispered, trembling with strong emotion. "I tried. I shouldn't be here now."

"Why not?" She clutched at him as if he would disappear on her.

"Because the Hatti are still looking for me." He touched her necklace before meeting her eyes again. "These pearls are secreted by oysters from their ancestral planet, one of the few non-edible items they cultivate without regard to culinary properties. They're only given to the most highly regarded chefs."

"They really are aliens from outer space?"

Her outraged and astonished tone caught him by surprise and he dissolved into laughter, holding on to her to keep from collapsing.

"What?" She shoved at him to get some space between them, but an unfamiliar smile made her face hurt. It had been so long since she had felt this carefree, and not even the knowledge of aliens in town could dull her joy.

"You have no trouble believing I'm from another planet." He struggled to get the words out between bouts of laughter. "But you're surprised the tall, bald guys with big heads and a food fetish are not from Canada?"

"I never thought they were from Canada," she denied. "I just... well, I knew they weren't local, but... I didn't want Kyle to be right."

Lateef sobered quickly. "What does that guy know about it?" He was serious, but underneath she could feel his undying love for her. She realized the emotion had been there for a long time, but she hadn't allowed herself to notice before now.

"I'm not sure he knows anything. He was here when Taltos came back a couple of days ago and..."

"The PI met the Hatti?" He interrupted her, all amusement fled from his face.

She nodded, surprised at his reaction. "I tried to get him to leave before they arrived, but he wouldn't go."

"You knew they were coming?" A puzzled yet pleased look on his face. "How long before they got here?"

She shrugged. "I don't know—long enough to get lunch ready."

"You fed them again?"

So many conflicting emotions swirled through her she couldn't tell if he was amazed or angry. "It's what I do, Lateef. Food kept them off balance before."

He stared at her and she blushed.

"Okay." She plopped back down in her seat and picked up her mug to hold like a shield as she avoided his eyes. "They enjoyed breakfast so much I couldn't resist the idea of getting such a great reaction again."

He snorted and she glared at him. "It's your fault," she countered.

"How do you figure?"

"You made me care again. If I hadn't met you, I'd still be wrapped up in my own little world instead of caring about what some random aliens thought about my cooking."

"Then I have done a very good thing." His voice dropped to a husky whisper and she felt his intense desire wrap around her body like a wildfire.

She met his heated gaze. The rush of emotions flooding through her was so intense she didn't know how to handle them. And some of them didn't feel like hers. She held one hand up to ward off the unfamiliar feelings and Lateef turned away. Her hand went to her chest as she felt muted and empty. Was this what her life had become?

Lateef refilled their mugs and then settled across the table from her. His hands shook, but his expression was blank. The next move would be up to her.

Dani stared into her coffee, trying to decide if she was willing to risk feeling again, no matter how wonderful it was. Life was too dangerous to care about people. *I don't think I can stand losing everyone again. It's so much easier to be alone.*

Chapter 16

I Promise You'll Never Be Alone Again

Lateef heard her internal anguish, despite his mental shields. The concern was so strong he had to reassure her. She was coming out of her self-imposed isolation and he couldn't let her slide back into despair. "You will never be alone again, Danielle, I promise you." He reached across the table to take one of her trembling hands in his.

"You can't keep that promise. No one can." Dani pulled away, taking several deep breaths as her face became a mask. "I didn't mean that to come out like an accusation. I know things happen beyond our control."

He held tighter as she tried to pull her hand away. *Can't let her back off now, or I might not ever get her to admit she needs people around. That she needs me as much as I need her.* "Dani, I promise you'll never be alone again. I have a large family and they won't abandon you either."

Dani snorted disagreement. "Hasn't been my experience. Families are the source of my problems, not the solution." She snapped her lips shut and pulled her hand free as she looked away from him.

Sweat beaded on Lateef's brow as the possibility of rejection grew. Dani wouldn't look at him. He longed to reach out for her mind with his. There was no room for misunderstanding with direct mental contact, but the next move had to be hers. He couldn't force her to love him. His heart hammered in his chest as the silence stretched.

She took a deep breath and met his gaze. "You were going to tell me who you are."

His pulse stuttered before settling back into a normal rhythm. He could sense no rejection in her posture. Hope began to flutter in his gut as he answered. "There's so much to talk about I'm not sure where to start."

"How about from the beginning?"

"But what is the beginning?" he countered. He looked over her shoulder to stare out the window, trying to get his chaotic thoughts in some kind of order. Despite the sudden lightness in her aura, he knew she was fragile.

"Tell me why you were in this area." Dani took another sip of coffee. "Then we can go from there."

She held the cup in both hands, but he could see the contents sloshing as her hands shook. He decided on a course of action and met her gaze. "I guess you'll have to find everything out eventually."

"Only if you want to stick around."

He grunted as the threat hit him like a physical blow. She couldn't deny him now, could she?

A frown furrowed her brow. "How are you doing that?" she asked.

"What?" Cautious optimism returned and he wiped off drops of sweat on his face.

"Making me feel your emotions?"

"What do you mean?" He stared at her intently, all thought of his own concerns gone. She had psychic potential and her aura had changed dramatically in the time he'd known her, but was that enough to allow her to fully live in his world? He'd happily stay with her on Earth, but options would be wonderful.

"Right now, I could feel a brief surge of panic and denial that wasn't mine. I could read the emotions on your face. I can't do things like that."

Relief flooded his system and he couldn't stop the huge grin hijacking his face. She had abilities that would help her fit in with his family. Not that they wouldn't love her for his sake, but she wouldn't feel like she was so different at family gatherings.

"And now you're pleased as punch about something. Spill." Her expression lit up her beautiful face.

"You'll love my family," he said. "They'll be crazy about you."

"Why do you think I want to meet your family?" A frown creased her forehead.

"Because you like me." His grin deepened. She wasn't ready to admit it yet, but she was his. He could afford to be patient.

"I don't know you, and knowing your name isn't enough," she said over his effort to introduce himself again. "I need more."

"But you already know more than you realize," he said. "You can feel my emotions—you know when I'm telling you the truth and you can tell where I am. And," he grinned broadly at her. "You miss me when I'm not here."

"You're impossible." Dani hopped to her feet to pace across the dining room. "For all I know you're a fugitive from justice and those sweet bald men are the police."

His mirth vanished and he suddenly sat straighter. *That was worse than a bucket of ice water. Step carefully.* "Do you believe that?"

She met his gaze. "No." She shook her head. "I don't seriously believe you could be a criminal. But you're asking me to accept an awful lot of things on faith."

"I'm Master Healer Lateef D'Oro." His pulse raced. All of his attention focused on her face as he fought for his future. He couldn't lose her. "I'm the youngest of seven kids. I'm a healer, but I also travel on business for my planet. My mother's currently the leader of Beryl, but all that means is I get in more trouble because we're all supposed to be perfect." He paused to give her time to digest this information.

She remained motionless, letting him continue.

"My people have been at war with the Falgarans for longer than I've been alive. We have allies, since the Falgarans tend to be pretty nasty to everyone they run across and I occasionally work to gain new allies. Sometimes things don't work out as well as I'd like." He broke eye contact and stood to pace himself. The next few moments could make or break him.

"I was invited to an event with the Hatti when things went sideways. While I was making a strategic retreat, I felt you and had to stop."

Her look dripped skepticism. "You felt me from outer space in a space ship traveling fast enough to travel interplanetary distances? I'm a sci-fi fan. I'm familiar with best guesses about planetary physics and how faster-than-light travel isn't possible."

"We were already in this solar system. The Hatti are returning to Earth for a visit. They used to live in the Middle East a millennium or so ago," he said. "And

I'm not an engineer, but travel between systems works fine. Doesn't even take years, but teleportation is much faster. That's how we usually travel."

"You can teleport? Why were you in a ship then?"

"The Hatti have developed a shield that blocks psychic abilities. While I was getting into a life pod, I was shot with a bolt poisoned with a drug that did the same thing, so I couldn't teleport or call for help until the drug wore off. You were the first connection I made."

Her expression clearly revealed her doubt. "So how did you 'feel' me? Especially when you were blocked and nowhere near this planet?"

He leaned on the table, staring into her warm eyes. "This is so not going where I expected. I'm trying to tell you who I am and why I'm here and you keep derailing me."

"How is any of this my fault?" Her cheeks flamed red. "I was running my business and all of a sudden I have some PI banging on my door like a stalker, a bunch of strange men bringing me extravagant gifts and you. It's a bit much to take in and all of your explanations create more confusion instead of answering any questions."

"What kind of gifts?" Dread stiffened his back. Could this situation get any worse? He thought she was done with the Hatti, but he had learned enough to know the strange, food-obsessed race was not free with praise. He had never heard of them giving out gifts.

"See?" She threw up her hands. "Always more questions instead of answers."

"What gifts?" He slipped into healer mode, determined to learn every fact he needed to fix the situation, no matter how reluctant the patient was to tell him everything.

She looked away and rolled her shoulders. "I'm not sure. Things got weird after lunch, so I stuck the boxes in the closet."

"Weird how?" He pushed, though he sensed her reluctance to talk about the situation.

"Kyle got pushy. He demanded answers I didn't have and then he said he…" She snapped her mouth closed and started to clear the table.

"What did he say?" Lateef was afraid he knew the answer and fought the urge to hunt the bastard down.

"It doesn't matter." She carried the dishes to the sink.

He followed, stopping just close enough their auras almost touched. Forcing all of his violent emotions down, he pushed calm at her. She needed his help to deal with the situation, not to have him storming around like a rabid bull. *I'll deal with Kyle later.* The promise made being rational easier.

"You had to have your friend come help you. You still jump whenever there's a sound outside. It does matter, Dani. Tell me why he has you so upset."

"He got obnoxious and wouldn't leave. I've handled the situation." Red color crept up her neck and her back was rigid as she loaded the dishwasher.

Lateef struggled for patience. This was not a fight he could drop. Whatever had happened was like a boil needing to be lanced. *How would Rissa handle this? She'd make a stupid comment and push until Dani threw things at her. Better think of a different strategy.* "Dani." He paused, his mind blank.

When the silence had hung for too long, she turned to face him, her complexion faded to her normal color as the angry tension in her posture subsided. "Yes?"

Silent, he took her hand and led her to the couch, tugging to overcome her mild resistance.

She perched on the edge of the cushion and he settled beside her, still keeping hold of her hand as he tried to figure out what he needed to say. Life was such a roller coaster. Had only five minutes passed since he was so happy?

"I can't let go, and not because I don't think you can take care of yourself."

She stirred, but settled again as he squeezed her hand.

"Dani, your pain is part of what pulled me here to start with. You never complain or let it slow you down, but I'm a healer. I can't help but notice. I've worked on the worst of your injuries since you brought me home." Sudden shame flashed through him.

"What?" She pulled free and held her hands, palms up with a frown. "Why are you so embarrassed now? I swear you're driving me crazy, Lateef. One minute you seem so aloof and condescending and then you practically melt into a puddle of need and then you act like a guilty child." She hopped to her feet and whirled to look down at him. "Answers, buddy boy. Straight and clear and no mystic healing crap. I'll let the alien stuff ride, because I have to, but tell me everything else about you now."

"Tell me about Kyle first. What did he do to spook you so badly?"

She threw her hands in the air and worried her lower lip between her teeth. "He tried to tell me he was in love. I told him to leave and he pretended he was so deeply in love with me he couldn't. He doesn't know me well enough to have those kinds of feelings."

He moved to stand in front of her, close enough their bodies touched. "Why did that scare you?" He searched her aura, catching spikes of some foreign influence he didn't recognize, but couldn't imagine was important. Not at this exact moment, anyway.

She vibrated with tension for a few seconds and then abruptly sagged, her head resting on his chest. "I don't know. Wasn't so much what as how he said it. His eyes went all weird."

Lateef's arms instinctively went around her. "I won't let him hurt you. I'm sorry I wasn't here when you needed me."

"It's not your job to take care of me. I appreciate what you've done so far, but you don't owe me anything."

Her words were strong, but she remained in his embrace.

"I still owe you for your help. You're in danger because of me. I tried to pay some of the debt by healing what I could of your old wounds, but I did that wrong, too." His arms tightened and shame heated his face. "I should have asked your permission before working on you, but seeing you hurt so much was more than I could handle. I limited my work to the worst of your injuries."

"I thought I felt better. Figured it was time and exercise like the therapists said." She stepped back and met his gaze. "Thank you."

He let out a relieved sigh. "I didn't realize I was so worried. I know you want answers, but honestly I don't even know what your questions are."

She shook her head. "I'm not sure I do, either. You keep saying the most outrageous things and I just nod and accept them. The Hatti are from Earth? There's some group of people trying to kill everyone else in the universe? We're not alone? You can teleport and have other psychic abilities? I feel like I've been in a dream, ignoring a bunch of weird stuff."

"Sit down and I'll try to explain." He pulled her back to the couch, continuing once they were settled beside each other. "The Hatti aren't really from Earth, but this clan spent some time here in the distant past. The clans live in city-ships, always looking for different foods. Occasionally they settle on a planet for a few years. No one's had contact with any clan for generations until a friend of mine ran across them. Even though they're primarily interested in food, they are vicious warriors and we'd rather have them as allies than enemies in our fight against the Falgarans."

She nodded at his pause, brow furrowed with concentration.

"The Falgarans are... I don't know how to describe them. Intelligent locusts with a nasty desire to play with their food maybe? They sneak onto a new planet and eventually take everything useful, leaving little beyond bedrock and salt water. If there's a sentient race on the planet they turn everyone against each other and once the civilization has broken down, they use or sell the people as slaves to their equally nasty allies. Their technology is better than ours, but they have never shown any psychic abilities. That's our advantage, and why the Hatti shield and the drug are so worrying."

"So why did you piss them off?"

His mouth fell open at her blunt question and then he laughed. "That is the real question, isn't it?" He settled back into the couch, subtly reassured by her sass. She would accept the truth. "I was tricked into entering a kitchen during feast prep."

"Wait a minute. All you did was walk into a kitchen and now the Hatti want to kill you? Are you sure that's all you did?"

Lateef rubbed the back of his neck and stared into the distance. "They're obsessed with food. Recipes are family treasures and a clan's reputation can be broken by one sub-par dish."

"Wow." Dani shook her head in disbelief. "That's a bit extreme. So, you think someone set you up?"

He nodded.

"Could these Falgarans be behind it?"

He shrugged. "I don't think so. To the best of our knowledge, they haven't spread to this area of space. But who knows?"

"So, what happens now?"

"I hoped once the Hatti searched and didn't find me, they would move on. I didn't expect them to come back and bring you presents." He pointed to the pearl necklace.

"This was the least of it."

"There was more?" He wheezed as the air left his lungs in shock.

"Come see for yourself." She led him to a closet by her workshop and began to pull out a dozen wooden boxes decorated with geometric patterns inlaid in precious metals.

He helped her stack them on the floor, numb with disbelief.

"I'm not sure what's in them. Taltos showed me, but I was too surprised to pay much attention, and then Kyle got weird and... well, I just shoved the boxes in here and forgot about them."

Lateef opened a box, speechless at the array of jewelry pieces revealed.

"I still don't understand why they brought any of this." She held up a beautifully filigreed pendant made of a metal that gleamed like fine silver yet had a much warmer glow. The figure looked like a dragon with sapphire eyes and was so finely done it seemed to move in her hand. "All I did was feed them breakfast. And I had to threaten to refuse the gifts if they wouldn't accept lunch."

His eyes grew wide and his stomach churned. "You threatened them?"

She shrugged. "Not really. I told them they had to eat since lunch was already cooked and then we could be even—they didn't owe me anything else."

He shook his head in admiration. "And they agreed?" This woman was a constant source of amazement. She was absolutely fearless at times.

"Taltos tried to argue, but I don't think the rest of the group was okay with leaving." She smiled in memory of the meeting. "Everything smelled good by then. I let him know if they didn't eat and take the rest with them, I'd have to throw the leftovers away. Got an immediate reaction."

"I bet." Lateef's knees weakened. He had seen the Hatti fighting demo. Any one of the soldiers could have killed her without breaking a sweat. "What happened then?"

"They ate, I packed up the leftovers and made up a plate for their Thane. I thought I owed him something special after he sent me these pearls." She once again fingered the strand, wonder in her gaze. "So, I sent them a local wine since they apparently sent me some of their wines." She pointed at the box full of metal containers. "I added a bottle of mead for the Thane and one for Taltos, since he had been so kind. Then they left."

"You make it sound so much like a tea-party in the garden," Lateef said. He was unable to tear his gaze from her. She had handled the threat so easily. Trevan had regaled him with numerous tales of bloody conquest, all set off with far less provocation.

"I didn't do anything special," she protested.

"Probably why you got away with it." He continued quickly at the flash of anger from her. "The Hatti are very, very serious about their food. Their sub-clans are headed by matriarchs who jealously guard the family recipes. Wars have been fought over attempts to redact a recipe and marriages are arranged as much on culinary prowess as genetics and clan ties. There isn't an equivalent concept in your world. Food is such an important thing to them the fact you took them in and fed them and asked for nothing in return—not even information—put them in your debt."

Dani gaped wordlessly at him for a long moment. "It was only crepes," she finally got out. "Not worth this!" she held up the dragon pendant.

"It was to them."

She had no response, so he showed her how the wine containers kept a preservative seal on the remaining wine. Another box contained bottles of liquors they uncorked to sniff. Rich odors of berries and licorice filled the air and they took turns tasting samples dripped onto their fingers. Every time their hands touched a spark passed between them, and those touches grew longer and the silences grew more and more heated.

"Danielle." Lateef took both of her hands in his and turned her to face him, unable to ignore the feelings any longer. Fear made his hands tremble, but he kept his shields up, afraid to find out what she wanted.

"Yes?" Her hands shook to the beat of her pounding heart.

"Do... Do you think we... Can it..." His voice trailed off.

She reached up and cupped his face with her hand. "Do I want to be with you?"

He nodded slowly, allowing her to see all of his fear and insecurity. She could so easily destroy him and the thought terrified him.

"Yes," she whispered. "I very much want to be with you, no matter where that might be."

He raised a hand to cover hers, closing his eyes. Relief made his muscles weak, but he pulled her in tight against him.

"Even if we are far away from here?" he whispered, his lips scant inches away from hers.

"Even if it's in another universe." She stretched forward, closing the distance between them.

Her lips were every bit as warm and soft as he imagined. His mind went blank as his nerves came alive, the fire growing with every touch until he wanted to pull her entire body into his to merge forever. His hands roamed across her skin, pushing aside the interfering pieces of cloth in his way. She helped, her excitement amplifying his until there was nothing but need. The two of them existed in a space beyond the physical, bodies entwined as their minds merged and they danced to the oldest music of all, lost to the flames of passion consuming them both.

Chapter 17

Don't Distract Me

"**G**ood morning."

Dani smiled lazily and stretched as she slowly opened her eyes. Lateef lay beside her, propped up on one elbow as he watched her. His expression moved from open and vulnerable to passionate in seconds flat.

"It is a good morning." She returned his greeting.

He laughed and leaned over to kiss her. The kiss deepened and she tangled one leg around his, pulling him off balance until he lay stretched out beside her, in contact along the length of their bodies.

Warmth bloomed in her belly as she ran her hand up and down the length of his toned body. Her breath came in pants as his hands made her skin heat with a delicious glow. All thoughts of her scars and imperfections vanished.

'You're beautiful exactly the way you are.'

Dani wasn't sure she heard the words with her ears or in her mind, but the emotion banished the final shadows from her soul. She could finally release the overwhelming sorrow that had dominated her life for so long.

Lateef paused with his lips inches above hers. "You bring me joy. I love you, Dani and I will spend the rest of my life making you happy."

Tears stung her eyes and she rose to meet his lips, kissing him with an intensity that left her shaking as he plunged deep inside her. Fireworks burst behind her eyelids as they moved together.

She felt his mental invitation to meld with him. After a slight hesitation, she accepted, and the universe exploded with so many different sensations it was impossible to tell where her skin ended and his began. Time slowed to a crawl as pleasure swirled throughout her body, pulling her to heights she had never imagined possible.

'You'll never be alone again.'

The absolute certainty of his love pushed her over the edge and she shuddered as an orgasm caught her.

She tightened her legs around his body as he followed her over the cliff of passion, secure in the knowledge that against all odds, she had found her soul mate.

An hour later Dani stood at the stove, flipping pancakes. She'd showered and dressed in comfy jeans and a loose sweater but was barefoot with wet hair trailing down her back like a thick snake. Lateef was in the shower now. They'd tried sharing one together, but the friction of soap and wet bodies led to more contact and... soon they needed another shower, and the hot water was getting low. So, they had finally decided to bathe separately. She hummed as she moved around the kitchen, more relaxed than she had been in years.

"You are beautiful!" Lateef's quiet comment from the doorway didn't startle her.

She knew exactly where he was now. In fact, she had to concentrate to completely separate her feelings from his. Except for the few things that she kept behind tight barriers. No one else needed to know those bad things. It had to be okay for her to forget about them, too.

He took several steps to close the gap between them and swept her body against his. "I don't think I'll ever get tired of this."

"Me either." Dani leaned her head against his shoulder, sighing with contentment, until a whiff of smoke broke the spell.

She squeaked and pulled away to drag the pan off the burner. "You are impossible."

He stepped behind her and pushed the thick mop of wet hair aside to nibble on the back of her neck as she poured more batter.

"That's my job," he said.

She twisted away with a fake angry growl. "And what are you going to say when the house burns down because you're distracting me?"

"I would never let anything happen to you." He took her face between his strong hands, forcing her to meet his eyes. "I'll always stand between you and danger."

"Don't make promises you can't possibly keep." Dani pulled away from him with a sudden twinge of foreboding. "I don't need protection."

"Can't help it." Lateef snuck in a quick kiss to her forehead. "I'll do my best not to be smothering, but I can't guarantee I won't occasionally slip into the heroic protector role."

"As long as you understand I'll do the same thing sometimes." She captured his lips with hers, sinking into his embrace.

Abby barked and they heard a car coming down the driveway.

"Who could be here?" She fought the urge to ignore the sound and drag Lateef back up to her room.

Lateef's eyes unfocused momentarily, then his gaze sharpened on her. "It's that PI."

"Kyle? Why is he back again?" Outrage warred with curiosity as she considered calling Charlie, but decided to see what he wanted first.

"He cares about you."

"I never wanted him to." She flipped the almost forgotten pancake. "I didn't encourage him."

"You didn't need to." Lateef caressed her face as he tugged her against his chest. "You are a beautiful, vibrant lady. All you have to do is smile and birds fly down from the sky to be near you."

She laughed aloud. "No more radio for you. I have to cut you off when you start paraphrasing song lyrics."

"But I'm serious," he said. "Maybe not about the birds, but to men like Kyle? You're catnip."

She rolled her eyes at him, refusing to pick up on his seriousness. "Do you have any idea how bad catnip smells?"

"Not to a cat." He stuck his nose on her neck and sniffed loudly before nibbling up to her ear.

"Such a cruel thing to do when company is coming." Dani clutched at the stove to remain upright as her knees threatened to buckle.

"I know." His quiet murmur was more in her mind than her ears. "But you are irresistible."

"We could hide upstairs and refuse to answer the door."

"He's determined to see you today." Regret and disappointment were obvious in Lateef's voice. He straightened, holding tightly to her until she regained her own sense of equilibrium. "Besides, the scent of burnt pancakes will give him a reason to insist."

She swore under her breath as she turned back to the stove to take care of the problem.

"You know, there was something to be said for being alone. I never used to burn food."

"But you were lonely, and now you'll never be alone again."

She nodded. Even if she found herself physically alone, she would never again have to endure the tortured emptiness of being utterly abandoned as she had since losing Caity. It seemed like a silly distinction, but it was huge emotionally.

She leaned against Lateef's warm strength, enjoying his physical presence for a few seconds, before Abby's renewed barking pulled her back to the present.

"I guess we should let Kyle in." Reluctance slowed her words.

"Maybe he'll go away happy if you feed him." Lateef dropped a kiss on the top of her head. "It worked for the Hatti." He gave her one final hug and stepped away. "Just remember I won't let him or anyone else hurt you."

"I'm not that delicate."

"But I am that protective."

"Then go get some plates and mugs." She tapped his chest playfully. "I'll get some pancakes ready. It's hard to argue with a full mouth."

She had a couple of flapjacks cooking away, flipping them as a car door slammed in the front yard.

"Do you want to get the door or should you stay out of sight?" She suddenly realized Kyle had never met Lateef.

"Too late to hide." Lateef gestured towards the large window on the side of the kitchen where she met Kyle's angry glare.

She sighed in resignation. This wouldn't be easy. She gestured with her head for him to go around to the back door and concentrated on cooking as Lateef showed the unwelcome visitor into her spacious kitchen.

"Will you tell me what the hell is going on?" Kyle snarled as he stalked into the house.

"Why are here when you've been told to stay away from me?" Her retort was every bit as quick, but without anger—an icy contrast to his incandescent heat.

She slid pancakes onto a plate and poured more batter onto the griddle. "Sit down and eat, Kyle." It was more order than invitation. "You'll feel better with a full stomach."

"I'm not one of your strays to be distracted with food."

"No." She whirled, pushing her anger down. "But you are an uninvited stranger who has forced his way into my home on numerous occasions, and who has refused to obey my explicitly stated desire to be left alone."

His mouth opened and closed several times as she glared at him. She turned and slammed the plate down on the table and then returned to the stove for another batch of pancakes. "Sit down and eat while it's warm. Butter and syrup are on the table."

Wordlessly he obeyed, all the while shooting daggers at Lateef who calmly poured coffee in three mugs. All three moved in silence until the rest of the batter was cooked and Dani couldn't put the confrontation off any longer. *Alone is so much easier than dealing with wounded egos.*

'But lonely. Being with me is better.'

She touched Lateef's back as they walked to the table, taking comfort from the contact hidden from Kyle's view. They took seats across the table from the sullen PI.

"Who is he?" Kyle gestured with his fork at the serene healer.

"Lateef D'Oro." Dani made the introductions. "This is Kyle Manning, Private Investigator."

"Nice to meet you, Kyle Manning." Lateef nodded his head and speared a couple of pancakes, transferring them to his plate. "Hope you don't mind if we go ahead and eat while you talk. Be a shame to let these get cold."

Kyle settled back, giving Dani a chance to slowly eat one pancake before she pushed her plate aside. Her appetite was gone. She realized she felt the anger in a way she had never felt someone else's emotions before. She shot Lateef a sideways look, aware his presence had changed more in her than she had realized.

"Ready to talk now?" Kyle was rigidly polite. "Or do you want to come down to Denver and be official?"

She shook her head, more in sorrow than anger. "What do you need, Mr. Manning?"

"I came up here to find... someone." He stumbled over the words.

Dani felt a flash of shame that made no sense to her, even as she saw Lateef stiffen and a barrier slammed between them. His expression turned hard and he put a few inches of space between them. She waited a few seconds for an explanation that didn't come, so she turned to Kyle.

"You told me you wanted to find Lateef. Then you wanted to know about the men looking for him. Who are you really searching for and why do you think I can help?"

"It's complicated." He reached across the table for her hand but stopped when Lateef twitched.

Nervous tension twisted in her gut as a nasty suspicion took root. He couldn't be working for Carl's father, could he? The absence of Lateef's now familiar mental touch bothered her more than expected. From the set of his jaw, he knew something about Kyle that pissed him off.

"Saying something's complicated generally means you won't tell me something you know will piss me off. Who are you working for, Kyle?"

Kyle's gaze darted between her and Lateef and several emotions crossed his face before he settled on indignation. His back straightened and he thumped both hands on the table, leaning toward her with a grim expression. "I need to know where those bald men came from."

She bit her lower lip, as the butterflies in her belly grew spikes. Changing the subject was not a good sign and Lateef was no help. He was like a black hole beside her.

"Why? My company is none of your concern."

"It is when they bring you something made of a metal that doesn't exist on Earth. Kind of makes it a matter of national security." His grin was smug as he leaned back in the chair, arms crossed in satisfaction.

Dani froze, cold fury slamming through her veins. "How do you know?" she asked.

"I had one of the necklaces analyzed." He blinked, as if surprised he had answered.

"You stole from me?" She leaned forward to glare at him. Lateef reached out to touch her leg under the table and she shuddered, trying to get her emotions under control. "When?" Her mind was on overload and she mentally reached for Lateef, only to meet a tight shield. *Fine. I've dealt with bastards before. Kyle's a kitten compared to Carl's dad. I've made it this far without help, so if Lateef has to hide behind shields, that's his deal.*

Kyle blustered for a few seconds. "You have to admit the whole thing was strange."

"When did you steal from me?" Dani snapped the question.

"While we were cleaning up after lunch. I only took one piece of jewelry."

"I want you out of my home. Right now." She bounced up, knocking her chair over and only Lateef's quick grab avoided a crash to the floor. "If you need any more information from me you will have to go through my legal representative."

"This isn't a legal matter." Kyle stood his ground.

"Then you have no right to be here. I want you to leave."

"You need to tell me what you know."

"I don't need to do anything." Dani started around the table, nearly tripping over the anxious dog.

"Dani, you need to calm down. I'm only trying to help you." Kyle raised his hand in a placating gesture.

"Don't," she interrupted. "I'm not your friend. You spent time in my home because I didn't have the energy to kick you out. Now I want you to leave."

Abby ran to the backdoor, barked furiously, let out a frightened yelp and ran to press her shaking body against Dani's legs.

A loud bang on the back door brought the argument to an abrupt end.

Chapter 18

Not This Time, Master Chef

"Taltos." Dani breathed the name as she locked gazes with the stern-faced warrior through the window of her back door. Her heart sank to her shoes then raced with a spike of adrenaline as her mind spun into high gear. "You have to go, Lateef. Run out the front door. I'll keep them occupied." She forced her head to turn to face her love.

"It's too late."

Lateef's tone was calm, but she could see lines of tension around his eyes. He lowered his mental shields enough to send a wave of soothing emotion at her, but there was an undercurrent of self-recrimination that made the hairs on her arms stand up.

He swallowed hard and nodded toward the door. "It will be okay. Let them in before he gets angry."

She stared at him until an impatient pounding at the door shook her out of her stupor.

"Go on," he urged. She walked slowly as Lateef quickly instructed Kyle.

"I recommend you say and do nothing to antagonize these visitors," he said. "They shouldn't cause you any problems as long as they get what they want."

"And what do they want?" Anger still bubbled underneath the PI's bland expression. Dani opened the door, and the men fell silent.

"Good morning, Taltos." She nodded at the familiar visitor. "I didn't expect you, but it won't take long to whip up some more pancakes. Would you like to come in and wait?"

"Not this time, Master Chef." The regretful look he shot at the nearly full plates on the table said more than words how sorry he was. "I cannot be distracted again. You must come with me and speak to Thane Hantili."

"Okay. I'll grab some shoes and we can go. Be right back." She started to close the door, but he stuck out a hand to prevent it.

"Your guests must also come." He gestured to the two men still near the table. "We have been searching for one of them for quite some time."

She frowned. "I don't think you want Kyle to go anywhere," she said. "He was getting ready to go back to his office. His boss expects him back soon."

"Then his boss shall be disappointed." The expression on the alien's face firmed as his companions reached for their weapons. "You will all come with me."

He took a couple of steps into the spacious kitchen forcing Dani back, but she could see the armed men in her yard, and she got a glimpse of the nightmare creature from several nights ago, at the far edge of her yard. She gulped, feeling the stirrings of panic in her gut.

"Why don't you go get your shoes on, Dani?" Lateef said. "No one will fight you, Sir Taltos. We are at your disposal."

"Yes, you are."

The anger in the gaze he turned on Lateef chilled Dani's marrow. She swiftly ran upstairs and pulled on thick socks and her most comfortable pair of hiking shoes, not truly wanting to leave the men alone. She wasn't sure what she would find when she returned.

She flew back downstairs to find Kyle and Lateef leaning against the kitchen counter, putting on an air of confidence. The alien men remained near the door watching. Abby was pressed tightly against Lateef's legs until she saw Dani. Then the dog shot across the room with a panicked whine, trying to climb into her arms. Dani knelt and gathered her shaggy friend to her in an effort to soothe the completely unnerved dog.

"I need to call a friend to take care of Abby." She looked up to meet the dark eyes of her captor.

"We must go now." Taltos stared over her head.

"I need to call Charlie," she pleaded. "I can leave her in the house and he'll come by and get her later."

The alien merely shook his head.

"I can't abandon my dog!" The raw pain in her voice made him meet her gaze. "She's my responsibility and I can't leave her locked in the house to starve or turn her out into the woods to be eaten by a bear or coyote."

Taltos considered for a second. "The furry one should remain in this dwelling. We must go." His tone was implacable as one of his men grabbed the doorknob.

"No." The agonized cry burst from Dani as she hugged the frantic dog. Lateef took a step toward Dani and three weapons cleared holsters to point at his heart.

"Be cautious, o defiler of kitchens. My Thane has requested your presence, but he did not care if you still drew breath."

Everyone froze. The only sound in the house was the quiet whimpers and yips of the terrified dog until Kyle let out a snort of laughter.

"Defiler of kitchens?" The look he gave Lateef was full of disbelief. "That's a thing?"

Taltos's face darkened and his aim shifted to Kyle.

"Whoa!" Kyle's hands flew up and his eyes widened in alarm.

Dani rose to her feet, speaking quickly to defuse the situation. "He doesn't understand, Taltos. Neither does Abby. Let me call a friend to take care of her and we'll go with you, no problem."

"We must leave now." The alien's jaw tightened belligerently.

"Dani's right. I have no clue what's going on here, but I know her. You'll get out of here faster if you just let her make a call. She doesn't lose arguments." Kyle's hands remained in the air, and he shrugged as all eyes turned his direction. "You know I'm right."

Taltos growled an obvious curse under his breath. "Quickly then. Do not reveal our presence."

"I won't. Thank you." She managed to get to the phone without tripping over the still frantic dog and dialed Anna's home phone.

"Hey, Charlie." Her hands shook when she heard the familiar rough voice, but she managed to keep her own tone steady. "No, I'm fine. There's nothing wrong, but I need a huge favor. I have to go out of town and I can't take Abby. Would you mind keeping her for a few days?" Her eyes shot to Taltos, hoping he would indicate the trip would be shorter, but the dark eyes gave her no information.

When Charlie reluctantly agreed, her shoulders slumped with a release of tension. She continued quickly before he could ask any questions. "Thank you so much. Tell Anna hi for me, will you? I'll see you in a few days. I'll leave the back door unlocked. Yes, I'll explain then. I promise. No—there's nothing to worry about." She glanced at Taltos and shuddered at the look of impatience on his rounded face. "I'm not sure when, but everything will be fine. I promise."

She pushed the disconnect button on the phone and gave the dog a final squeeze. "You be good for Charlie and Anna. He'll be here as fast as he can."

She followed the men out the door, her heart breaking as she shut the frantic dog in. When she caught another glimpse of the feathered creature moving in the distance, she knew she'd done the right thing. Abby was a great companion, but she was no adventurer. She would not do well exploring strange new worlds. When you came right down to brass tacks, Dani wasn't much of adventurer herself. But then she felt Lateef's feather light touch on her mind and she knew it would be okay. Somehow, her life would all work out. It had to. She couldn't stand to lose everything she cared about again. They would all have to survive this confrontation.

Dani shivered as a gust of cold wind tugged strands of hair out of her ponytail. The sunny morning sky had been replaced by dark storm clouds and she was glad she had taken the extra few minutes to put on sturdy boots and grab a jacket.

"It is not much farther." Taltos slowed to walk beside her as the strange group started up yet another steep hill. "Our transport is on the other side of this rise."

Dani winced as Kyle's feet slipped out from under him and he fell heavily to his knees. The PI had arrived at her door in his expensive suit and slippery, leather-soled shoes completely unsuited for their present situation. She was relieved when the alien guard helped him to his feet and made sure he was okay before urging him on again. *Maybe this won't be too bad?*

A quick glance at the aliens around Lateef trashed that idea. They all appeared to be contemplating throwing the healer down the hill once they finally reached the top. And then maybe dragging him back up to toss him down again. She hoped he didn't slip on his own.

"Where are..." The words stuck in her throat as she topped the rise and saw two obviously alien craft parked in the wide valley below. She froze in disbelief.

Taltos grabbed her arm and urged her to continue walking. "You must hurry, Chef Danielle Hamilton. We must be aboard the shuttle before the Jangxing crew arrives. It will be eager to return home and is sometimes... careless and hard to control. My job is to ensure you arrive safely."

Dani's feet moved faster in spite of her shock at the undeniable reality of spaceships in front of her. The colorful, triangular shapes perched on tall, thin legs with no obvious sign of any kind of engine or windows or any sign of life, until the back end of the nearest ship slowly extended a ramp. *Crap. Guess I didn't really believe they were aliens. This has got to be one of those bizarre dreams.*

Lateef made a final plea as the group bunched before entering the ship. "Sir Taltos, I beg you to leave the Terrans here. Their planet has not yet developed true spaceflight and they are not aware of our customs. I will go with you willingly."

Taltos glared at the shorter healer, obviously struggling to keep his rage under tight control. "You will come with us, willing or not, you defiler. We have a shield which blocks your teleportation so you shall remain until honor has been restored."

Kyle let out a sharp laugh. "Now I know this all a nightmare. Teleportation and blocking shields, my great-aunt Matilda." He tried to sit on the damp ground, but his guards grabbed his arms to drag him up the ramp.

Lateef planted his feet as he drew near Dani, bringing his escort to a halt. "I beg you to release them, Sir Taltos. I will not try to escape. My people are not your enemies."

"That is for Thane Hantili to decide." Taltos gestured and the guard knocked Lateef's feet out from under him, and grabbed his arms to drag him onto the ship.

A burst of static hit Dani as Lateef crossed the threshold and her knees wobbled at the flash of pain. She reached for the lost contact with Lateef, but felt only a cold void.

"Madam Chef?" One of the crew members held out a hand to help her up the steep ramp and she accepted with a mental sigh of resignation. Her eyelid twitched and her brain itched as she passed an invisible barrier. She paused near the top of the ramp as a rank smell assaulted her nose. Near the top of the hill she saw a group of the alien men herding the Jangxing toward the other, larger ship and was glad they would not be sharing a ride.

Dani allowed her escort to help her into one of the padded, reclining seats that filled the large space like the seats on a more familiar airplane. Kyle and Lateef were already strapped in and all three of them were as far apart as they could be in the space. She nervously ran the black pearls of her necklace through her fingers, trying to relax as her guard adjusted her harness and made sure she was comfortable.

An alarm blared and Dani jumped.

"Don't worry." Her guard reassured her as he finished buckling his own harness. "Yanok is a very good pilot."

She grinned weakly before a sudden burst of acceleration pushed her back into her seat cushions. Her vision blurred and she mentally reached out for Lateef, but felt static instead of the warm mental presence she craved. She must be fated to be alone.

A seeming eternity later the heavy force eased. She turned back to her guard, proud her voice sounded normal. "Where are you taking us?" Very little time had passed in the real world, but those seconds of high acceleration had felt endless. Anxiety gnawed at her gut.

"To the *Alalakh*, our city-ship, Madame Chef. Thane Hantili wishes to meet you. *You* have no need to fear."

"What about my companions?" Fear gripped her with his emphasis on the word you.

She caught the hard look the man shot in Lateef's direction and groaned internally.

"They will get what they deserve. Thank you for the meals. I was lucky enough to partake in both of them. My cabin mate is very jealous."

She blushed at the compliment, hearing the capital letter on the word meal. "You're welcome. But I didn't do anything special. There wasn't enough time to get fancy."

The man shuddered. "The food was appropriate for a Middle Festival at the least. You are truly a modest Master. Again, I thank you for the incredible experience."

Dani continued to run her pearls through her fingers as she tried to process the inexplicable admiration. "What did you like the best?" She wanted a distraction from her dire thoughts. She tried to check on Kyle and Lateef, but they were hidden by the tall seats.

Her seat-mate considered her question seriously and she found herself interested in his answer despite her fear.

"I think the potato dish was my favorite," he finally answered. "Although the grilled fish was a close second. Your family must be very powerful to possess such recipes. Would you ever consider merging with another Clan?"

Her mouth gaped and her eyes widened. Only half of what he had said made any kind of sense. *Merge with another clan?*

"I don't have a recipe for either one of those." She would ignore the merger question in case it was some bizarre, alien marriage proposal. "I just kind of throw things in a pan and hope for the best."

The look he gave her screamed disbelief.

"I swear. I chunk up some potatoes and throw them in a pan with some butter and onions and garlic and add a bunch of seasoning. Fresh herbs are better, but dried will do in a pinch."

He gaped at her.

"That's all there is to the dish." His reaction increased her anxiety. "I usually use the potatoes I grow in my garden, but you can use any low to medium starch variety. My personal favorites are the Klondike Gold's mixed with some Purple Majesty and Colorado Rose, but it works with anything. You can change things up by substituting some turnips to cut down on the carb count. And if you really want to jazz it up, you can throw in some crumbled bacon and gorgonzola cheese."

"You are truly willing to share your secrets so freely? Will your clan not lose status?"

His scandalized tone and the shocked glares of the nearby Hatti momentarily glued her tongue to the roof of her mouth. *Careful, stupid. These guys don't see the world the way you do.*

"My family was killed several years ago, so there's no one to lose status." She closed her eyes against the pang of remembered pain. "And I don't have any cooking secrets." She opened her eyes to meet her seat-mate's distressed gaze.

"You are clan-less?" Horror and astonishment battled on the alien face, but Dani felt nothing but sympathy from her odd companion. "You are truly a strong Master Chef, Danielle Hamilton. Perhaps Thane Hantili may find…" His sentence cut off abruptly as a companion poked him from behind and he abruptly changed the subject. "Do you grow all of your own vegetables?"

Dani was baffled, but went along with it, describing her garden and the intricacies of ordering food online as the nearby aliens joined the conversation. Soon there was a lively debate pitting her dishes against some of their own favorites.

The announcement they were ready to dock ended the conversation. All of the crewmembers settled back into their chairs, and Dani copied them, prepared for another burst of massive acceleration. She was pleasantly surprised to feel no more than a gentle nudge before a loud clang reverberated through the passenger cabin. The three prisoners were quickly escorted off the transport and guided between several parked shuttles into a wide corridor.

"Can you believe this?" Kyle's amazed whisper was magnified by the immense space.

Dani tried to slow her steps to let the PI catch up with her as they approached a branching corridor, but her escort gently took her arm.

"Please come with me." Her former seat-mate's grip provided a not-so-subtle reminder she was not exactly a guest. She threw one last glance at Kyle and Lateef, receiving nods of reassurance from each and then followed into the wide, featureless corridor without protest.

Chapter 19

Time to Meet the Thane

Dani followed her escort through a labyrinth of identical corridors apparently designed to confuse visitors. Junctions were marked by stylized icons that vaguely resembled flowers, but the only place labeled with anything close to words was a double-door with round windows like an elevator or subway train. She'd been hurried past before getting a close enough look to see if the door hid some kind of transportation system.

The soldier opened an unmarked door in a short hallway full of identical doors. The small, featureless room revealed contained a table, two chairs and a tall stool with a back. All of the furniture was functional, but the lines held a simple elegance at odds with the space, which reminded her of a police interrogation room.

Dani sat in the indicated chair. A shorter, more feminine alien appeared with a pitcher and two matching cups on a beautifully decorated tray. She placed them on the table and shot Dani a shy glance, full of curiosity before the guard herded her out.

The door closed behind them without a sound. Dani sat alone, trying to make sense of recent events and her place in them. *Wish I knew if I was guest or prisoner.* She glanced at the door, considering the look from the alien woman. *Maybe I joined the freak show? Although, in that case, they would have kept us together.*

She rubbed her leg, which ached from the unaccustomed walking. *Not as bad as it should be.* She shifted cautiously, realizing none of her old injuries bothered her as much as they had before Lateef had come into her life. Her back hadn't spasmed on her in weeks. He really had been working on her injuries. Her mood lifted, and anxiety shifted to boredom.

The silver pitcher on the table caught her eye and she studied it, with her hands clasped behind her back. These people were so extremely touchy about food she didn't want to assume anything. The gleaming container was beautifully embossed with geometric shapes and the cups reminded her of Japanese tea mugs. Finally, she could not resist touching one of the cups. The surface was warmer than she had expected. It fit her hand as though designed for her and she reveled in the pleasure of the simple joy of seeing beauty.

A sound at the door broke her out of her reverie and she swiftly replaced the cup, retreating back into her chair. Her face heated at the nearness of being caught. She wished Lateef was with her. She had no idea of what was going on and what she should do to stay out of trouble so they could all get home again in one piece.

Briefly she wondered how Kyle was handling things. She hoped he would be tactful and curb his temper. Lateef—well, he had already managed to piss this group off somehow. For that matter she hoped she could handle whatever came up correctly.

The door opened and the tallest, biggest, bald guy she had seen yet entered the room. His muscles had muscles and his round face was set into a permanent sneer. Yet his beautiful, dark eyes shone with a kindness which belied the angry expression. He settled his graceful bulk onto the stool opposite her and placed his hands on the table in front of him, precisely folding one over the other. His plain, dark-blue uniform fit him like a second skin, emphasizing his well-developed musculature.

"Are you comfortable, Master Chef Hamilton?"

Dani gaped at him, momentarily unable to process the perfectly under-standable words spoken in one of the most beautiful bass voices she had ever heard. His brow lifted in a question and she shook herself out of her daze.

"Yes." A blush burned across her face. "I'm fine. Would rather be home, though."

"Hopefully you will be returned there soon, but we must learn of your association with the Beryllian."

She fought the fascination of his velvety tone, struggling to pay attention to what he was saying. She took a deep breath and concentrated on blocking out the confusion muddling her thoughts. She straightened her shoulders and gave him a level look. No reason to be deferential.

"Why is anything I do any of your business?"

"Were you not thirsty?"

His question threw her off again. She tilted her head and frowned at him.

"You did not drink any of the offered water." He indicated the pitcher.

"I wasn't sure I was supposed to."

"And yet you touched a cup?"

She buried her face in her hands. "I couldn't help it." Her resolution to stay in charge of the conversation crumbled under the accusation. She looked back up. "It was so pretty my fingers itched. I had to get a closer look." She had subconsciously been aware she was being observed, but had tried to deny it. *Glad I didn't scratch any embarrassing places while I thought I was alone.*

She caught a pleased look in his eyes and relaxed minutely. Apparently, she had passed a test of some sort. Dani attempted to reach for Lateef, hoping for guidance. She expected to feel nothing but a vague reassurance as she had on the shuttle. Instead she felt an empty numbness that rattled her further. She hoped the silence didn't mean something bad had happened to her new love.

"Would you like some water to drink?"

She nodded. Things couldn't be too bad if this guy was serving her, right?

He deftly poured, handing the mug to her ceremoniously. She accepted it, cradling the cup in the palm of her hand to admire the craftsmanship.

"Thank you." The interior was silvery and the water brought out patterns she hadn't noticed before. A faint scent tickled her nose and she paused, trying to identify the floral fragrance.

"What's wrong?" Dark eyes stared unblinkingly at her.

"This isn't plain water, is it?" She met his gaze.

He shook his head. "No. *Obosa* is a flavored water offered only to special guests."

And what does that mean? I can see special as a bad thing. Dani set her expression to skeptical, yet friendly. "Special guests who were abducted and held against their will?" She was still determined to be polite and non-confrontational, but she wouldn't play stupid. All the weirdness was reawakening her self-protective instincts, knocking her out of the unfamiliar daze.

He studied her for a long moment and then filled a cup of his own, holding it up for her inspection before taking a long sip. The challenge was so obvious she had to copy him. The taste was indescribable—perfectly cool, thick and flavorful without being syrupy. Her eyes rolled closed and she took a deep breath, savoring the sensation as a sense of immense well-being spread through her body.

"That's incredible." She breathed as her eyelids fluttered opened. She stared into the cup as if she could figure out exactly what the drink was, then took another small sip, this time prepared for the explosion of taste and beamed at her interrogator.

"You like the *Obosa*? Even if it is only given to involuntary captives?"

Her smile grew rueful. "If you treat captives like this you can't be too bad."

"Your companion does not seem to think so." His expression sharpened.

"Which companion?" Her imagination painted all sorts of pictures of Kyle protesting his treatment and being roughed up.

"The defiler." His sharp snap conveyed contempt.

"Lateef?" She was surprised at the intense hatred from the man in front of her. Her body felt light and focusing grew difficult. "He never said anything bad about you guys."

"What did he say to you?"

The heated blush instantly covering her face surprised them both. "Oh, my goodness," she muttered as scenes from their night of passion flashed through her mind. "I can't believe this."

Judging by the extended silence her captor didn't believe her either.

"Before he left, Lateef told me someone might come looking for him and if they did, I should tell them the truth. That's pretty much the only thing he ever said about you." She stared at the table, unable to meet his steady gaze.

"So how did you know about our patrol?"

"It wasn't exactly a secret that a group of men were wandering around town." She couldn't stop the snarky tone in her response, but she tried to temper it. "They knocked on my door one morning." The very normal questions allowed her to regain her composure and she looked back up at him.

"What else did you talk about?"

"That is none of your business." She felt the flush creeping across her face again and rose to pace. "I don't like being put in the middle of something I don't understand."

"That was not our doing. You chose to hide and aid our enemy." His words were angry, but his face held an unexpected defensiveness and maybe guilt?

She took several steps toward him, one hand tangled in the black pearl necklace she had been fondling unconsciously. "Let's get something straight. I did not aid your 'enemy'." She put air quotes around the word. The need to look up to the seated man sapped some of her anger. "I found someone who was hurt and needed help. And when your men came to my door, I shared my food with them. I didn't ask for anything in return from any of you."

"And when my men returned with guest gifts?"

She had to look away. "Okay, I did make demands then. Taltos was going to drop off stuff and run away. And that was after he had showed me some of the incredible gifts. So, all I did was tell the truth—the food would be wasted if they didn't eat. It's not like I held anyone down and forced them to eat."

He stared at her thoughtfully, intense suspicion slowly fading into surprise.

"It truly is so simple to you?"

She frowned. "Nothing about this situation is simple. If someone'd told me last week I'd be taking a trip in a flying saucer surrounded by foodies I'd have called for a padded truck– and yet here I am."

"What is a foodie?" He stumbled over the unfamiliar word.

"Someone fascinated by food. The whole trip here was spent talking about food. I've never been around so many people who all have a favorite ingredient or technique but are so ridiculously secretive at the same time." She shook her head and began to pace again. "The way they talk you'd think they were nuclear scientists trying to give you hints about what an atom bomb was and let you know how incredibly intelligent they were without telling you anything useful."

He watched as she babbled on, still as a statue except for dark eyes tracking her every move.

"They all talked about different dishes, but none of them would list ingredients or explain some of the more difficult techniques. And when I asked a question, you would have thought I was asking for some state secret, not what kind of onion they like."

"You asked for details about a family recipe?" He went rigid, pinning her with an intense glare.

"No." She froze. "Or at least I don't think so. I asked if he preferred red, white or yellow onions in general."

He relaxed again and she leaned against the wall to stare at him. "You didn't bring me here to talk about food." Her head was suddenly clear and she felt focused. "And your little drink wasn't plain, flavored water."

His eyes widened briefly in surprise and she knew she was right.

"You could have just asked me whatever it was you wanted to know."

"Would you have told us the truth?"

She looked up and shook her head, muttering under her breath about the bone-headed stubbornness of men, no matter the species. She dropped into her chair and smacked her hands on the table. "Would you believe anything I did tell you?"

He studied. "Why did you not answer questions?"

"No one asked any questions I haven't answered." She bit the words off, glaring at the much larger man.

"None?" he prompted.

She growled wordlessly. "No. And when everyone finished eating, I packed up the leftovers and they went home."

"You were so willing to share food with strangers who unexpectedly appeared at your door? Many of your neighbors commented about the food you provide for their events, even though you do not attend."

"You talked to my neighbors about me?" She frowned. "When?"

"The people with the goats mentioned you allowed a stranger to stay with you and tried to sell our team some cheese. They praised your cooking abilities."

"The Saunders ratted me out?" she exclaimed.

"Were you trying to hide?"

She slumped in her chair. "Not really. At least not from you. I don't like attention."

He gazed at her thoughtfully, his head tilted as if listening to someone she couldn't hear.

"What do you know about the Beryllian?"

"Depends on your definition of 'know'." She muttered under her breath, unable to face her interrogator as memories of bodies moving together heated her skin.

"What was that?"

"I don't know much about him." She felt absolutely chatty and wondered if the *Obosa* was like sodium pentothal, lowering her inhibitions and making her say far more than she should. She got to her feet to restlessly pace. "He's a healer and has several siblings and isn't from Earth. Oh, and he can barely boil water without setting off the fire alarm."

"How do you know he's a healer?"

She leaned against the cool metal wall of the small room as she shot the man a glance under her eyelashes. "He saved my life after your little bloodhound scared me half to death."

"Explain." His gaze sharpened and he leaned forward.

"I was in my shop late one night and saw your feathered creature staring at me. It scared me and I sliced open my arm instead of my soap. Fortunately, Lateef was in the kitchen and managed to stop the bleeding before it was too late."

The bare bones of the story still made her heart race.

"I am sorry our Jangxing frightened you. It did not report the encounter."

Dani shrugged and looked away. She was ready to go home. Her energy faded as her head cleared.

"What of this other man who was with you?"

She blinked at the subject change. This was so surreal. Maybe she had died that night in her workshop–or maybe she'd never woken up from the car accident. Her breath caught in her chest at the fleeting thought that if she could open her eyes she would see her baby girl again. If only that were possible!

'I'm sorry.' The thought whispered through her mind, wrapping her in warm, ethereal arms. The presence vanished and she sagged against the wall. Lateef's brief message meant this whole bizarre situation was real. She blinked rapidly, holding back the tears that threatened to flow down her face before feeling able to answer the question.

"Kyle Manning is an investigator who was searching for someone." She shrugged, unwilling to go into any more detail or express her doubts. "I guess he thought I knew more than I did because he spied on me."

"So, he did not know the Beryllian?"

"They met for the first time this morning, right before Taltos arrived and bundled us all up for this little joy ride."

"Have you told me the complete truth?" The words seemed formulaic, like some kind of ritual.

"I haven't lied to you about anything."

"Is there anything else about the Beryllian you wish to disclose?"

"No. Absolutely nothing I want to talk to you about. Why?"

"Are you aware of his crimes against the Hatti people?"

She shook her head. "And unless he's some kind of serial killer, I don't want to know."

"You do not wish to know what kind of a person you are intimate with?"

She groaned as embarrassment pulled her out of the black pit of depression she was circling. "Can we stop with the questions about my personal life? Lateef has been nothing but kind to me and everyone I've seen him interact with."

"And what do you think about us?"

She opened her mouth and then closed it again, searching for the right words. "I don't know. I still wonder why you gave me such extravagant gifts." She absently fingered the pearls. "But everyone I've met has been extremely friendly."

"So, you count us as friends?"

She looked directly at him. "I don't know you well enough to answer yet, but I most definitely wouldn't put you in the enemy category."

"In spite of the fact we brought you to our ship against your will and administered a truth serum?"

She looked away from him, muttering a few imprecations under her breath. "I can't say I appreciate any of this," she finally replied. "Even though there was a lot of gun-waving, Taltos let me take care of my dog. I don't know what would have happened if we'd resisted, but, well, your crew was unfailingly polite to me. Kyle might have a different story, but I have absolutely no complaints."

"And if we detain you for a long period?"

"Then we'll have a problem." Anger burned away the last of her lingering sadness. "I have a business to run and animals to care for. What is this all about?" She pushed to her feet again, pacing with an agitation she had not felt before.

"Just because I helped someone, you're trying to tell me I might be kept captive on some spaceship?" She turned her outraged look on him. "There better be one very good explanation."

He watched her expressionlessly as she continued to stalk from one end of the small room to the other.

"If only I could be assured you are hiding nothing."

"What could I possibly be hiding that would be of any interest to someone from another planet?"

The two locked gazes, neither one giving an inch. Abruptly he came to a decision and rose to his feet. "We shall see," he said. "Someone will come for you shortly."

Before she could object, he was gone. Minutes later another crewmember escorted her to yet another featureless room furnished with a small table, two padded benches complete with a small pillow and blanket, and an obviously inebriated Kyle Manning.

Chapter 20

I'll Watch for Pod People

"What do you think they're doing out there?" Kyle's worried question broke through her mounting anxiety.

"I'm not sure." She strained with every sense, including her new psychic one to get some information. From the empty cavern in her belly, hours had passed since the interrogation. Several times through the long day she had felt Lateef's mental touch, but the contact was always short and full of static—barely enough to reassure her he still lived. But not nearly enough to let her know he was okay.

Kyle grabbed one of the remaining round bread loaves from the table. Their only contact with their captors since their questioning had come in the form of a single visit from a silent woman laden with a large pitcher of cool water, two mugs and the bread containing chunks of cheese. She had indicated they were welcome to eat, shooting Dani an encouraging look and a secretive wink that left her oddly comforted.

The bread was good, but her stomach was so tied up in knots she couldn't force herself to eat much more than enough to avoid offending her prickly captors.

She turned to look at Kyle. He seemed to be handling all the weirdness pretty well, now he was sobering up. "Why don't you try to get some rest?" He looked a bit green around the gills, but she wasn't sure if it was from the odd illumination from the four walls, or because he had been so affected by the *Obosa*.

"Maybe falling asleep isn't such a good idea under the circumstances." Kyle rubbed at his temples. "No guarantee we'll wake up."

She chuckled. "I'll watch out for hatching pod people. And I promise to wake you if I hear anyone coming." Their last visitor's footsteps had preceded her by a good minute, and they had heard nothing through the door of their cell since then.

Kyle's eyes were still glassy and his gaze unfocused. As she helped him remove his suit coat and shoes she wondered if she should encourage him to eat and drink some more. But the obvious exhaustion on his face convinced her to loosen his tie, push him down and cover him with the silvery blanket.

"Don't worry," she admonished as she tucked him in. "I will definitely let you know if anything changes."

He tried to fight, but exhaustion won as his eyes drooped. She sat beside him until his breathing deepened to snores then resumed her pacing near the door, pausing every once in a while to listen.

When the light dimmed to a comfortable level for sleeping, Dani sat on her own bench with her knees tucked to her chest and rested her head on them. She reached with her mind, trying to contact Lateef, but felt absolutely nothing. She held back sobs of frustration by sheer will power. He had to be okay—he had to be. She couldn't lose him so soon. She couldn't survive that kind of loss again.

Lateef stumbled to his knees as Taltos shoved him into a small cell containing a low bed and a chair.

"You are fortunate Thane Hantili wishes to question you, otherwise I would have put you in the shuttle with the Jangxing, you defiler of kitchens. I still may lose my way and send you through an airlock."

Lateef used his bound hands to pull himself up to sit on the bed. His expression was calm, although the thought of Dani at the mercy of these food fanatics curdled his stomach. He prayed she had not endured an interrogation session with the formidable Madame Tamarra like the one he had just finished.

"I have tried to apologize, Sir Taltos." His words were slurred and he closed his eyes only to open them quickly as the floor moved beneath him. *Obosa really packs a punch. Tastes great, too.* A chuckle burst out at the absurdity of praising the taste of the truth serum.

Taltos's face darkened and he loomed over Lateef. "Barbarian. You sully your apology with laughter?"

Lateef sobered quickly, forcing his whirling thoughts to slow. "I am truly sorry for entering the kitchen of Madame Amman uninvited. I made a grievous mistake, not a deliberate insult."

"Then why do you laugh?" The alien was not placated.

Lateef let his head fall forward and shrugged, unable to stop babbling. "Because, Sir Taltos, the Hatti are the only civilization in the entire universe who care enough to ensure their drugs of interrogation have an incredible flavor."

Taltos drew back, confusion obvious on his face. "Do not mock me, Beryllian."

"I meant it as a compliment." Lateef gripped the soft blanket with both hands as the bed shifted underneath him. He couldn't decide if closing his eyes made the motion better or worse, and swallowed heavily. "The Hatti clans are unique in their appreciation of fine cuisine. No one else would care how their interrogation drug tasted. The Falgarans sure don't. Those bastards wouldn't even give a prisoner a sip of ditch water if they were drying up and blowing away in the breeze."

Lateef's eyes went wide in dismay as he realized he had said too much.

"You are free with your insults." Taltos' tone was calm.

Lateef could see ambivalence in the man's expression and tried to get his thoughts in a coherent order. Now was not the time to show weakness. He had apologized enough. "I've already lost three siblings to the war, and most of my patients come from unprovoked Falgaran attacks. They declared themselves my enemy, and I won't apologize for responding appropriately. I understand empty compliments and apologies made to win favor. That is not what I offer you or Madame Amman."

A knock on the door interrupted his story, and Lateef was grateful for the mug of warm broth a young Hatti female thrust into his hands. He sipped slowly, feeling the floor settle beneath his feet. He eyed the plate of bread left on the table, but wasn't sure if Taltos was ready to allow him so much freedom. *This is why I went into the Healer Hall instead of becoming a Field Agent or diplomat. I can't believe Rissa's so eager to jump into situations like this.* He swayed and shook his head, trying to force away the dizziness.

"Eat." Taltos gestured at the tray. "Amman will not appreciate an untouched plate, and food will ease the after-effects of the *Obosa*."

Lateef hesitated and then met the alien's hostile gaze. "I honestly don't mean to cause offense, Sir Taltos. I'm a healer, not a diplomat, and that means I speak my mind before I can consider all of the ramifications."

"So much is obvious." Taltos glared at him for a long moment and then turned away. "Eat, Beryllian. The details will be sorted out later."

"Thank you." Lateef drank the warm broth and nibbled at the delicious bread filled with chunks of cheese. *I am in so far over my head. Rissa would never have gotten into this much trouble. Damn Trevan and his dinner invitations! I wouldn't lose any sleep if they dump that lying Kyle Manning out a convenient airlock, but I can't let Dani get hurt.* His fingers tightened around the mug.

"Sir Taltos, do you know what happened to Ambassador Trevan? He invited me to the feast, but he was not responsible for my getting lost."

The Hatti soldier jerked, several emotions flowing across his face before the impassive mask slipped back into place. "Ambassador Trevan has not been seen since the feast."

Lateef considered the information as he finished the roll of bread. *Would Taltos lie to me about that? Could Trevan be a prisoner? Would the Falgarans be bold enough to kidnap an ambassador in such a public manner?* Possibilities whirled in his mind, none of them good.

"We are not responsible for his disappearance."

"I don't believe you are, Sir Taltos." Lateef considered his words, and decided to take a chance. "I don't think your clan would take the coward's way out. If you say you don't know where he is, I believe you."

Taltos was motionless, only his eyes moving as Lateef took another bite of bread.

"I think our relationship has gotten off on the wrong foot. If you'd like, I can call for a team to come help straighten everything out. The Falgarans are good at promising friendship, but they usually follow up with violence." Lateef snapped his jaw shut. *Idiot. Lesson number one – never show a hint of criticism, especially when you are dealing with a new ally.* His heart sank as Taltos stiffened. *Never should have mentioned the Falgarans, even if you are worried about Trevan.*

"Thane Hantili will speak with you later." Taltos stalked out of the room.

Lateef leaned his head back against the wall. *Just had to push, didn't you? You almost had everything worked out and then you had to bring up the farging*

Falgarans. Chains rattled and he growled under his breath. *Could have gotten these cuffs off, too, if I hadn't let my mouth run off.*

He sniffed at the water on the tray, relieved at the lack of scent and took a cautious sip. When no unexpected explosion of flavor followed, he drained the cup and settled back on the bed, dropping into a light trance to wash the residual effects of the truth serum from his system.

'Lateef!' His sister's mental voice eased into his mind. *'Are you okay?'*

'Rissa, I'm glad to hear you.' He quickly filled her in, hoping the interfering shield would stay down long enough to plan an escape.

'We're coming. Hang...'

Silence descended abruptly and Lateef jerked upright. Nothing in the room had changed. He was still alone, but far more optimistic about the situation than he had been before the brief contact. He had even sensed Dani's presence on the ship. She was angry and confused, but not afraid. He got comfortable on the cot, draping the handcuff chains over the edge of the bed as sleep made his eyelids heavy.

Glad I don't have issues with being rescued by my big sister.

Chapter 21

Rescue

Kyle's head felt as though all seven dwarves were mining for diamonds in it. He licked his lips and groaned at the grungy feel of his teeth. He must have gone on some kind of bender last night, although he didn't remember going out.

"You alive?"

Kyle froze at the undeniably female voice. He never brought anyone to his apartment. On the rare occasion he did have overnight company, they always went to her place or a hotel. Although, the senator's niece, Mandy, might be the one to change that rule. Happiness at the thought of being around the vibrant woman eased some of the ache in his head.

"Here, have some water and go back to sleep."

Gentle hands held a glass to his lips and he drank, relaxing with a contented sigh. Memories of aliens and spaceships and horrible dragon-type creatures flitted across his mind and he sat up abruptly, reeling as his head spun.

"Take it easy."

"Where am I?" His voice was slurred.

"On board the Hatti spaceship. Do you remember how you got here?"

Kyle forced his mind to focus on the whirling memories. The trip in the shuttle, the walk through endless corridors and the pitcher of flavored water. His head popped up and he stared into Dani's concerned eyes.

"I was drugged!"

She watched him closely and then removed her hands from his shoulders, standing as he remained stable. "Yes. They gave us a truth serum."

Kyle hunched over and rested his elbows on his knees as he rubbed his temples. "Feels like a wicked hang-over."

"It was good though, wasn't it?" Dani plopped onto the opposite bed, hugging her legs to her chest.

"Yes," he agreed. "But I finished the whole pitcher before they came to talk to me."

Her eyebrows lifted in an expression he couldn't read.

"Seeing the way you feel, I'm glad I only took a couple of sips."

"Did you get any sleep?" He squeezed his eyes closed for a long moment before slowly straightening up with a muffled groan. He finger-combed his short hair and brushed at the wrinkles in his rumpled shirt.

She shrugged and rested her chin on her knees. "I dozed a bit."

"And no pod people?"

"No people period," she said. "It was quiet the whole... I was going to say night, but I have no idea what time it is. My watch quit right after they picked us up."

Kyle checked his wrist, held his watch to his ear and then shook it. "Mine too." He stretched again before putting his shoes back on and stood with his ear pressed against the stubbornly silent door for several minutes.

"There's nothing out there making any noise," he complained. "You don't think they locked us in here and forgot about us, do you?"

"I doubt it," she said. "They did feed us."

"Yeah," he said with disdain. "Bread and water. Nothing even close to what you made for them."

"Shhh." She hissed, raising a finger to her lips with a warning glare.

Kyle slapped a hand over his mouth, eyes wide with shock. He hadn't meant to say anything, but his tongue had a mind of its own. "It was very good bread. I really liked the cheese."

She rolled her eyes and leaned against the wall. "Why are you here, Mr. Manning? Why couldn't you have left me alone?"

Kyle flinched. "I needed to make sure you were okay. You wouldn't talk to me."

"I didn't have to talk to you. Why would you think I did?"

"I'm a private investigator." He bit his tongue, closing his eyes as he mentally berated himself for babbling. If he wasn't careful, he'd tell her all about the senator and how sorry he was for blowing her cover, even if he hadn't told the senator about her. He took a deep breath and glanced at her out of the corner of his eyes. "I couldn't leave you alone to deal with all the strange things going on. I had a duty to…"

"Stop it." Loose strands of hair covered most of Dani's face, and her expression was decidedly unfriendly. She sat up straighter, trembling with intense emotion. "You don't know me, I don't know you. I don't want to know you. I did not invite you into my life, and don't appreciate your interference. You're under no obligation to protect me and I would appreciate you forgetting the way to my house once we get home."

Kyle slowly backed away from her anger until his legs bumped his cot and he sat with a thump. His yelp of surprise broke her mood and she clenched her jaw a long second before dropping her head back to her knees.

He tried to gather his scattered wits. He'd never seen this side of the normally placid woman. *Could the senator be right? Was Dani responsible for her family's death?* Maybe she was showing guilt, not profound grief.

"I'm sorry." The quiet apology was barely louder than the roaring of the blood in his ears. "You didn't deserve an attack right now. Things are weird enough."

Kyle rubbed at his temples again. "What do you think is going to happen to us?" He could pretend this was a normal conversation.

"Who knows? I think we'll have to wait and see. It's not like we can exactly climb out a window and run home."

Kyle snorted, laughing harder as she raised her head to glare at him. "Oh, come on, Dani. Even you have to admit that was funny. Climbing out the window of a fricking spaceship?"

A wan smile flitted across her lips. "I can't say I ever imagined being in a situation like this."

"At least these guys love you." Kyle was surprised at the bitter anger in his tone.

Dani looked at him for a long moment before dropping her head back to her knees. "You're here with me. Lateef isn't. Has to mean something."

"Crap, Dani, I didn't…" He snapped his mouth shut and took a deep breath. "I'm sorry. You're right. We humans have to stick together, no matter what." He raised a hand as she glared at him. "I don't know what's going on. I don't know if Lateef is the evil man these bald guys think, but I trust you. I'll follow your lead, but I have no clue how to proceed."

He raked his fingers through his hair again. "There's no chance NASA or any other Earth organization can help us. I don't think we have any cell reception up here, even if I had a satellite phone. Whatever happens is up to us. These people like you, so work with it. Answer their questions and ask them to send us home."

Dani stared at him, and he noticed the dark circles accentuating the haunted look in her eyes. He no longer knew who to trust, but his heart leaned towards her instead of his arrogant client.

"How long have you been awake?"

She blinked in surprise at his question. "I don't need much sleep."

He barked out a laugh. "That's what they all say, but science isn't on your side. Everyone needs shut-eye time, even superwomen like you." He overrode her protests. "Lie down for an hour or so. We'll hear anyone coming down the corridor and I promise to wake you if anything happens." He pulled the blanket down and swung her folded legs to the side, leaving her with no options.

"Okay." Her shoulders slumped as she gave up the fight. He pulled her shoes off and sat beside her on the narrow bench after pulling the light blanket over her shoulders. A huge yawn shook her thin body and a faint red hue flushed across her face. He laid a hand on her arm. "Get comfortable and don't worry. I promise I'll wake you if anything comes."

Her body tensed and he moved to his own cot to give her space. He hadn't given her any reason to trust him. He remained alert for any change in their surroundings as her breathing slowed and deepened. They had to figure out a way to rescue themselves since there was no one he could imagine able to rescue him, even if they did know where he was.

On a freaking spaceship. Kyle's mind shied away from the knowledge. If he got home, he'd never be able to tell anyone where he'd been. Not unless he wanted a stay in a padded room.

Suddenly Dani sat upright and reached for her shoes, moving with her eyes closed.

"What?" Kyle demanded. "What's going on?"

"Don't know," she said breathlessly as she fumbled with the lace of her shoe. "I'm not sure, but someone's coming. We need to be ready to go."

She rubbed the sleep out of her eyes and retied her ponytail to recapture the loose strands wafting around her face. Kyle took a position by the door with his ear pressed against the crack straining to hear the slightest sound. The only sound louder than the blood pounding in his ears was the faint roar of air in the ventilation system which had not changed in the entire time he had been on board the ship. The longer everything remained quiet the more he began to think maybe Dani had hallucinated as she lay on the edge of sleep. She began to pace. Kyle was on the verge of telling her she had imagined things when he heard stealthy footsteps.

"Someone's coming."

They both moved behind the door, trying to prepare for whatever was going to happen. *Those aliens wouldn't be stealthy, so this has to be a rescue, right?* The door slowly inched opened and a quiet, very non-Hatti voice called out, "Is anyone there?"

Dani pulled free of Kyle's warning grasp to dart forward and yank the door wide.

"Where's Lateef?" she demanded of the young woman peering into their cell.

"You must be Dani." Large green eyes dominated a face surrounded by a mass of curly auburn hair reaching nearly to her knees. "Brandon and I are here to get you two," she said. "I'm Rissa, Lateef's big sister."

"One of his big sisters." The man who remained on watch in the hallway added as his steely gaze took in everything about the cell and the tired humans. His expression softened when he looked at Rissa, showing a tiny hint of the love he obviously had for her before once again watching the sterile corridors for trouble. "We need to get going, Riss," he added. "They'll be here soon. Those damned shields of theirs made our camouflage pretty iffy and it took forever to get here from the transport bay."

"Who are you people?" Kyle demanded. His body was rigid with anger and distrust and his hand unconsciously reached for the gun that wasn't at his waist. "And what do you mean about shields and allies and Falgarans? What the hell is a Falgaran?"

"We're friends." Rissa confidently reached out to touch his hand. "We've come to take you home."

Kyle felt his suspicion melt away, replaced by a warm, fuzzy feeling of safety as he followed her without a question, uncharacteristically confident this short stranger would keep them all safe.

Chapter 22

Run for Freedom

Rissa led the four of them in a mad dash through featureless hallways. Dani felt like a hamster running in circles through the endless series of identical corridors. Fear squeezed her chest, slowly tightening its grip every time Rissa or Brandon uttered a muffled curse under their breath and guided their charges into an empty room to hide for a few moments.

"Nearly there." Rissa's quiet statement could have been a signal.

Klaxons blared an alarm. The sound of running feet grew more frequent as those empty rooms grew scarce. More than once Kyle's panic threatened to overwhelm Dani as they heard the Hatti soldiers draw closer to their exposed position. And when they did dart into a room barely ahead of the Hatti crew, Dani's heart pounded so loudly she couldn't believe their pursuers didn't hear it. Rissa's encouragement and air of calm competence did little to ease the worry growing into terror.

Brandon gently touched her hand and she felt a wave of calm wash over her. She took a deep, shuddering breath and gave him a quizzical look.

"Most of the panic isn't yours," he said. He glanced at Kyle then back to her. "But you haven't learned how to block outside emotions yet, have you?"

Dani gaped at him. "What do you mean? I still don't know how I can hear Lateef in my head."

The blare of the klaxons halted, and their ears rang with the memory of the loud noise.

Brandon shook his head and continued the conversation. "Sorry," he said. "I know this is all weird and none of us have time for the explanations you deserve." They all froze as the rapid clomps of many booted feet shook the thin door. Rissa stood with her hand on the doorknob, eyes closed in intense concentration until the sound faded.

"I promise to get Lateef to explain everything as soon as we get off this ship," Brandon said. "And he'll find someone to help train you to use whatever abilities you end up having. But I can show you a quick trick to help you block stray emotions until then. At least the few you can get through this damned shield."

Dani listened to his instructions, grateful when the noisy babble receded. Maybe she was getting the hang of this? Or maybe she was in a mental health facility, drugged out of her mind and hallucinating.

"Let's go!" Rissa's command had them on their feet and at the door in seconds.

The nerve-racking game of cat and mouse continued until the little group finally reached the room full of brightly-colored transport ships the two humans recognized from their arrival on board this alien ship.

Rissa and Brandon exchanged glances and Dani's brain itched, even through her new mental shield. She strained to hear any sounds, but there was only the sigh of air moving through the large space and a distant clang of metal on metal. The breeze carried the mingled scents of fuel and metal and some other smell she couldn't place. It was pleasant and brought to mind fresh bread and hot chocolate.

"Let's take a break." Rissa broke the spell and nudged Kyle to sit on the floor as Brandon took off. She took a post at the bow of a bright blue transport, gaze moving constantly.

"What's up?" Dani asked quietly as she stood back-to-back with the shorter woman. She had noticed a distinct chill in Rissa's attitude towards Kyle, but didn't have the desire to figure out why.

"What's the delay?" Kyle's question broke the tension.

"We're waiting for Lateef and 'Rantha." Their rescuer's attention was far away from them. Dani could feel a tickle in her brain and she was almost able to catch words, but they remained tantalizingly out of reach. She stretched her own senses out, reaching for Lateef. She managed to catch a brief contact—enough to know he was alive and preoccupied, but not enough to exchange any information. She took a deep breath and realized Rissa was staring at her with an odd expression.

"Lateef was so right about you." Rissa shook herself and resumed watching their surroundings. "Johfrit will be p… irritated."

"When did you talk to him?" Dani whirled to stare down at the auburn-haired beauty. She wondered who this Johfrit was and why he mattered.

Brandon reappeared suddenly. "Gotta run." He yanked Kyle to his feet to drag him deeper into the maze of parked Hatti transport ships, Rissa and Dani hot on their heels. The sound of pursuit spurred the four of them to greater speed.

"Chef Danielle Hamilton."

Dani stumbled at the sound of her name. It seemed more like an offer of protection than an angry demand, but that made no sense. *Who's that? If I ignore everything, will I be back in reality?*

"Wouldn't recommend it," Rissa whispered.

Dani shot the other woman a startled look.

"This is as real as life gets."

"How?"

"Mind reader, remember? The shields aren't as effective when we're close." Rissa lifted her head in a listening attitude then grinned broadly. "Amarantha has Lateef."

Dani nearly tripped over her own feet before she could get her coordination back.

"They'll meet us at the ship." Rissa urged her to run faster.

Dani halted abruptly with the sudden certainty Lateef was close. She darted to the left, ignoring Rissa's hissed command to stop. A door opened and he was suddenly there. She flung her arms around Lateef, spinning them both with the wild energy of her greeting.

"I couldn't find you," she whispered in his ear.

"I know." He hugged her tightly. "But I'm here now."

"No time for a long reunion." A tall, dark-haired woman joined them. She looked at Danielle, but did not make eye contact. "Company's right behind me."

Lateef threw his arm around Dani's waist and they all ran. Their camouflaged ship was in sight when a large group of Hatti burst out of an adjoining wall of ships. They changed direction but everywhere they turned a new group of heavily armed, bald men faced them.

"This way, Chef Danielle Hamilton. Come to me."

Dani looked to her left to see Taltos holding out a hand, beckoning her as he pointed a weapon at her companions.

"We will keep you safe!"

She recognized three of the men who had come to lunch with her at his back, including her seat-mate from the shuttle ride up.

"I don't need to be rescued." She clutched Lateef's hand. He tried to step in front of her and the Hatti group raised their weapons threateningly until Dani pushed Lateef behind her.

"We will keep you safe," Taltos repeated. "You must come with me."

"I am safe," she said.

"Not with them." The venom in his tone startled her and she looked back at Lateef's family. The sentiment was apparently mutual. The three Beryllians faced the Hatti soldiers with their own weapons drawn and Kyle in the middle of their protective circle. Rissa motioned for her to join them as Lateef tugged at her arm.

"You people are nuts," Dani muttered before raising her voice to address both groups. "This really needs to stop right now."

"This battle is not our choice," Taltos said.

"You attacked a guest at an official diplomatic function without provocation," Rissa retorted. "Then you made demands for our Embassy to hand him over without any explanation of what he had done or what you intended to do to him."

"Okay." Dani held up a hand to stop the escalating argument. "You guys need to sit down and talk. There's obviously a whole bunch of misunderstanding going on here. Why don't we go back to my house for coffee, crumb cake and a nice long chat?"

A wave of agitation started near the wall and everyone fell silent as the crowd of Hatti parted to reveal the muscular man who had interrogated her stalking through the hanger toward them. He towered over the much shorter throng bowing as he passed, rippling like wheat in the wind.

"Thane Hantili." The whisper ran through the crowd like a prayer.

'Be ready to run.' Lateef spoke in her mind.

She shook her head in denial. She was going nowhere until the situation was resolved. Otherwise she would never be able to return home with the man she had come to love. She knew she'd follow Lateef if he had to go into exile, but there had to be a middle ground. She ignored Lateef's continued telepathic pleas as the Thane's arrival made his arguments moot.

"Greetings, Danielle Hamilton." He nodded his large head respectfully at her.

"So, you're the Thane?" She recognized her interrogator. "Thank you for the exquisite pearls." She pulled her hand free of Lateef's and took a step forward. Everyone in the room tensed and she halted, shooting a withering glance around the gathered crowd of anxious soldiers.

"Mellow out, guys," she snapped. "What do you think I'm going to do? Gnaw on his kneecaps? You know I'm not armed and I have given you absolutely no reason to think I'm an enemy."

"But now we know you are friends with them." The shout came from somewhere near the back of the room.

Dani looked back at Lateef. "What else did you do?" she asked. "Insult someone's family recipe?" He blushed and she turned to face him fully.

"I told you I was tricked into entering a kitchen during feast prep."

"Seriously? That's the only reason Taltos has been chasing you all over creation?"

He shrugged minutely and she gazed heavenward, begging for patience as the wordless muttering nearly drowned out his explanation.

"I had awful timing. I walked into the kitchen when one of the Matriarchs was finishing a dish. I tried to apologize, but..."

Dani caught a flash of movement from the corner of her eye. Time slowed to a crawl as she realized the metallic glare came from a weapon that looked like a small spear gun aimed directly at the Hatti Thane. She blinked and a gory horror movie played across her closed eyelids. The enraged warriors ripped Lateef and his family to shreds as the Hatti leader died. It wouldn't matter if the attacker was one of theirs. These warriors were already primed to believe the Beryllians were evil savages who deserved death. She had to stop this. She yelled a warning as she flung herself at the alien Thane, hoping to knock him out of harm's way. White hot pain plowed through her back, shoving her into a dark chasm as she heard Lateef scream her name.

Chapter 23

I Can Save Both of Them

Fury roared through Lateef as he saw the silver bolt pinning Dani to the Hatti leader. Time warped as he watched them fall in slow motion, her scream of pain reverberating in his mind as several soldiers blocked his view.

"Dani!" The anguished cry ripped from his throat. He lunged toward the fallen pair. Two beefy guards grabbed him before he could take more than a single step and twisted his arms behind him, forcing him to his knees in spite of his frantic struggles. All of his self-defense training vanished from his mind.

He was hyperaware of his surroundings yet removed from everything. With his attention focused on Dani's pale form he could hear his companions and the muttering Hatti, but nothing mattered except her.

"Don't resist," Brandon told Kyle as angry soldiers advanced on them.

"But we didn't..." Kyle tried to argue.

"Doesn't matter." Brandon interrupted the human. He went to his knees with his hands on his head before he could be thrown down. "Don't give anyone a reason to overreact."

Kyle slowly copied the submissive posture, resentment plain on his face.

Lateef tried again to get to Dani, but his captor shoved his head to the floor with a curse.

'She's alive. There's still hope.' Brandon's reassurance helped him get his panic under control as Taltos stomped up to him, black eyes cold with a fury so deep his body shook.

"I knew you were trouble, Beryllian." The voice was soft, but the dark promise of imminent death cut through the confused babble filling the transport bay. "We were warned about your kind. We would have disposed of you long ago if Danielle Hamilton had not vouched for you. But if our Thane dies..."

"We were not involved in this attack." Rissa's soothing voice, rich with deep undertones of grief, cut through the babble. She was the only member of their group to remain upright. A single soldier pinned her wrists behind her. She was obviously a captive, yet she radiated an aura of calm that spread to the aliens around her. She shot a glance to the side where a cluster of angry men pinned the shooter to the floor.

"Your soldiers have detained the one responsible. I am certain you will learn he is either a Falgaran in disguise or a traitor working with that contemptible race." She paused, waiting for some sign from her audience.

Lateef strained to reach Dani any way he could. Although he was only a few steps away, the distance felt immense. He could sense the spark of her life fading. He squirmed against his captor. For the first time in his life he wished he had worked on a martial art. *I can't let her die.*

Rissa continued to speak, dominating the large room. "Lateef is a Master Healer. If it is possible to save your Thane and Chef Danielle, he will do so."

Lateef jerked out of his daze at Rissa's words, but forced himself to be still as Taltos glared at him. *I can save both of them. Danielle's tough enough to give me the time.*

"Brandon is also a healer," Rissa said. "And I, too have some healing talents. Please allow us to help them."

She looked small and frail in front of the tall soldier holding her captive, yet Lateef knew she was anything but.

"I fear it will take both of them as well as your own medics. You need to decide soon." She looked away, giving the alien soldier space to decide.

Silence began in the far corner, slowly spreading through the hanger. A path opened in the milling soldiers, and two elaborately garbed women, every bit as hairless as the men, strode the length of the long room. A dozen squat, white-robed technicians followed them, bearing stretchers and medical equipment. Whispers followed their progress and the tension in the room decreased. Silky gowns, bordered with elaborate designs brushed the floor as the Matriarchs split up, each heading for a different trouble spot. The first woman in royal purple sank to the floor near the stricken Thane and the crowd shifted enough for Lateef to get his first good look at the aftermath of the attack.

"Dani!" A hard yank on his twisted arms cut his shocked shout short. His nightmares would forever be haunted by the vision of his love stretched face down across the much larger Thane. A short metal dart protruded through her lower back, pinning the two together.

"Shit." Kyle's inelegant exclamation reverberated behind him and Lateef clenched his trapped fists to avoid attacking the human. *Can't trust him not to betray Dani for a fee. I'll be happy to take care of the bastard once...* Lateef sagged as the knowledge he might lose his love hit him.

Taltos joined the Matriarch who sniffed at the bolt sticking through Dani's back as the technicians examined the Thane.

"Madame Amman." Taltos bowed deeply before holding out a hand to help her to her feet. She accepted his help and brushed imaginary dirt from her full skirts as she composed her expression.

"The bolt is poisoned." Horrified anger laced with despair dripped from her clipped words. "I do not recognize the toxin. Hantili is..."

"Can you save him?" Taltos asked after a long, tense silence. His pale green face lost all color and he swayed as the woman gave a sharp shake of her head. "There must be something we can do!"

"Let me help!" Lateef begged. "At the very least I can keep him stable while you interrogate the assassin and find out what poison he used."

Amman and Taltos exchanged wary glances. Dani's arm brushed against Taltos's leg. He fell to his knees and clasped her hand.

"Why did you sacrifice...?" Deep emotion clogged his throat.

"Let. Lateef. Save. Him." Each word came on a separate breath.

Ammon jerked with surprise at those words, crouching to study the wounded woman intently before turning her attention back to Taltos.

"Dare we take the chance?"

Taltos lifted his shoulders in a resigned shrug. "We are lost if we do nothing. We owed Danielle Hamilton a debt before this." He closed his large eyes for a long moment. "He can do no more damage."

Amman abruptly motioned for the guards.

Lateef raced over the short distance, falling heavily to the floor. One hand went on Dani and the other on the unconscious Thane, heedless of the green and red blood soaking into his rumpled jeans.

He closed his eyes in concentration and Dani gasped in relief, opening her eyes to look at him.

"You have to save him, Lateef."

"I will." Lateef cut her off as he concentrated. "I know what I have to do." His breath caught as he realized how precarious the situation was. He would have to give up his last few certain moments with her on the slim chance he'd be able to neutralize the poison and heal the damage from the bolt. He ignored the agony of his heart, praying Dani would understand.

"I need Brandon's help." He appealed directly to Amman, allowing his fear to show in his eyes. "The poison is too strong for me to save both of them. And I have to…"

The Matriarch nodded and Brandon rushed over as Dani's breathing grew more ragged.

"Stay with me, Danielle Hamilton. I can't lose you now." His voice faded as the Thane's heartbeat stuttered to a stop. "Keep her stable, Brandon."

Dani jerked as pain flared from her lower back for a split second as Lateef passed her care to Brandon.

'Don't let her die.'

'I won't.'

Lateef buried his fear beneath the routine of healing a critical patient. He couldn't afford to worry about what happened around him. Fear sapped the healing abilities, and the poison flowing through the pinned bodies was nasty. The Thane took a deep breath and Lateef realized several hands held his patients steady as the clan leader's body shook.

"We won't let you hurt." Lateef was dimly aware Rissa had joined them, lending her healing energy as she reassured Dani. "You have to trust us. Lateef and Brandon are both very, very good at what they do. You have to relax and work with us, Dani."

"What do you need from us?" Taltos spoke and Dani moved.

"Hold still!" Brandon snapped.

Lateef's breath caught harshly in his throat. He shared the bright shaft of agony in her back that traveled up and down her spine in sharp, spiky waves. Her back arched and convulsions shook her entire body, nearly ripping her away from the hands trying to keep her steady.

Several people yelled simultaneously. Bodies shifted toward them, radiating confused anger. Lateef tightened his hold on the Thane, calming his tremors and spared a tiny bit of concentration to help Brandon block Dani's pain. Their situation was precarious. If the Hatti felt the Thane was lost, they could all still die.

"Got it!" Brandon's triumphant shout cut through the confusion and Dani gasped.

Rissa knelt between Brandon and Lateef and gently took one of Dani's hands in hers as she sent waves of calm through the physical link. "Okay, Dani. Brandon had to put an extreme block on you. You won't feel any pain. You can't sleep until we know how much damage there is. But you have to stop fighting the healing."

Most of Lateef's attention was focused on the Hatti Thane, but he thought he sensed a shadowy presence watching Dani. His patient shuddered convulsively, and he had to concentrate on the delicate task of chasing down all of the poison, ignoring his sister's muttered comments about heroes being bad patients.

Sweat plastered Lateef's hair to his face. His eyes remained closed in intense concentration as he ensured the blood vessels near the bolt were sealed. "It's time to move her." He trusted his companions to prepare Dani.

Once Dani had been lifted away from Hantili, Lateef sank deeper into a healing trance. His head bowed in concentration as he pressed his hands on either side of the metal shaft, healing the pierced organs so the Thane would not bleed out.

Rissa wrapped a cloth around the exposed length of the bolt. At Lateef's unspoken signal she pulled the metal shaft straight out before handing it to a waiting white-robed Hatti medic. Lateef immediately shifted his hands to cover the wound, stemming the welling of rich, green blood following the metal shaft. Sweat dripped from his brow, and his entire universe tightened to the battle to keep Thane Hantili alive.

Kyle knelt beside Dani, one hand lightly touching her shoulder. "You okay?" He struggled not to look over his shoulder at the alien guard watching him so closely. Dani's act of heroism had given the rest of her group a reprieve, but they were not yet out of the woods. Something unexpected had happened to the assassin and the aliens were not too happy about it.

"Lateef needs help," she repeated. Her words slurred, but she was insistent.

"He has help," Kyle said. "There are a dozen medics over there. Everyone seems calm. Stay with me, Hamilton," he said firmly as her eyes started to glaze over. "This party is just getting started. You wouldn't want to miss anything." Kyle glanced at Brandon.

"Keep her talking." The words were strained.

Beads of sweat dripped down the healer's furrowed brow and Kyle's heart slammed in his chest. This was so not a good sign.

"The leader guy seems to be okay. The medics around him are calm." He was babbling now. Dani's face had lost all trace of color and though her eyes tracked him they did not focus. He looked over at Brandon and saw more sweat beaded on his flushed face.

Amarantha stalked over, cursing up a blue streak as she approached. She paused briefly in her litany when she noticed the strain on Brandon's face. "The thrice be-damned-goat-loving-worthless-waste-of-skin died," she said. "He screamed like a girl and croaked the second Madame Tamarra started to get something useful out of his worthless hide. Way too bloody convenient if you ask me. Her methods weren't even that harsh." She shot an admiring glance back at the Matriarch in question. "I think his boss is still around, though I'll be damned if I can figure out how he's getting any kind of reliable psionics through the fragging shield and all electronics can be tracked. Security claims everyone in the hanger belongs, except for us."

Kyle gulped at the callous remarks. *Every death deserves some regret, doesn't it?*

"What's taking so long over here? I've seen this guy re-grow entire limbs in less time than this and she still looks like utter crap." Amarantha pointed her chin in Dani's direction.

Kyle blinked at the dark-haired woman in surprise then shuddered at the coldness lurking in those eyes. This beautiful, alien creature was definitely a candidate for some serious mental health help.

She gave him a wintery smile and he immediately felt like a lamb staring at a hungry wolf. "I've had lots of therapy," she said. "Turns out I have trouble dealing with assholes who hurt other people. I'm also extremely good at holding grudges."

The chill fury radiating off the tall figure made him shudder convulsively. He vowed to do anything he could to stay on the lethal woman's good side.

"Don't worry." Her toothy smirk didn't reassure him. "I didn't kill the assassin. Did confirm he was a mother-loving Falgaran disguised as a Hatti guard. Can't believe we didn't figure out the how or why before the bastard croaked. Would have reported events to my handler, but can't get through the fracking shields these people have. Can barely get anything from Rissa when we're practically touching, and can't teleport an inch. Glad the healing isn't affected"

Kyle had no idea what the odd-woman meant and trying to understand was making his brain hurt so he asked the most important question.

"Can you help Brandon?"

Amarantha snorted derisively. "I can't even heal my own injuries. I'm not one of those fancy, multi-talented field agents. I'm a soldier." There was a hint of bitterness in her voice as she observed Lateef and Rissa who still hovered over the Hatti leader.

Suddenly a huge smile lit up Dani's face.

"Caity," she whispered. "I missed you, baby-girl!"

"Shit!" The exclamation seemed to explode from the frazzled Brandon. "I need Lateef."

"Hold on, Dani!" Kyle grasped her chin in an attempt to make her focus on him instead of ghosts from her past. "You can't leave us."

Amman and Taltos hurried over at Brandon's exclamation. Amman gently pushed Kyle aside to grab Dani's chin to sniff her breath. One side of her mouth lifted in an involuntary snarl before she nodded sharply at her companion.

"You may call for more help," Taltos said. "We will not block your healers." He spoke quietly into a communicator as Amman took a small bottle from a pocket and dripped three careful drops into Dani's lax mouth.

Brandon unsuccessfully stifled a protest.

"This will strengthen her," the Matriarch said. Her stare was merciless. "The other healer found it useful." She straightened and nodded her head at Brandon's whispered thanks then returned to her leader.

"I'll call," Amarantha said. "You want Mellora?"

Brandon nodded, most of his attention focused on his patient.

Kyle waited until the lethal woman opened her eyes again and then exploded when nothing else happened.

"I thought you were getting help? How is someone supposed to get here in time? Shouldn't we leave for a hospital instead of standing here?"

"Why would you want to do that?"

Kyle whirled to see a new woman glaring at him. She wore brightly-colored scrubs capable of passing at any medical office or hospital on Earth. Icy blue eyes dominated a heart-shaped face framed by thick, black hair pulled in a ponytail.

"How did...?"

Her icy glare intensified and Kyle raised his hands and backed away with his question unfinished.

"I was expecting to find Rissa in trouble again." She ignored everyone as she sank to her knees beside Brandon. "As usual, our 'Rantha was a bit short on details."

"It was a bloody emergency, Mellora. You always ask the exact same fracktastic questions again when you get here so why waste time repeating things?" Amarantha grabbed Kyle's shoulder and began edging away.

"Still haven't improved your vocabulary, I see." Mellora shot her a single glance before placing a well-manicured hand on Dani's head. "What are we looking at?"

Brandon began his report as Mellora closed her eyes. "Unknown poison on a dart..."

Chapter 24

You Saved Our Thane

Lateef extended his exhausted senses in one last scan through the Hatti leader's body.

'It's all good, 'Teef.' Rissa's equally exhausted mental voice chided him. *'Let the man wake up now. His people are getting worried.'*

He obeyed, withdrawing his senses as the Hatti Thane began to stir. Settling back on his heels he watched as the leader sat up, aided by the formidable Madame Amman and a med tech.

A flurry of activity erupted when the man rose to his feet.

Lateef's head fell forward and he tried to convince his body he still had some energy.

'You okay?' Rissa's mental voice was barely strong enough for him to hear.

'Will be. The poison was nasty.' He briefly wondered why his sister was helping out at the Hall, but then hoped his assistant would have a mug of restorative broth ready. Then he could collapse in bed to ride out the inevitable migraine. It had been a long time since he had needed to extend his abilities so close to the point of burnout, but this patient was important. A week of sleep would do wonders. Maybe someone could drop him off on Earth and he could recover with Dani. Her presence would do more good than any of Mellora's herbal concoctions.

Suddenly the fog lifted and he remembered where he was.

"Dani." His eyes popped open and he stumbled to his feet, only to fall to all fours as his exhausted body failed him. His mind reached out, but there was nothing but silence.

"Steady there." Kyle grabbed him around the waist and helped him to sit on a gurney.

"I have to get to Dani." Lateef fought to stand.

"You need to rest at least a couple of minutes." Rissa's voice was barely louder than the background noise. She allowed one of the hovering medical technicians to help her onto another gurney.

Lateef groaned. "I abandoned Dani. I have to help her." Each breath felt like an ancient massvore sat on his chest.

A Hatti crewmember appeared with finger foods and mugs of rich broth. Amarantha helped Rissa drink the broth, ignoring the agent's tired protests she'd rather sleep.

"Drink this," Kyle said as he held a mug to Lateef's lips.

He swallowed automatically, hands rising to help hold the cup. Welcome warmth flooded his system and the fog swaddling his brain thinned.

"Dani." Lateef renewed his struggles to get to his love.

"Dani has help. You need to eat and then we'll go check on her." Kyle popped a piece of cheesy bread in Lateef's open mouth.

He chewed and swallowed, accepting several more chunks even as he complained about being restrained.

"Enough," Amarantha snapped. "You can't do anything right now, Lateef. Brandon and Mellora have it under control, but if you collapse or continue to cause a scene, then one of them will have to come deal with you instead of working on her. So, shut up and eat."

Lateef glared at her, guilt gnawing at his gut.

Taltos approached and Lateef tried to struggle to his feet, only to have the soldier wave for him to remain where he was.

"Thank you for the sustenance," Lateef inclined his head respectfully. "I look forward to the opportunity to repay the favor."

"And I wait with impatience for the opportunity to join you at your table." The formal phrases were stilted and Taltos looked uncomfortably around the room, unable to meet the Beryllian healer's eyes for a long moment.

"Thank you for saving my Thane. Our medics tell us he would not have survived without your help." The words came in a rush.

"He wouldn't have lived long enough to hit the floor if Dani hadn't absorbed most of the poison." Lateef's voice caught, and he blinked, struggling not to shed the tears that wanted to fall. He looked at the cluster of people around

Dani's gurney, needing to do something. He couldn't feel her but wasn't sure if the silence was because of the shields on the ship or because he was so wiped. He refused to consider the possibility she was dead. No one would be around her if she was gone.

"Master Chef Danielle Hamilton is very brave," Taltos said. "It is hard to believe she lives so far from civilization and yet..." His voice trailed off as he apparently remembered his audience. He took a deep breath. "Her small body contains a huge life-source. I would not yet give in to despair."

An awkward silence took hold as Kyle continued to hand him bits of food he wolfed down unconsciously, distantly aware Rissa was up and walked to Brandon's side with the aid of the medic.

"Did you figure out what this assassin was trying to accomplish?" Lateef asked. "Or how he got on board?"

The bald man flushed a dark shade of green and looked at the floor. "He was in disguise as a crewmember. He joined us when we met another clan-ship a few weeks ago. No one ever knew much about him, beyond the fact he was vocal in his opposition to listening to what he called the Alliance propaganda."

"The Alliance?" Kyle repeated.

Amarantha grunted loudly and moved to the far side of Kyle as she explained. "The Falgarans are evil bastards, destroying what they don't eat just to keep anyone else from using it. They provoke all sorts of wars and crap to create havoc. The more pain and misery they can generate the happier the fracking jerk-offs are. They've made a lot of enemies over the years and we've banded together to make them pay."

"So, what happened here?" Kyle looked confused, or in shock, but he continued to hand Lateef food.

"The goat-loving Falgarans aren't imbeciles," Amarantha said. She tossed her long hair back over her shoulder and shot Kyle a look saying he was stupid beyond belief. "They start with a con game. Seems like getting a race to give up peacefully really gets their rocks off. Slime molds have managed to get us to play their sicko game with them. Damn parasites have a list of rules and rigid job descriptions for diplomats and field agents." She shook her head in disgust. "And we follow those ridiculous rules for what they can do and what can be done to them, but they stretch those same damn rules out of shape."

"It's given us a chance to defeat the Empire." Lateef protested, feeling a bizarre need to defend the policy. "They outnumber us, even with our allies."

Amarantha snorted, the expression in her cold eyes growing wilder. "The mother-loving-eat-their-own-young slimy bastards always break treaties and we do nothing but send polite protests to Tarnkappe. And then apologize for the disturbance. How many of our women are missing, leaving a trail directly to the Empire, and yet we won't begin to pursue clues for fear of creating an 'incident'?"

Kyle looked between the two Beryllians, his eyes wide.

Taltos broke the tense silence. "Before he died, we did learn this assassin was responsible for the event that made us think you were less than honorable." The admission was obviously hard for him. "Madame Tamarra confirmed he deliberately directed you to the kitchen at the worst possible time."

"That's good news." Lateef let his frustration at Amarantha go. She was irrational where the Falgarans were concerned. Her mother was one of the missing. And he had to admit he was not exactly in his own right mind right now. For the first time he felt the tiniest bit of sympathy for her erratic behavior. If he lost... He refused to allow the thought to continue. "I hated to think I was so clueless. It was never my intent to cause offense."

"We understand." Taltos said. "And for our part, we are sorry to have reacted so strongly prior to an investigation. We are not normally so... excitable."

Rissa suddenly appeared and dropped to her knees in front of Lateef to take his cold hands into hers.

His heart thudded to a stop and sank down to his shoes. "No." He protested loudly as the blood drain from his head. "You can't tell me..." He tried to pull free and get to Dani, but Rissa tightened her grip.

"She's not dead."

"Then what?" Fear tightened his throat, choking his voice as terrifying scenarios flooded his mind.

"She's badly hurt." Rissa held a finger to his lips to keep him silent. "And she was so much weaker than anyone suspected before she was shot. Most of the poison on the bolt ended up in her, and you know how hard the drug was to neutralize in the Thane. Mellora isn't sure how much of the damage will be permanent, but they are optimistic."

"Then I..."

"You are too exhausted and too upset to do anything right now," Rissa said. "Brandon and Mellora have already taken Dani and a Hatti medic team to Healer Hall. Amarantha will take a Hatti delegation, including Madame Amman to Beryl when they're ready. The Thane will have to prove he's okay before Amman will leave, but she insists she's the only one who can take care of Dani properly." A bemused look crossed Rissa's tired face. "She flatly refused to allow a Clan member to recover in some heathen place all alone."

"We guard our own, Healer Lateef. Chef Hamilton will recover. Amman shall ensure it." Taltos nodded his head and walked off as if there was no question everything would go as expected.

"See? She can't help but get better." Rissa touched his shoulder and his rigid control broke. She held him tightly as grief racked his exhausted body.

Chapter 25

Foolish LIttle One

That was a foolish thing to do, little one. You ruined several years of planning with your impetuous action. You are to become an Apirri, not die in place of a worthless animal.

My Apirri tells me you will survive with the Beryllian scum's help, but I must leave you in their hands for longer than I wish. But maybe I can turn this to my benefit. It is obvious the healer won't let you go. He would also make an excellent slave.

His family connections would cause even more chaos to the Alliance. Hmmm. I believe this could work. Maybe your punishment will be much lighter than planned. I will not allow you to remain a couple, though. I have much bigger plans for you, my sweet.

Chapter 26

Dani Isn't Home Yet

Kyle waited on Dani's porch as the Sheriff's car pulled to a stop. The passenger door opened and Abby bounced over Anna White Bear to tear across the yard to greet him. The dog sniffed excitedly at his shoes and up his leg before sneezing and barreling around to the back yard, where sounds of construction filled the quiet afternoon. The sheriff and his wife followed more slowly, their measured tread filling Kyle with dread. *Can't believe they left me alone here.*

"Mr. Manning." Charlie nodded his head with a frosty politeness. Anna's head barely reached her husband's shoulder, and thick black hair with a few silvery strands hung to her waist in two fat braids. But the frosty look in her brown eyes made Kyle's reptilian brain gibber in fear.

Kyle's heart sank to his toes. *They know. Anna'll gut me like a fish. That's why I'm here instead of one of the aliens. I thought they forgave me.*

"Care to explain the current situation?"

The sheriff's question froze the babbling in his mind and Kyle opened his mouth, hoping coherent words of explanation would miraculously pour out.

"You okay?" Confusion slowly replaced some of the anger in the sheriff's tone and he removed his hat and swiped his arm across his forehead. "You keep your mouth open like that much longer and you're going to catch some flies."

Kyle snapped his jaw shut and took a deep breath. Maybe he would have a chance to explain before Anna passed judgment again. His ego still burned from the last confrontation, but Charlie was a rational man. Words miraculously gushed out of his mouth. "Hi, Sheriff White Bear. Dani isn't back yet. Some friends are taking care of her house until she comes home. She wanted me to thank you for watching Abby, and I don't know how long she'll be gone."

He could see the older man's expression change from mild interest to anger as the words tumbled from his lips in a torrent he couldn't slow.

"Where is Dani? Who are these friends, and how are you involved?"

Kyle shivered and tried to get his mind focused. *I'm so not ready to explain all of this. Where's Tamarra or one of the others? Isn't that why they came? At least I hope it was to take care of the house, explain shit to the locals and not to start a new settlement here to take over the Earth. Focus, Kyle.*

"I don't know where Dani is at this exact moment. There was an… incident and Dani got hurt. Lateef took her to his clinic until she was healthy enough to come home."

"What do you mean she's hurt and you can't tell me where she is? And why did that stranger take her somewhere?" The deceptively mild expression could not hide the barely leashed fury in the man's dark eyes. "Two weeks ago, I get a call out of the blue from Danielle asking me to take care of her scatter-brained mutt and she's gone by the time I get here. She left food on the table and dirty dishes in the kitchen. That girl has never left a room with a single object out of place! And then we find your car in the driveway, but there's no sign of you. And neither one of you could be bothered to answer a phone call. Dani doesn't have a cell phone. What's your excuse?"

As the muscular lawman loomed over him, Kyle wanted nothing more than to find a quiet spot to sit and think while tossing back a cold brew. The last thing he wanted to cope with was trying to explain things he couldn't understand.

"I thought you understood you were to stay away from Dani."

Anna's mellow contralto froze the marrow in his bones. His life passed before his eyes and he hoped whoever cleaned out his apartment would be discreet when disposing of his magazine collection. *Playing with a grizzly bear cub would have been safer than talking to Anna. Why couldn't Charlie have come alone? How could he explain the bizarre situation to this woman who could flay him with her tongue?*

"It's not my fault." He cringed at the whiney sound of his voice. How could this woman make him feel like a toddler with only a few words? He sucked in a lung-full of air and gathered the tattered remnants of his courage. "I needed to apologize, we ate pancakes, and then there was a knock on the door and things got out of control. Honestly, Sheriff, I don't know how to tell you where

Dani is." He ran a shaky hand through his ragged hair. He needed a shave and a haircut. And coffee. *Pots and pots of coffee – maybe an IV drip. I'll never get used to teleportation and alien civilizations.*

"Give the poor guy a break." Amarantha strolled around the side of the house. Her eyes constantly swept her surroundings, always watching for danger, even as her body appeared relaxed. "He's had a rough couple of weeks."

"Who are you?" Charlie stepped back, one hand reaching automatically for his weapon.

Abby tore around the side of the house, nearly knocking the wary Amarantha off her feet as she bounded onto the porch. The dog bounced her front feet off Kyle's stomach, forcing a grunt out of him before dancing around the Sheriff in canine excitement. She stuck her long nose to the ground, sniffing at the front door and then darted out into the yard before returning to the porch to whine at Kyle.

"She's not home yet, girl." Kyle crouched to ruffle the anxious dog's fur. "She still has some healing to do, but she will be here as soon as possible."

The front door opened and Charlie and Anna gaped at the greenish-skinned, bald woman standing there in an outfit reminiscent of ancient Rome.

"Okay, Kyle. You need to explain who all these people are and why Dani isn't home yet." Anna's tone held a brittle edge that scraped Kyle's nerves.

"I think Madame Tamarra will do a better job than I can." Kyle shrugged, ruffling Abby's ears. "She actually understands what's happening."

"Come inside, please. I have food and beverage prepared, although the conditions here are beyond primitive." Tamarra shuddered before gesturing for the humans to enter Dani's house.

Amarantha walked up the porch stairs, sending a final searching glance around the quiet mountain. "I'd recommend obeying Madame Tamarra's request," she said in a stage whisper when Charlie balked. "The food's awesome, and we can bring you up to speed."

"I can't believe how much you've changed the house, Madame Tamarra. Dani'll be so surprised. The floor plan is very different from what she had before." Anna exchanged a glance with her husband.

Kyle's stomach churned with angst at the knowledge the alien Tamarra was trusted more than he was. Ever since the White Bear's had learned of the Hatti's existence Kyle's reputation had diminished. He was no longer welcome in the small mountain town. Three weeks ago, he wouldn't have cared, but now he longed to be a part of this growing community. He was amazed at how quickly the town had welcomed the alien Hatti without too many questions. The few people who resented the new buildings and increased population had been won over by the freely provided food and the swarm of well-behaved children or were just willing to give the strangers a chance, no matter where they came from.

"Do you have any word on when Dani will be home?"

Kyle heard the tension in Anna's voice. Apparently, there were limits to her trust. He wanted to hear the answer, too. He should report back to his office. The senator had filled his voicemail with demands for answers after he had told his assistant, Judith, to return the retainer and fire the client. Maybe Mandy could run interference for him. Surely the man had a soft spot for his only niece? *Judith'll call the men in the white suits and butterfly nets when she gets her hands on me. I'll have to come up with one great story before I think about going home.*

That was a problem for later. He couldn't concentrate on anything until he knew Dani was okay. Then he could deal with his obnoxious, should-be-ex-client and get on with his life. Amarantha reported Dani was improving but provided no details. And he wasn't sure he totally trusted the bizarre woman who seemed to teeter on the brink of insanity.

"I have heard she is expected tomorrow." Tamarra flicked imaginary dust off her rich robes and motioned for a helper to refill everyone's coffee mug.

"Why didn't anyone tell me?" Kyle half-rose from his chair, subsiding as both women glared at him.

"There was no reason to." Tamarra's flat dismissal stung him.

I should have left days ago. These people all think I'm little better than pond scum. But he couldn't leave before finding out Dani was okay. Pretending he understood the supposed telepathy, interplanetary travel, and psychic healing was one thing, but he had to see Dani for himself, if only to say good-bye. Then he could pretend all the rest had been a bad dream, and he hadn't let jealousy goad him into being a jerk.

"Is there anything you need us to do to get ready?" Anna asked, pointedly turning her back on him.

"Her room is freshly cleaned, and the healers will send any special supplies she may require. Amman says she resists the healing, and they hope coming home will force her to be sensible."

Charlie let out a laugh he quickly stifled as Tamarra turned her glare on him. "Sorry." He pretended to cough as Anna smacked his leg under the table. "You gotta admit the idea of our Dani being sensible about taking care of herself is pretty funny. You know she'll try to catch up on her business and the garden and anything else she can as soon as she walks in the door."

"There is no reason for her to fret." Tamarra sat up straighter, gazing down her nose at the sheriff. "She provided us with excellent instructions. We have filled all of her orders and found new customers and her garden was prepared for the season. She need do nothing more than rest and regain her strength."

"And maybe convince Bob Saunders you don't intend to take over his herd of goats." Kyle couldn't resist the dig, although the flash of anger in the alien eyes did give him second thoughts.

"I would not steal from a neighbor."

He could hear the longing in her tone, and knew the prickly alien had been smitten with the funny creatures.

"Nobody thinks you would, Madame Tamarra." Anna soothed the foreign woman, shooting the men a withering glance.

Kyle knew his time with these people was coming to a close. He realized with shock he would miss them, even the terrifying Amarantha.

"Okay, Manning." Charlie got his feet and dropped a not quite friendly hand onto Kyle's shoulder, urging him out of the chair. "Why don't you and I go for a walk while the ladies chat?"

Kyle allowed himself to be guided out of the newly remodeled house. He was certain Dani would miss the open floor plan, but the first thing the Hatti crew had done was close off the kitchen from the rest of the floor, hanging heavy curtains across the picture windows to get the privacy they considered proper for food preparation. The thought of the conniption fit the sedate Matriarch would throw if she found out about the Gourmet Foodie Network made him chuckle. Maybe it was a good thing Dani didn't have cable. And that the aliens were too busy to investigate the internet.

Abby bounded up, dropping a soggy ball on his shoe as he stepped off the porch. He groaned as she gave him a quick canine grin before focusing intently on the ball, waiting for the slightest movement. He pretended to kick it, laughing as the dog followed his feints before he booted the ball across the yard. Abby took off, skimming the ground as her fur flowed behind her.

"That dog is crazy." Charlie's expression was distant as he stared into the heart of the Rocky Mountain Range. "Dani won't believe all the changes. Not sure how she'll handle these Hatti being in charge of her space."

"The Clan take good care of all of the animals." Kyle heard the bitterness oozing out of his tone. "They'll do the same for Dani until she's able to take care of herself."

"And then what?"

Kyle took a deep breath before kicking the ball again. He watched the dog running, so happy and carefree and felt a smile on his lips. "I don't know." He turned to meet Charlie's bland expression. "I really don't. Even after being around these aliens for several weeks I don't know what to think about them. The Hatti owe Dani big-time for saving their Clan. The Beryllians... I don't know." He shook his head and kicked the ball again, taking several steps down the driveway in an unconscious desire to get away from the strangeness in the house.

"Lateef seems to care for Dani, but he left her to die so he could cure the Hatti guy, and his sister helped him do it. Brandon's nice enough, but he's not in charge, and that Amarantha lady—well, let's say if she snaps and kills everyone here, I won't be surprised."

"So, you don't trust any of them?" Charlie gave him no clue about his own position.

"I don't know." Kyle kicked the ball farther down the drive and walked after it. "Why did any of them drop everything to move to a foreign planet to make things easier for Dani? Could this place be a base to use to take over the world?"

"What about you?" Charlie fanned himself with his uniform hat before resettling it on his head. "Why are you still here?"

Kyle's stomach clenched. He did not want to have this conversation. "I want to make sure Dani gets home safely."

Charlie stared at him a long moment. "That's all? Why'd you show up here to begin with?"

"I told you I was looking for someone, and she was my best lead." Sweat trickled down Kyle's neck, and he resisted the urge to allow his gaze to swerve away. He had to stick around long enough to make sure Dani was okay. Then he could throw the senator off her trail.

Charlie's tone hardened and the temperature around them dropped into the distinctly frigid zone. "Don't you think it's time to come clean, Mr. Manning? Confession can be good for the soul."

The ground underneath them began to shake and Abby zoomed up to plaster herself against Charlie's legs.

"What in the..." Kyle's exclamation was cut short as the entire compound of people streamed out to stare into the sky where a Beryllian space transport slowed to hover over the front yard.

Chapter 27

Homecoming

Dani stared out of the shuttle window, shocked at the changes to her home. There were too many buildings, including a huge greenhouse and more people than she could easily count on her front lawn.

"What's going on?" She didn't realize she had spoken aloud until Lateef took her hand and raised it to his lips.

"The Hatti are determined to take care of you until you're back on your feet. Madame Tamarra and her crew moved in to keep your business running, and apparently brought the family with them."

Dani tore her gaze away from the window to stare into Lateef's eyes. Her surprise melted in his warmth and she leaned into his embrace, shaken at the strength of the love surrounding them.

"I can't believe you literally fell out of the sky to meet me."

He lifted her hand to his lips again. "I can't believe I had to go to another planet to find the half of my soul I didn't know I was missing." His smile faltered. "Or that I'd abandon you to save a stranger."

Dani lifted a hand to cup his chin. "You did exactly what I asked you to do—what you had to do to save everyone. If you hadn't healed Thane Hantili, your sister would've been killed and the whole clan would have slowly died out."

"I know." He stretched forward to kiss her gently and she leaned into him.

"It's all good, Lateef. And I'm almost home. Abby'll be nutso."

"That dog's always nuts." He sat back, making sure she was settled into her seat as the shuttle drifted to the ground.

"Do you think landing in the front yard's a good idea?" Dani took one more look out the window, wondering if she was ready to face so many people.

Lateef remained silent.

She tore her gaze from the window to stare at him. "What're you trying to hide from me this time?"

He bit his lip, closing his eyes with an expression of pain for a long moment before meeting her gaze. "It's the safest way to do a stupid thing."

"Don't give me any more of the 'you're too weak to go home crap'. I got more than enough from your boss." Dani felt the heat rise in her face.

"You won't let us help you…"

"Enough, children." Amman's sharp retort carried over the whine of the shuttle's engines, making both of them throw guilty glances over their shoulders. "Blame is pointless. Danielle Hamilton is back to her home where she *will* allow us to ensure she is returned to good health. Further discussion is unnecessary."

The Hatti Matriarch sniffed and settled back into her padded seat, shooting Dani a final warning glare before ostentatiously turning to stare out of her window.

"Yes, Madame Amman." Dani resisted the urge to stick her tongue out at the overbearing woman. Rebellion was futile. She might as well save her energy for a fight she could win. Like coming home when everyone told her she couldn't. Satisfaction flitted across her lips.

"I would've teleported you home, if it wasn't too dangerous." Lateef captured her hand and whispered his confession in her ear. "I'll do anything to make you all better."

Dani relaxed into the shuttle seat with a sigh. "I know. Thank you."

As hard as she still found belief in teleportation and other psychic abilities, Dani had been forced to admit they did exist. The fact she could feel her legs, much less walk after her spine had been shattered, made any denial stupid. Unfortunately, the poison that had nearly killed the Hatti Thane had made her ultra-sensitive to the psychic energy used to teleport. That's why she was on a space shuttle, exposing all of her friends to potential scrutiny by the US government.

"Don't worry about the military." She met Lateef's amused glance. "I don't have to read your mind to know you feel guilty, my love. It's your normal condition. Your government doesn't have the technology to track the transport. There's nothing to worry about."

She rolled her eyes and turned her head to watch their final descent. He was only partially correct. She had worried about the military, but her biggest fear was what Anna and Charlie would think. Would they hate her for unleashing this alien horde on their small mountain town?

Dani shook her head, clasping her hands firmly in her lap to avoid any misunderstanding. "No thank you, sweetie. I've had more than enough tea. If I drink any more, I'll float down the mountain." She smiled to take the sting out of her refusal to the helpful Hatti adolescent holding out yet another mug of 'restorative' tea Amman insisted she drink. She and Lateef sat on the front porch rockers as the impromptu party that began with her arrival a couple of hours ago continued around them. "I would like some more of those spice cookies, though."

The youngster's expression changed from disappointment to happiness before he tore off in the direction of the kitchen, carefully holding the untouched mug of tea.

"Kid's got talent. I'd be wearing tea if I tried that." Lateef reached over to hold her hand, subtly monitoring her pulse.

"I'm fine, Lateef." Dani gently took her hand back. "I've got another hour or so in me. Especially if I get more of those cookies. I can't believe how many people have moved in here."

Madame Amman strode up the porch steps, a swarm of assistants trailing behind her. "We are clan, Danielle Hamilton. We take care of our own. The tea will do you more good than cookies."

"I'll spend the night in the bathroom if I drink another drop." Dani fought the urge to squirm like a guilty schoolgirl. She didn't know if she could handle much more help as she recovered. It would be so much easier to just curl up in her bed and sleep instead of trying not to offend the wonderful people who cared so much about her for reasons she still couldn't fathom.

"Your color is still off." Amman peered into her face, lifted her eyelids and then sniffed her breath.

"That's because I should be more pink than green." Dani fought the urge to pull away, knowing such an action would insult the woman. This time she welcomed Lateef's hand sliding into hers.

Amman grumbled under her breath. Her ears turned a darker green as she stepped back and adjusted her gown. Dani couldn't believe she had made the outspoken matriarch speechless and decided to press her advantage.

A commotion started in the yard before she could open her mouth. The partiers turned to the long driveway, pointing at the cloud of dust from a black town car driving down the freshly graded dirt lane.

Dani's heart raced as she recognized the far too familiar vehicle. She was dimly aware of Kyle erupting into a long string of swear words that would have impressed her at any other time. She knew who was in the car and her reptilian hindbrain screamed at her to flee. Her muscles quivered as she tried to decide which impulse to obey. The car made the final curve and glided to a halt in the circular turn-around. The Hatti surrounded the vehicle as she twitched, praying to awaken from this nightmare.

'You're not alone anymore.' Lateef's mental voice slid under her shaky shields and her muscles abruptly relaxed as he squeezed her hand. She stared at her lap, taking several deep breaths as the crowd around the car began to mutter angrily. She took great comfort from the strength, love, and acceptance that flowed from the brief contact with her soul mate. All things she'd never felt from Carl.

"Thank you." She let her love shine in her expression, then settled into her chair, as rigidly upright as any queen on her throne, hands on the armrests and every trace of emotion wiped from her face. *Don't give the bastard anything.*

Lateef gave her one startled glance as she pulled free and then copied her posture, waiting for the action to start.

Amman stepped to the side, making a brief gesture and the crowd parted, leaving a clear path between the car and the porch. The driver stepped out, nervously adjusting his blue uniform jacket, looking at the crowd before giving a minute shrug and moving to open a rear door. He held his body in a rigid half-bow as the other rear door popped open and a young woman hopped out, sweeping her phone camera across the surroundings.

"You've got to see this, Uncle Howard. These people are greenish!"

A male voice boomed from inside the car. "Enough of your foolishness, Mandy. Indulging your imagination will keep you from success."

Dani bit her tongue to keep from reacting. Mandy was Carl's only cousin, all grown up. The last time Dani had seen her, Mandy had been a gangly teen, all arms and legs heading to college, but this young lady was poised and confident. *Hope he hasn't turned her into a jerk like the rest of the family.* Those fears vanished when the young woman bounded across the yard to give her a gentle hug and whisper into her ear.

"Missed you, cousin. Glad the rumors were wrong."

Before Dani could do more than return the embrace, Mandy pulled away and bent down to introduce herself to the dog bouncing around her feet.

What rumors? Dani's eyes were drawn to the car where long legs clad in immaculately pressed slacks swung out to place highly shined shoes on the dusty ground. Pale, well-manicured fingers grasped the edge of the car door. Dani's heart hammered in her chest as the man rose to his full height, staring across the gathered crowd of people as if he owned the world.

Sweat gathered under Dani's hair, trickling down the back of her neck in a sticky rivulet of fear, chasing all other questions from her mind.

'You got this, my love. You're so much stronger than you think.'

Dani shot Lateef a quick glance, but he watched the intruder, inscrutable as the Sphinx. She appreciated the current of support he held, available for her use whenever she needed it. She no longer had to face this particular demon alone. Her back stiffened and she sat up straighter, suddenly confident she would not be the one disappointed by today's encounter.

The front passenger door opened and the senator's long-time aide popped out, his nervous gaze darting between the crowd and the smartphone in his hands as he pranced around the car to join his boss.

"We have to hurry, sir. You're live on the news tonight."

The distinguished man nodded and gave a final glance around the crowd before sniffing disdainfully and striding towards the front porch. Agitated murmurs made him halt and glance at Dani.

She stared back, still as a grave, giving the man no emotion.

He took a tentative step forward, then resumed when nothing happened.

She saw the unaccustomed hesitation in his gait, but his face revealed only prideful arrogance. He placed his foot on the first step to the porch, but backed down as Madame Amman swayed toward him, a fierce look of determination on her round features.

"I see you have made some... interesting new friends, Danielle." The politician smoothed the sleeves of his expensive suit coat, looking down his patrician nose at her.

She suppressed a snarky comment, realizing her continued silence made him far more uncomfortable than any words. Her spirits rose when she noticed the tiny beads of sweat around his hairline.

"Pretty neat, don't you think?" Mandy elbowed Kyle and he jumped before giving the young woman a long, considering look.

Anna and Charlie pushed past the senator, unapologetically bumping into him as they came to stand at Dani's side.

"Why are you here, Senator Weatherly?" Kyle stepped forward.

His shoulders were hunched, and he rocked onto the balls of his feet, as if preparing for a fight.

"I could ask you the same question, Manning. Have you forgotten you work for me?" Weatherly looked Kyle over then dismissed him as irrelevant.

"I returned your retainer. And I never gave you any information about this place." He waited for his statement to sink in and then continued. "So why are you here?"

"I hired you to find my daughter-in-law. You did, and that's all you need to know." He glanced at his aide busy on his phone.

"The check was returned, Senator, but we declined to release him from the contract."

Kyle let out an exasperated snort. "You can't force me to work for you."

"Should I authorize the investigation? The DA sounded very interested when you spoke with him." The aide continued as if Kyle hadn't spoken.

"I haven't done anything wrong." Kyle clenched his fists. "But I'll fire the ass of whoever leaked this to you. Who was it?"

"What do you want, Howard?" Dani interrupted and everyone froze, the ping of the cooling engine the only noise to break the sudden silence.

"I am your father, Danielle. I wanted to be sure you were okay after the…" His voice stuttered and he closed his eyes briefly. When they opened his gaze was hard and bitterly cold. "You unexpectedly disappeared from the hospital and there are things you need to deal with."

Anna stirred, but Charlie laid a hand on her shoulder. Kyle remained tense, ready to throw himself between Dani and the threatening interloper.

"You made it perfectly clear I wasn't needed for anything, Howard. If I recall, you told me in that same hospital I should've had the good grace to die and save you the trouble of dealing with me. Seems you'd planned on Carl being a widower."

He flinched when she used his name, and his mouth opened and closed as his eyes darted around at her accusation.

"Thought I was unconscious for that part, didn't you?" Dani caught the flash of red on his assistant's face, though her gaze never left Howard Weatherly. "I'm sorry to have disappointed you yet again, Dad, but you must be aware I took nothing with me, not even photos or my personal jewelry."

Her voice caught at the unfairness of losing those memories, but she refused to let the odious man see her grief. The brief flash of satisfaction in his cold eyes reaffirmed her determination to end whatever game the bastard was playing.

"I don't want you here, Howard. We used my name and my money to keep you from finding out about this place until Carl was ready to tell you. That means you have no claim to anything."

He sputtered again. "Enough of this nonsense, Danielle." He pulled his composure together, regaining his haughty expression. "Like it or not, you are a member of my family and still have obligations."

Dani tipped her head to stare at him, frost dripping from her words. "You lost any claim on me when you buried my baby without me."

His lip lifted in a sneer. "I took care of the funeral arrangements for *my* son and *his* daughter because you were incapable of making decisions at the time. Don't try to make that my fault. Your foolish decision to travel in bad weather caused the tragedy."

Dani swayed, and felt Lateef's mental touch lending her strength. She fought the overwhelming desire to scratch the bastard's eyes out. Howard could never know how much he affected her, or he'd continue to attempt to control her. She forced her tone to sound bored, rather than giving in to her fury. "I'm positive you have better things to do than annoy me, Howard. You should go now if you want to get back to Denver for your TV appearance. The weather can be pretty iffy this time of year. I'd hate to hear you crashed driving down the mountain."

The tension in the air ratcheted up as her friends prepared for a fight. Weatherly's assistant let his phone hand drop to watch the action in disbelief, his gaze darting back and forth like he was watching a high-speed tennis match.

Her father-in-law took one step forward and her anger morphed to fear. She resisted the urge to run, fascinated by the flush of anger slowly creeping up the man's neck.

"You listen to me, you low-born guttersnipe. The only reason I'm here is because I wanted to extend you the courtesy of being present when Carl and his daughter are moved to their final resting place. The world would be a much better place if you had died instead of my son."

A roaring filled Dani's ears and she rose, only to be stopped by Anna's hand on her arm. She took a deep breath as her head threatened to explode.

"How dare you disturb..."

"I've attempted to contact you." Howard interrupted her. "I hired a private detective to inform you of the necessity of moving the remains." The look he shot Kyle should have incinerated the man on the spot. "But apparently you managed to wrap the bastard around your finger, just like you twisted Carl..."

"That is enough from you." Dani's cold words cut through the growing babble. She was hyperaware of her surroundings, knowing the Hatti were at the limit of their patience, Kyle wanted to sink into the ground and Howard Weatherly felt he was the injured party she owed utter obedience to. He sincerely believed she owed him an appearance to boost his ratings in the polls. That's why he was here. Well, that and a need to prove something? *I can't know any of this!* She shook off the obvious fantasy, concentrating on the despicable man in front of her.

"You need to come with us for the ceremony, Danielle. It's the least you can do to honor the memory of your husband. We need a public appearance to prove you're still alive." Weatherly gentled his tone and took another step onto the porch, attempting to intimidate her into obedience. "You can stay at the Palace with me tonight and we'll have appropriate clothes brought in. The gossip rags are full of ridiculous stories of your murder as part of some conspiracy."

Now she understood exactly why he'd spent so much effort to find her. He didn't need her to play the pitiful widow. He needed the cloud of suspicion removed. "Sounds like your problem to me. I don't care if strangers think I'm dead." Dani looked up at the taller man, drawing courage from Lateef's silent backing. "Your son was a bully exactly like you. I can't believe I spent so many years terrified." She shook her head in disgust at her own fears. "You're here because you have another election and are behind in the polls because people think you had me killed. Everything Carl did was based on those damned polls. The only reason he agreed to have Caitlin was because he thought a grandchild would help your election chances." She saw the barbs hit home and pressed her advantage. "I loved Carl, but he was every bit as incapable of the emotion as you are. Don't try to tell me you're acting out of grief, Senator." She made the title a sneering insult.

The crowd in the yard stirred, and she saw his assistant sidle around to the open door, looking for a quick escape.

"How dare you speak to me like that? You are nothing but a trailer-trash, gold-digging, sorry excuse for a human being, willing to use the death of her own child as way to cash into my family's wealth."

Dead silence greeted the harsh words. Dani felt the blood drain from her face as fury slammed through her veins. She could feel Anna's overwhelming desire to wipe the smug grin off the man's face, nearly as strong as her own.

The sound of clapping drew all eyes to her cousin moving closer to the pair, her phone aimed at the senator as Kyle clapped. "Can I quote you, Uncle Howard? This'll go viral. I can't believe I didn't want to come with you. This is so much better than that crazy woman at the last rally who accused you of being an alien."

Silence descended until Dani spoke.

"I don't want anything from you, Howard. I won't be your prop." She stumbled back to her chair, weariness weighting her limbs. "Carl and Caitlin are gone." She closed her eyes against the old pain wrapping cold fingers around her heart. "They're beyond your control. It doesn't matter where their bones rest.

You do whatever you need to give your twisted soul some peace, but I won't play your game."

"But you owe Carl…"

She opened her eyes to meet his gaze. "I loved Carl and would've loved him if he was a dead-broke nobody. I don't regret a second I spent with him. I can't regret the time I had with Caitlin, the grandchild you never had a use for unless there was a photographer present. Don't try to lecture me about familial obligations. Just go and don't come back."

She watched as the man slowly gathered his composure, pulling the tattered threads of his dignity around him like a worn coat. He glared at her as if studying some noxious creature and straightened his tie before dismissing her as if she had never existed. Kyle made a move and the senator turned on him with a snarl.

"You're fired, Manning. Do not think about sending me a bill."

"I wouldn't dream of it, Weatherly. If you recall, I fired you last week. And I have the documentation to prove my case if you try to cause problems for any of us later. You won't win this fight."

Senator Weatherly glared at the PI for a long moment.

"Come on, Uncle Howard. Your assistant's about to have a coronary. We'll be late if you don't shake a leg." Mandy stuck her phone back in her huge tote and gestured at her uncle.

Weatherly shot Dani a final, unfathomable glance and stalked through the gathered crowd as the driver scrambled to get the door open.

Mandy gave Dani a huge wink, miming a phone to her ear once the man was in his car, stuck a card in Kyle's hand with a breathy command to call, then scrambled to reach the vehicle before the driver peeled off in a spray of gravel.

Dani remained tense until the car pulled out of sight in the distance.

"I can't believe that horrid man still wins elections." Anna placed a warm hand on Dani's shoulder.

"He must be doing badly in this one. That's the only reason he'd track me down like this."

"Well, honey, he'll to have to figure out how to win without you. You did good, Dani. I don't think he'll be back. He doesn't strike me as someone used to hearing the word no."

Dani patted Anna's hand, glad for the support. "I'm not sure anyone ever told him no. He wanted Carl to follow in his footsteps, and that meant having the perfect family. I think I was Carl's one attempt at rebellion, since I was so obviously the wrong person for him."

"Looks like that young lady is a force to be reckoned with." Charlie continued to watch in case the car returned.

"I can't believe she's related to that bastard. She's so… nice." Kyle stared at the card in his hand, desire obvious in his eyes.

"That's Mandy, Howard's sister's only child. She seems to have escaped the family evilness. Maybe she can balance out some of the damage Howard's done in this world." Dani sagged, as the adrenaline high wore off. Pain radiated from the area on her back that was still not healed.

"I can't believe I spent so long hiding from that man." She shook her head, speaking mainly to herself. "I crawled into a hole and pulled the dirt over me so he wouldn't find me, when all I had to do was tell him no."

"I think the recording and the unfriendly audience had a lot to do with his quick retreat." Charlie's deep voice resonated in her chest. "Standing up to him took courage, Dani. I'm proud of you."

"You must rest." Amman was in front of Dani as quickly as if she had been summoned, peering into her eyes and resting a hand on her forehead. "Your room is prepared. I will bring you broth as soon as you are settled."

She gestured to her people, but Lateef scooped Dani up before anyone else could move, walking through the door Kyle held open.

"I'm sorry, Danielle."

She reached out for Kyle's hand, urging Lateef to stop. "It's not your fault, Kyle. You took a job and your client ended up being kind of evil. Howard's good at sounding reasonable until you cross him. When you found out the truth, you didn't turn me in. No need for you to be sorry."

Kyle squeezed her hand, but she could tell he couldn't forgive himself. Maybe he and Mandy would find an opportunity to exchange notes about the Weatherly family that would give Kyle some peace. In spite of the reason he had come into her life, she wanted him to find his happy ending. Maybe Mandy?

Exhaustion swept over her in a wave and she leaned her head against Lateef's shoulder as her eyelids grew too heavy to keep open. Could her long nightmare really be over? Even Howard would have to understand she hated him enough to make her presence in a campaign ad more of a problem than a positive. Maybe she'd have some lawyer release a statement that she was alive and living on the other side of the world to remove Howard's last excuse for using her.

'Rest, my love. You're home with people who love you.'

She sank into Lateef's unconditional love, content, for the moment to keep breathing, though she once again felt the presence of the shadowy figure from her dreams. She ignored the ghost's threat.

'You are mine, Danielle. No one will keep us apart.'

Chapter 28

Party Time

Lateef hesitated on his way down the stairs, watching Dani and Anna at the dining room table discussing the final details of the big party about to start. The main floor of the house was so different now. The living room was connected to the dining room and had been expanded with a bay window and skylight. The dining room still contained the large, wooden table where Dani had served the memorable meals to the Hatti search party, but now a wall separated it from the kitchen. A door to the kitchen was always guarded by one of the junior members of the Hatti clan. The only concession Dani had won was a drink and snack bar set into an alcove in the dining room. The women of the clan did their best to ensure Dani had everything she needed. However, sometimes she needed something as simple as getting her own cup of coffee to boost her self-esteem.

If she'd let me heal her, she could be totally independent. All of the Hatti could move into the other buildings, or even go back to their ship. Lateef let the thought slide through his mind, taking care Dani couldn't pick any stray information from behind his mental shields.

He remembered the reason for the party and sighed. With any luck Amman wouldn't have to drug Dani to force her to do what everyone knew needed to be done. Dani was fading in spite of everything they tried in the seven months since the incident on the Hatti ship. She had to return to Beryl and cooperate with Mellora so they could heal her completely. They needed to learn what was draining her strength and why she blocked their efforts to fix it.

He shook off his morbid thoughts, trotted to the kitchen door and knocked, expecting to see one of the Hatti youngsters. There was absolutely no chance he would ever again enter Hatti food prep space without an escort.

Instead, Madame Amman opened the door and shoved a tray into his hands.

"Make sure Danielle Hamilton drinks all. This is too much excitement, Lateef. I do not agree with this party. We should have returned her to the Healer Hall months ago, whether she wanted to go or not."

Lateef agreed with the formidable matriarch. "Dani won't let us heal her until she's ready. You were there when we tried." He swallowed his fear. She had tolerated their efforts to heal her spine and the nerves and muscles around the injury, but when they attempted to flush out the remnants of the poison, Dani had absolutely refused to cooperate. The one attempt to force her had set her condition back far enough to make him stop trying. Even Mellora had been forced to acknowledge the futility of continuing. "We have to convince her everything here is good before she'll let us help."

"I do not know what else to do. Her business and home are thriving, and she has dealt with the man she feared. There is nothing left for her to worry about. We have even started preparing the garden, although this warm spell shall prove deceptive. Our botanist is surely competent enough for her to trust."

Amman's dark eyes snapped with irritation and Lateef ducked his head to hide his smile. Dani had slapped the bastard down all by herself. Probably one of the only times the senator had to accept defeat. The rumors they'd released of her presence in several foreign countries set off a media frenzy that had finally died down. Enough photos of her had been manufactured by the Hatti that the mystery of her disappearance was considered solved. Howard had won the election without Dani's endorsement. That kept him too busy to worry about an unwanted daughter-in-law. *Silver linings to everything, if you look hard enough.*

"You know what she's like, Madame. Dani still grieves and feels responsible for everything. She'll never agree to leave for an extended length of time, no matter how much she trusts us. But your potions, and my healing can no longer keep the poison at bay. She must return to the Healer Hall."

The Hatti sniffed and Lateef inclined his head to her. "I know you can convince her to do what she needs to do. She thinks I'm too protective."

"You do coddle the girl, but such is to be expected when one is in love." Her expression softened as she continued. "I do hope Taltos and the crew arrive in time."

"I thought they weren't due back for another month?" Lateef caught the fact she wanted a certain man, rather than the entire clan. *Can Amman be in love?* The thought was comforting and made him feel a bit closer to the stoic leader.

A greenish blush crawled up the woman's neck and she stared into the distance. "Thane Hantili learned of our success in acquiring the goats, and decided it was worth returning to add the goat and the sheep cheese to our trading inventory."

Lateef bowed his head to hide his mirth. "I'm glad Madame Tamarra came to an understanding with the Saunders. He was ready to retire, and she seems happy with the goats."

Happy was an understatement. He'd always considered Tamarra the enforcer of the clan and yet the tall woman was giddy every time he saw her in the field attempting to train Abby in the finer art of goat herding. The poor dog had been an utter failure with the sheep. He always got the impression the trained sheepdogs just laughed at the sheltie whenever she got near the flock.

"It'll be good to see the Thane again, if he gets back before we have to leave." His mood quickly sank. He'd put Dani into a deep coma, if that was his only option.

Amman touched his shoulder and he looked up at the uncharacteristic contact. "You will heal her completely. You succeeded with Hantili."

"He didn't fight me at every turn."

"I have confidence in you. Now, go make sure she drinks her medicine, and be prepared to be firm if she becomes too excited. Do not let a sweet face distract you." Amman turned away, slipping the door shut before he could reply.

Guess I've been told. Joy lifted his spirit as he carried the tray to the table where Dani chatted with Anna.

Dani picked up the mug with a smile of thanks that turned to a grimace as she noticed the light green color. "I was hoping for coffee."

"I tried," he said. "But Amman was adamant you had to drink your potion first. Otherwise you'll miss some of the party."

"Potion is right," she muttered. But she took a tentative sip, knowing argument was pointless. "This one isn't bad."

"You don't need quite as much medicine." The lie slid easily from his lips. There was no reason to dampen her spirits. For a few hours they could pretend all was okay.

"Is everything ready?" she asked. "I feel odd throwing a party and not doing anything. I want to cook."

"Amman's crew has the food covered, and Charlie and the teens have everything else under control." Lateef took the empty seat beside her and ran a hand along her hair. "Today is for you to allow us to pamper you. Arguing will only make you look ungrateful."

She shrugged. "Can't dispute that," she said. "Want to help me go outside?"

"Not until you finish your drink."

She grumbled under her breath but obeyed. "I heard from Kyle. He's bringing Mandy. I can't believe those two are still in touch."

"That was unexpected. Is she still with the senator?" Lateef shook his head in disbelief.

"Not much. The marketing job in Denver keeps her busy. Reconnecting with her was almost worth dealing with Howard. I still don't believe his complete denial about the origins of our guests. Mandy believes they're from outer space, but Howard insists they're foreigners. When he'll talk about that day, anyway. According to Mandy he prefers to forget he ever came up here."

Lateef snorted. "I bet. Getting that man out of your head was worth the show-down. Mandy was a bonus. And I'm sure it's easier to ignore a bunch of people who might not belong instead of giving future opponents an excuse to question his sanity."

She shrugged and finished off the warm drink. "Are Rissa and Brandon coming?"

He nodded, refusing to meet her eyes. "Mellora, too."

Before she could dig for more information the front door flew open and a veritable herd of children poured in. The human and Hatti mixed with no distinction, all talking happily at the top of their lungs. Abby circled them, trying to influence the direction of the swarm, but it was a bit much to expect of one sheltie. They circled the table and converged on Dani, all babbling excitedly about something that had happened outside where the adults were already gathering.

Anna took advantage of the distraction to pull Lateef into the living room.

"Okay, pretty boy," she said. "It's past time for some answers. And I'm not interested in the story you've been peddling to everyone else. I want the whole truth."

Lateef studied her and then nodded with resignation. "Okay."

Anna's expression immediately became suspicious, her gaze intensifying.

"You're Dani's best friend," he said. "She trusts you more than anyone. You deserve the truth. But you'll be the only one besides Kyle to know."

Anna snorted.

"I'm serious. I'll tell you the whole story and you can decide who else needs to know." He looked at Dani, feeling Anna's scrutiny for a moment.

"I'll let Charlie in on the secret."

"That's okay." His attention remained on Dani and the children and a smile tugged at the corners of his lips. "It's not good to have secrets between spouses."

"And yet you're trying to keep a secret from Dani?"

He blushed and turned back to the older woman. "Sometimes it's necessary."

"Dani doesn't like secrets."

Lateef returned the woman's intense scrutiny, looking for clues his trust was misplaced without invading her thoughts. "I know," he admitted when he could find only genuine concern. "But she still isn't convinced she deserves to live. She's an incredible woman, but I haven't been able to convince her yet. Until she releases the stupid guilt she carries, she won't recover."

Anna studied him for a few moments and then nodded her head decisively. "I knew I liked you. What's your secret?"

Lateef laughed. "I think I'll put off introducing you to my mother. I'm not sure the universe would be safe with two of you in the same space."

"It's good to know there are more sensible people out there." Anna waited.

"Okay," he held up his hands in surrender at her impatient look. "You've realized most of the people living here are not really natives?"

Anna rolled her eyes. "Tell me something I don't know. We all saw the spaceship, and no one bought the lame story about an experimental helicopter." She snorted in derision.

Lateef stared at her in shock. "And no one cares?"

Anna shrugged. "The kids are polite, well-behaved and so far from evil, how could anyone mind? And what invading army would bring along their children?"

"I'm a little surprised," Lateef stuttered. "I thought it would make a difference."

"I'm sure to some people it does," Anna admitted. "But the human brain is capable of ignoring information it doesn't want to process. People tend to believe what they are able to handle. Unless they pose a threat, our visitors are welcome. What are you hiding?"

Lateef chuckled. "I thought that would be the hard part."

"No," Anna insisted. "The hard part is telling me what's wrong with Dani and what you're going to do about it."

He stared at her for a long moment and then sighed. "Dani doesn't remember much of what happened."

"I gathered." Anna sat down on the couch and patted the cushion beside her. "She hasn't talked much since she came home."

He sat beside the dark-haired woman who had been a surrogate mother to his love and gathered his thoughts, listening to the happy shrieks of children as Dani teased them. "She stopped a war before it could start."

"Sounds like a good story." Anna's eyes popped wide for a moment before she patted her thick braids into place and settled in to listen.

"There was a... situation at an official banquet." Lateef could feel his face warm as he admitted his part in the disaster. "I was set up by someone who wanted to be sure those problems were magnified and like an idiot I stepped into the trap."

"And that's how you ended up here?"

Lateef nodded. "My ship crashed nearby, and Dani found me, gave me a place to recover and I fell in love. I tried to stay away from her. I didn't want to get her tangled up in my problems, but the Hatti were so close on my heels, I couldn't abandon her. Not when they started interrogating people. Then Kyle showed up and I..."

"Noticed Kyle was handsome and moving in on your girl?"

Lateef felt his face grow hotter and looked away. He'd hoped she wouldn't pick up on his jealousy. "Something like that," he muttered. "But I would have stayed away if she'd chosen him."

Anna looked at him with raised eyebrows.

"I would have," he said. "I wouldn't have liked it, but you've got to admit someone from her home planet was probably a better choice."

Anna shook her head. "The heart goes where it will, no matter what the obstacles."

Lateef nodded. "I warned her about the Hatti on my trail. I was pretty sure if they knew the truth, they'd ignore her and keep following me. I did not expect her to impress their socks off." He gave Dani an admiring glance. She was still surrounded by the children while the dog bounced around their feet. He was relieved to see Tamarra stood watch, making sure no one got too rambunctious.

Anna snorted. "You shouldn't have been too surprised. She has that habit."

He nodded his agreement. "The Hatti party felt they owed her for her hospitality and returned, not expecting the new feast she prepared with very little warning."

"You're stalling."

He nodded. "When they came back, they saw a plant I'd given her. It's only found on my home planet, so they knew I'd been here. They kept her house under surveillance and managed to catch all three of us here." He glossed over those events as his heart pounded at the memory. *Stupid of me to be caught.* "And once they took us to their ship for questioning, well... she managed to impress the Thane. The second in command was already a big fan of hers, so when my family came to rescue us, the Hatti thought Dani was being kidnapped and the whole thing degenerated into a dangerous comedy of errors."

"How did she get hurt?"

"There's a nasty race of people known as the Falgarans. They attacked my people years ago and we've been at war ever since. We both spend time looking for allies—or new victims in their case. My friend thought he'd met the Hatti before they had contact with the Falgarans, but he was wrong. A Falgaran agent infiltrated the Hatti ship and when he saw the opportunity to kill the Thane, he took it. On top of creating a huge amount of chaos, it had the added advantage of making my people look guilty." He stared into the distance as memories of the horrible events danced across his mind. Remembered fear knotted his stomach. He had come so close to losing a love he had never imagined he could find. Everyone thought he would spend his life in the Healer Hall with only a steady stream of patients for company.

"But Dani stopped him?" Anna prompted when the silence continued too long.

Lateef looked at her. "The assassin took the shot, but Dani jumped in front of the Thane. He was badly hurt, but Dani slowed the bolt enough he didn't die immediately. She gave us the time to heal him."

He thrust the memory away as a chill shook his body. "I thought I'd lost her. There was so much blood and you could see splinters of her spine around the metal bolt pinning the two of them together."

Anna placed a warm hand on his leg, giving him comfort. "But she didn't die."

He pulled himself out of the memory and his face went bleak. "No thanks to me," he denied. "I knew the Thane had to be stabilized first. If he died the entire Clan would go with him. I had to choose, and although Brandon is a good healer, he's nowhere near what Dani needed. And I knew that." His voice grew harsh with self-anger and his hands tightened into fists in his lap as he looked away, unable to bear the condemnation he imagined in her eyes.

Anna reached over and covered his fists with her hands. "But she is alive, and this Brandon was good enough. You have to know by now Dani wouldn't have forgiven you for doing anything else."

He slowly allowed the tension to ebb from his body. He glanced at Dani, once more marveling someone so incredibly perfect could love him, the clown of his large family.

"Why would the Clan die with the Thane?" Anna's quiet question pulled him back to the present. He was stunned at her casual acceptance of his explanation and use of odd terms and relationships. Not to mention the easy acceptance of alien civilizations and visitors to Earth. Dani had remarkable friends.

"The Hatti... I'm not really sure what they are." He struggled to explain a species that looked so similar to human but was so different in many big ways. "They're a bit closer to a hive mentality, but not really. Each Clan has a leader who is the..." He racked his brain to find the correct term. "Heart? Center? I don't know how to explain, but they are necessary for the health of the clan. He's not directly involved with reproduction, but if the Thane is lost before a replacement is at a certain level of preparation, the Clan dies. They don't drop dead where they stand, but the end result is bad enough. The previous Thane died under suspicious circumstances, so Hantili was rushed into a leadership position. There's no one else even close to ready to replace him, so he had to survive."

Anna patted one wrinkled hand against his cheek. "Sometimes you have to make impossible choices," she said. "You had to pit the one life against all the others. Dani couldn't love you if you'd made any other choice."

"But I left her alone, knowing how badly she was injured and how much pain she was in. Right after I'd promised to keep her safe."

"You did not leave her alone," Anna denied. "There were other healers there. She loves you, pretty boy."

He had to laugh at the nickname, breaking him out of his self-anger. "I hope so."

"So, what are you planning to do?"

"You are persistent." As much as he admired the loyalty Dani inspired, he wished he wasn't getting this interrogation. He could feel Dani's exhaustion and looked up to see Tamarra shooing the children out. He took a deep breath and faced Anna again. "We got her stabilized, but she fought our healing. So, we decided to bring her home and get things set up so she wouldn't have to worry. There's still a lot of nerve damage that's progressively getting worse and the poison is slowly causing her organs to fail. She'll be unable to walk at all before much longer, if her heart doesn't give out first. She has to go back to Beryl no matter what she wants."

"And today is the day?"

He stared into the distance for a few moments. "It wasn't supposed to be," he finally said. "We thought we had more time."

"But she won't agree to let you fix her up?" Anna asked.

He looked at her with a wry grin. "You know our Dani. She just keeps saying soon. If Amman hadn't insisted her honor demanded she take charge of things, Dani would be in the kitchen right now trying to make sure everyone eats, even if she had to crawl to do it. Amman kind of took over without any of us realizing what was happening." His brow wrinkled. None of the Beryllians understood how the whole situation had worked out, but Amman was responsible. No one was upset about it, other than Dani, who missed her kitchen. "While we were at the Healer Hall, she sent Tamarra and her family to take care of things here, and when more help was needed they contacted the teen shelter in Denver, thinking kids would be easier to work with and ask fewer questions and before we knew what was going on we had a whole compound growing up."

He shook his head wonderingly. *So glad she's on our side now. Can't imagine that woman as an enemy.* "I'm kind of surprised there hasn't been an official investigation." His look sharpened at Anna's smug grin. "What do you know?"

"All of the necessary permits have come through the town and we all approve of what's happening out here. Even Bob Saunders admitted he's glad to turn over his herd to someone who loves the stupid creatures as much as Tamarra does. And no one'll go around screaming about a real alien invasion—not if they want to be taken seriously."

He leaned over and planted a kiss on her forehead. "You are a good and incredibly devious friend," he said. "So, I hope you'll forgive me for stealing her away."

"As long as you return her healthy and happy," Anna said. "And I do mean bring her back. You do not have permission to keep her on some foreign world out of touch with us. Especially if you haven't made an honest woman out of her yet."

He felt his brow furrow with confusion. "An honest woman?"

"Do you intend to stay with her forever?"

"Yes." He didn't need to consider his answer, surprised she would feel the need to ask.

"Then you need to marry the girl," Anna said. "Especially if there's a chance you'll have kids at some point in the future."

Lateef laughed. "Okay, I take it back, you're not persistent, you're pushy."

"Just looking out for my girl." Anna was unrepentant.

"As far as my family is concerned, we are married," he said.

She punched his arm. "Boy, you didn't invite any of us to the ceremony? And never gave us a chance to celebrate?"

"I didn't realize I needed to."

"Does Dani know you consider yourselves married?"

He started to answer and then stopped. "I'm not sure."

Anna shook her head. "Men. You're the same no matter the species. I think you need to go have a chat with Dani. I'll line up things on our end."

"Line things up?" His head pounded and the room appeared to be revolving slowly around him as he tried to process what she was saying.

"We have to have a wedding before you drag her off to parts unknown."

"A what?"

She patted him on the shoulder at the look of panic he knew covered his face. "You go make sure Dani is okay with being stuck with you and I'll take care of the rest." She pulled him from the couch and gave him a push toward the table as she hurried outside.

Chapter 29

Plans Change

Once the kids ran off, Dani slumped into her seat, wishing she had time for a nap. *This exhaustion is getting old, but there's no reason to go back to Lateef's planet.* There was no reason to believe they could do anything there that couldn't be done here, where she felt comfortable. All the hard work was done. She could walk when she had the energy. The miraculous nature of that fact amazed her whenever she thought about it. She didn't remember much about the accident beyond a sense of terror followed by searing pain. She'd picked up a few flashes of images from Lateef on the rare occasions his mental shields slipped. Her injuries had been extensive, but she was okay now. *Need a little bit more rest. Or a chance to pour some of my own soap. Then I'll be worn out from exercise, not from being lazy. I can't wait to play with the sheep milk as an ingredient. Wonder if the soap will be as creamy as the goat milk?*

The shadowy figure that had moved from her nightmares to random waking moments nodded in agreement. The shape slipped away as she focused on it. *Has to be a figment of my imagination. Surely Lateef would have noticed something real.*

Lateef plopped down on the chair beside her as if summoned. His eyes were wide and his forehead wrinkled as he stared into the distance. Abby shoved her nose under his hand and he stroked her without thought.

"You look confused," Dani said. "Everything okay?"

He shook himself out of his bemusement and reached out to touch her face, sending healing energy through the link.

She started to pull away but stilled at his stern look. *Can't believe I'm so tired after listening to the kids babble. Wonder if my imaginary stalker has anything to do with it?* She did seem to be more drained each time she saw the lurking shadow. But that was a stupid idea. How could an imaginary shadow hurt her?

Lateef smiled. "You're learning."

"Don't have much choice yet," she said. She sat up straighter as he restored some of her energy reserves. "Give me a couple more weeks and I'll show you who the boss is."

He leaned over and planted a gentle kiss on her lips. "That's always been you." Her return kiss deepened until a sound behind them broke them apart with a guilty chuckle.

One of Amman's many helpers stood waiting impatiently until they noticed her. She held a tray with sandwiches cut into bite-sized squares and yet another mug of something warm. "Mistress Amman requires you to eat and drink before the party may start. I shall return in a few minutes to see you have obeyed."

She set the tray onto the table with enough force the drink sloshed over the edge, glared at Lateef, and stalked off with a stiff back.

As soon as they heard the click of the kitchen door latch the pair burst into muted laughter, ignoring the dog's low growl. "She's new," Dani explained. "Definitely hasn't loosened up yet."

He stared in the direction of the kitchen with a puzzled frown. "She looks familiar, but I can't place the face." After a moment of thought he shook his head. "Drink it down. Don't want Amman sending you to bed without a party."

A burst of music came from outside as one of the guests slipped through the living room.

Dani forced herself to pick up the mug. She wanted to be in the fresh air to see the performers and feel the joy of all the guests in person. In spite of avoiding most entertainment for the last few years, she did enjoy the music of *Bluesy*, a local band who were regulars at all the community gatherings. The lead singer always made her laugh. With a sigh she took a cautious sip of the warm drink. Her lips puckered as her tongue tried to push the vile substance out, but she swallowed quickly.

"That's foul." Her body shuddered and she tried to put the cup down, but Lateef gave her the look. The one that made her heart melt and her brain turn to mush with a desire to make him happy. With a roll of her eyes, she stuck her tongue out at him and then chugged the rest of the liquid and plopped the mug back on the tray. Most of Amman's potions tasted far better. *I'd better be ready to dance all night after drinking that nasty crap.*

"Good job."

Her reward was a tiny bit of heaven in the form of a sandwich bite. She savored the taste, glad it wiped some of the nasty off her taste buds. A look at the plate made her heart sink. She'd never be able to put a dent in the huge stack, but Amman would be insulted if she didn't. *Distract Lateef and slip some to Abby.* The optimistically watching dog wasn't supposed to get people food, but exceptions could always be made for a good cause.

"What were you and Anna talking about? Looked pretty serious."

"I thought you were too busy with the kids to pay attention to me." He handed her another sandwich bite.

"I'm never too busy to pay attention to you." She returned his happy grin. "The kids are a lot of fun. I never imagined how entertaining an entire herd of rug rats could be. My parents were older when I was born, so I never spent much time around other kids. What about you? You have lots of siblings."

He looked away and she slipped the food to Abby. The dog inhaled the treat, wriggling with uncontainable excitement and plopped down closer to Dani. The long tongue slid over sharp teeth, licking her lips as she begged for more.

"There was such a large age difference between all of us that most of them were gone before I was old enough to care. I was with Rissa more than any of the others, but she was out for training before I got through school. I missed having her around."

"I always wanted a lot of kids." Her thoughts were more on how to sneak some more sandwiches to the dog than on what she was actually saying. "Holidays were always missing something, you know? No aunts or uncles or cousins to play with."

Lateef handed her another tid-bit.

"You're aware my family runs to the large side, right?"

She paused with her hand half-way to her mouth and tilted her head to stare at him. This wasn't idle chatter. She needed to understand him, but the only word that would come out of her mouth was, "What?"

"You know I love you, right?" he asked and she nodded, absently raising her hand to keep it away from Abby, who stealthily inched forward.

"I love you, too."

He threw his arms around her, squeezing her as tightly as he could without hurting her. He then kissed her most thoroughly.

"Oh, my goodness." He sputtered and pulled back to stare at her, wrinkling his nose. "That is one nasty drink our cooking guru gave you."

"Told you." Dani smirked and tugged on his shirt to pull him closer. "I think you need to try again. The taste might get better with time."

He wiggled his eyebrows, making her laugh and kissed her chastely on the lips.

"So, did she say yes?" Anna asked.

"Haven't asked her," Lateef muttered, burying his nose in Dani's neck.

"Asked me what?" she pushed him back enough to meet his eyes. "What were you two cooking up?"

"Anna reminded me our relationship has not yet been formalized."

"What do you mean?" Her heart raced as her brain bounced between thoughts of joy and despair. He couldn't say he loved her and then leave, could he?

He took a deep breath. "Will you be my spouse, Danielle?" The words poured out in a rush, and anxiety filled his eyes. "My family to be your family, my life your life until time ends, no matter what the universe shows us?"

"Yes," she whispered through sudden tears of joy. "Oh, yes, Lateef."

They embraced again, oblivious of their growing audience. She was aware of a sense of triumphant anger coming from someone, but was too happy to try to pin it down. Maybe she could have a happily ever after despite what she had done.

"Have you eaten food yet?" Amman broke the charged silence.

Lateef sat up abruptly, his face blazing red. But he didn't release Dani's hand.

"Relax, Madame Amman," Anna said. "We're going to have a wedding today."

"Today!" The normally unflappable Matriarch yelped, horror mixing with anger on her face. "Such is not possible! There are weeks of preparations to be made before such a momentous occasion. I cannot possibly prepare a wedding feast with little more than a wave of my hands. The cake alone will take a week, not to mention the seven required courses. Hantili will have to send a hunting party to procure the albino Jangxing mascots for the ceremony…"

"It's okay," Dani said quickly, light as a feather with joy. "Don't worry, Amman. We're already having a party—that's more than enough. I don't need anything formal." *And I really don't want to see an albino Jangxing.*

"But you deserve more," the distraught alien said. "You are Clan!"

Dani reached a hand out to touch the tall matriarch's arm. "Amman, you've already given me more than I could possibly need. You've left your own home to come to a strange world to care for me. You can't possibly think you owe me anything else."

"But you are Clan and deserve to have your union celebrated in the proper manner. Hantili must be here to officiate. Taltos will be devastated to not act as sponsor. You young people are so very hasty!"

"Then we'll wait." Dani fought to hide her laughter. "We have time. Nothing has to happen today."

"But…" Anna blurted out a protest, shooting Lateef an unreadable look.

"Neither one of us is going anywhere," Dani said. "And no lack of ceremony will ever change how I feel about Lateef."

Dani's head spun with so much information coming at her. She was barely accustomed to feeling Lateef in her mind, even when his thoughts were shielded, but all of a sudden, everyone in the room was shouting at her. She looked over and saw Lateef slumped in his chair, pale as a ghost.

Dani's hands rose to cover her ears before her head fell forward to rest on the table. Her breath came in short pants and she was aware of her friends' panicked questions, but unable to respond, even when Charlie stormed in, responding to Anna's panicked call.

"What is wrong?" Amman rolled Dani's head to peer into her eyes carefully before turning her attention to the tray on the table. "Who is responsible for this food?" Amman picked up the mug and sniffed before throwing it across the room to shatter against the wall. Her nose wrinkled with disgust. "Tamarra!" The angry matriarch's command carried through the entire house and several of the guests appeared in response to the commotion.

"We need an ambulance," Anna said.

Dani fought to raise her hand to touch Lateef, as her chair seemed to dip and move erratically underneath her. She stretched her senses, straining to contact Lateef or Rissa as she had on board the Hatti ship so many months earlier. She felt a brief whisper of a familiar voice and then the connection collapsed. The abrupt silence after the cacophony of moments earlier was an almost physical shock.

"Lateef." She whispered his name, only vaguely aware of Amman's strong hands on either side of her face coming close to smell her breath.

"They have been drugged." The tall woman held a finger to the rapid pulse in Dani's wrist as she snapped out orders.

Tamarra appeared at Amman's side and they conferred quietly as Dani continued to try to reach the motionless Lateef only inches away. Anna took her hand.

"He'll be okay," Anna tried to reassure her. "Help is coming."

Dani jerked as a sudden premonition cleared her head for a few seconds. All the weird happenings suddenly formed a pattern. She gathered every ounce of energy she had left. "He's here." Tears stung her eyes. Terror wrapped skeletal fingers around her heart and she struggled to speak through chattering teeth. "Get everyone away, Anna. The shadow's coming!"

"What shadow?"

Dani's eyes fluttered shut as she tried to catch her breath and get her racing heart under control.

"Dani, what are you talking about? Who's coming and what are they going to do?" Anna's tone was calm, but she could sense the fear underneath.

"He's so angry. He'll kill everyone." She shook her head as she tried to figure out how she knew disaster was closing in on them.

"How do you know?" Anna asked.

"Get the children away, please? Take them down to the Saunders." Dani pulled the strength to beg from a reserve she hadn't known she possessed. "Go with them and keep them safe! Hurry!"

"I'll send them." Anna pushed to her feet, obviously reluctant to leave her young friend alone. She threw a concerned look at the pair slumped at the table as she grabbed Charlie and ran out of the house. Dani sagged with relief and allowed her eyes to drift closed with the exhaustion that suddenly overwhelmed her fear. Charlie and Anna would keep the children and other guests safe. She could count on them. She heard a labored breath and her heart stuttered. Lateef! She tried to turn her head and reach out to him, but moving was too hard. Her body betrayed her as she clutched at the memory of the brief contact with Rissa and the belief help was on the way.

Chapter 30

Invasion

"I 've waited so long for this moment, my sweet. My leader will be surprised to learn how successful our little experiment has been. I have proven the Apirri are not the only weapons we have."

The possessive tone in the unfamiliar voice pulled Dani out of her stupor, although the words made no sense. She forced her heavy lids open at the touch of cold fingers on her arm. Dark, pupil-less eyes of evil set in the face of a gaunt giant stared back.

"I'm glad you're finally awake." He stroked her cheek. A false look of sympathy was plastered on his triangular face that had the remorseless, predatory look of a praying mantis.

"My associate overestimated the dose and I thought you would sleep through this party as you have done so many nights lately. I enjoy our time together so much more when you actively participate."

His look turned her bones to rubber. *Who is this guy? Can he be the figure haunting my nightmares? How is that possible?* Dani tried to speak, but her muscles refused to obey.

"Nothing to say?" The creature gave her cheek one more caress, then turned his attention to Lateef.

The healer's head rested on the table. His dark hair covered his face like a curtain.

The creature poked him with a long finger. When he got no response, he swung his fist, delivering a vicious blow to the side of Lateef's head. The healer flew off the chair, landing in a senseless heap on the floor at the feet of Anna and Charles who stood against the wall along with several of the human and Hatti guests, all with their hands bound behind them. Amman was tied hand and foot to a sturdy chair. Her face was darker green than normal and a cloth napkin was stuffed in her mouth.

The monster growled and turned to someone behind Dani. "How much did you give him?"

"I dosed only the girl," a familiar voice retorted. "You said to give her the drug. You said nothing about him."

Dani recognized the Hatti woman who had given her the drink. Red haze filled her vision and she took deep breaths. *I swear neither one of those bastards will walk out of here on their own.* Her mind refused to consider the possibility Lateef didn't move because he was dead. She would know if the unthinkable happened. All she had to do was stall and keep the monster's attention on her until help came. Then everyone would be safe.

"This so-called master healer is such a weakling. I shouldn't be surprised a small amount of the drug knocked him out. He's nothing like Rissa." He took a shuddering breath as a strange emotion crossed his alien face. "I would give much to own her. Surely Wendar will allow me to be in charge since I have proven the drug effective." The last sentence was whispered.

"I gave the boy nothing," the Hatti woman insisted. "He kissed this one and collapsed."

"That was enough." The tall man leaned over to pull Lateef's eyelid open. He grinned at the hugely dilated pupil. "Even his human girlfriend has more stamina. You did well, Bilal. The clan will be yours once the Thane has been made to see reason."

Amman let out a strangled protest and rocked her chair.

"What do you want?" Dani asked through dry lips. He couldn't intend to destroy Amman's clan, could he? She couldn't imagine the prickly matriarch without the rest of the Hatti around her. *Damn it, I've stopped one disaster already. I can't let this fracking insect destroy an entire clan because of me.*

The monster stiffened, as if he had heard her internal thoughts, then continued to examine Lateef. His indifference to her increased her fear. She somehow knew the reaction would be worse the longer the delay. *Why didn't I mention the nightmares to Lateef? Maybe he would have known it was all real and not my imagination.*

"This healer interfered with my negotiations, and then you..." The alien turned on her with a fury that left her bones quaking. Long fingers curled into a fist raised in an unconscious gesture before he took a deep breath and obviously composed his features back into a semblance of calm. "And then you, the treasure I have been cultivating for many months, threw away your life by taking the bolt meant for the leader of those foolish Hatti. All of my work killing the old Thane and gathering allies was gone. Poof! That one act turned the entire Clan against me after all I had done to make the Beryllians take the blame!" Anger radiated from the tall figure as his fist opened and closed and his breath rasped in his narrow chest.

"I didn't do anything." Her denial was barely louder than the scraping of feet on the floor as a captive shifted position.

He closed his large eyes for a few seconds as he visibly fought to control his temper. He plastered a smile on his alien face that shook her to the core. "It doesn't matter what you believe." His liquid velvet voice rasped along the inside of her brain as he ran a long fingernail along her jaw line. "What matters is you got in my way. You should have known better after all the time we've spent together. And after I learned your barbaric language. I am terribly disappointed in you, little one."

Dani's pulse accelerated to scary levels. She closed her eyes, trying to slow the racing of her heart. She had to stall. Rissa's team couldn't be too far away. How long had she been unconscious? Her mind was clearing almost as fast as the drug had knocked her out. If she could delay this monster, maybe she could regain her newly acquired psychic abilities and give Rissa an idea of what was happening. That would help, right? Dani, the Typhoid Mary of destruction, didn't deserve to live. Not while Caitlin was gone. Eventually Lateef's refusal to see the awful truth about her would crash into reality. *I'm not the type to get the fairytale ending, but Lateef and the rest of my friends have to live.* She concentrated, stuffing her fears into a tiny corner of her mind. She could have an amazing case of screaming meemies if she survived this, but until then she would be calm. *I can do this. I just have to be brave for a few minutes at most.* She opened her eyes to stare calmly into the soulless gaze of her enemy.

"Fine." She was proud her voice shook only slightly. "Sorry for screwing up your plans. I thought you were a figment of my imagination I'm just a dumb human, remember? If you want me to help, you need to be a little clearer about what you want me to do."

The bald man held her gaze for a long moment, trying to understand her change from timid to confident.

"I won't interfere again, but please don't hurt anyone else here." She projected a calm she did not feel. "This is my fault. Give me a chance to make it up to you?"

A slow look of happiness built on the alien features. "You continue to exceed my expectations. Even so, you must be taught a lesson. I had to leave my slave aboard ship, but she will explain the rules to you. You still care too deeply about these pathetic creatures." He waved a hand carelessly at the humans lined up against the dining room wall. "It is a fitting punishment for you to know you alone are responsible for their misery."

"I'm not responsible," Dani said. She struggled to keep her tone subservient, yet confident, though her confidence ebbed as she took in the sight of her friends under the watchful eye of the monster's Hatti accomplice. "This is all on you. I can be your excuse, but I'm not doing anything. The karmic debt is yours."

The bald man studied her. "Intriguing." A puzzled look passed through his dark eyes then settled into a pleased gleam. "I shall enjoy breaking you, little one. We will have years to explore the limits of the foolish bravery you wear so proudly. Wendar thinks he is close to perfecting the..."

The wail of a siren in the distance cut his sentence off. Dani ruthlessly squashed the glimmer of hope trying to break through her calm shell. There was nothing the local rescue squad could do except get hurt.

"You need to leave now." Charlie's deep voice made Dani jump.

"You don't think I came alone do you?" The monster took a step toward the Sheriff with an upraised hand.

Dani forced a snort of laughter out, desperate to keep his attention on her. "Of course not," she said. "We all know you're too afraid to go anywhere alone. You might run into a weak human who kicks your butt."

She didn't see the blow, but suddenly her face was on fire and she fell to the floor with a loud thud. Blood dripped from a split in her lip. The unexpected pain helped to clear her mind. As her tormentor buried one hand in her shirt, lifting her to slap her several more times, the fog broke. She called for Rissa at the top of her mental lungs.

"We're coming!" Rissa's calm mental reply steadied her. *"Hold on for a few more minutes, Dani. There's a shield blocking us from teleporting, but we're close."*

The beating stopped. She could hear the horrified gasps of her friends. A hum filled her ears, loud enough to drown out the grumbles of anger as she stared directly into the enraged Falgaran's eyes. *No point in playing safe now. See how pissed you can make the bastard.* She spit out a blob of blood. "Oh wait. It's a not a weak human beating your butt. I'm a girl. That's even worse than losing to a Beryllian healer. What do you...?"

Suddenly she was flying through the air. She hit the wall with a thud and slid bonelessly to the floor. Slowly she forced her eyes to open then tried to sit up.

"Stay still." Anna crouched beside her and hissed the command. "You're hurt."

"Have to keep his attention," Dani's tongue felt like a giant slug with a tang of rust. Her ears rang so much she wasn't certain she was actually making any sound. "Help's coming."

The Falgaran stalked over to tower above Dani, and Anna let out a startled yelp.

"I am the victor." He bent over and grabbed Dani's long hair, yanking her to her feet. Anna yelled and kicked the scrawny leg, but he casually batted her aside, ignoring Charlie's bellow of anger.

"That's what I want you to think," Dani sneered. Blood dripped onto her shirt. Her head ached so fiercely she shook to the throbbing pulse in her skull. "How's it feel to be beat by a girl?"

She was flying through the air again, certain she had lost a few seconds. She was going to hurt like hell when this was all over. She hit the ground with a thud that shook the house and was immediately hauled back up to her feet.

"Had enough?" The tall alien shook her like a rag doll.

"You're still afraid to tell me who you are." Blood filled her mouth and she let some dribble out.

A growing blood-lust mixed with anger rolled off her tormentor. She wasn't certain which emotion would win, but she was keeping the brute off balance. *I can live with that. As long as he hates me, he'll leave everyone else alone.*

Her back slammed into the wall. His large hand tightened around her throat and the world went dark.

A calm voice in her mind comforted Dani. Help was here. Her nightmare would all be over soon. She opened her eyes.

"You lose," she whispered. The taunt pushed the creature past the boundaries of his control.

Her captor roared and tightened his grip around her throat.

Dani's smile remained on her face as her fingers clawed at the restraining arm in a desperate attempt to get air into her starving lungs.

Her captor bellowed in pain as she drew blood, but the pressure on her neck never eased.

Dani's vision tunneled and her soul felt light. She reached for Lateef, expecting to find a void. Instead she got a response. His touch was light and confused, but alive.

'Hang on, Dani.' Rissa's command rang in her mind.

Dani relaxed and her arms dropped. Lateef was alive. Help had arrived. She could let go.

Chapter 31

Happy Endings

She floated on a cloud, calm and peaceful, with no pain or anxiety. She could hear someone calling her name, but responding was too much effort. So, she didn't. She wasn't sure who she was. She recognized her name, but it felt detached from her. She relished the liberating feeling. Subconsciously she knew she was guilty of some great crime and soon she'd face her punishment. Then the agonizing wait would finally be over. She was ready.

The sound of sobbing broke her resolve. She wasn't certain where the sound came from, but the person was heartbroken. She had to help. She was responsible, somehow. All bad things were her fault. She was heavy now, no longer floating. The light dimmed, and the clouds no longer glowed. Slowly the sobs faded. She became aware of air moving in and out of her lungs, and the slow thud of her heart in her chest. She concentrated on those familiar sensations and gradually settled back into her own aching body. Memories sluggishly rebuilt. Her eyes drifted open to a muted light. She felt a weight on the bed and knew without looking Lateef was beside her. He had called her back. A hand touched her forehead and she forced her eyes to focus on the face hovering over her.

"So, you're finally awake," Mellora said.

Dani licked dry, swollen lips, too confused to respond.

"I hope this isn't going to become a habit with you," the dark-haired healer said. "Rissa keeps me busy enough. I don't think my nerves can stand two of you with a hero complex."

"Lateef?" She tried to speak, but no sound escaped.

"Lateef is okay," Mellora reassured her. "So is everyone else. A bit banged up, but in far better shape than you. The Falgarans are in Alliance custody, the Hatti woman working with them is in Clan hands and there's a line of people waiting for you to wake up so they can swarm in here and exhaust you again, all because they won't believe me when I tell them you'll be fine."

Dani caught the note of righteous indignation in the healer's melodic voice.

"We're still in your little mountain house for now," Mellora said. Then she paused and looked away, a tinge of red flushing her cheeks. "We found out the Falgarans have begun to exhibit some psychic powers. Apparently this one tied his mind to yours and siphoned off some of your energy. That's why we couldn't get you healed. Never expected to run into something like that. War's about to get really interesting."

She shook her head and stared directly at Dani. "Regardless, you are not to worry about anything and you will not fight me about healing or returning to Beryl for as long as I need you to. When I do finally release you, it will be because you have followed all of my orders without argument and are completely healed. Do you understand?"

Dani nodded meekly. This beautiful healer was far more intimidating than the monster who had thrown her across the room and tried to choke her to death.

"You shouldn't scare her, Mellora," Rissa said, laughter bubbling in her tone. "She'll do what needs to be done. Otherwise she'll have to answer to Anna and Amman and Lateef and..."

Mellora shook her head. "Get her up to speed and I'll let Amman know she's ready for some broth or something. That should get the fanatical cook off my back." The delicate woman shuddered.

"Finally met someone more pigheaded than you?" Rissa batted her eyelashes in surprise.

"Try not to wake up Lateef." Mellora's tone was sharp. "I had enough trouble getting him to sleep in the first place. Dani has a pain-block on, but if she does much more than breathe, I'll take the block off." The healer stared directly at Dani. "That's a warning to you. Don't overdo things. I don't want to have to redo a bunch of healing because you get too eager to play hero again. Give someone else a chance."

Mellora left and Rissa gently settled onto the bed and took one of Dani's hands. "I get to play Lateef." She smiled. "This is what he usually does for me.

It's kind of nice to be on this side of the bed for a change." She shot her sleeping brother a warm glance and continued.

"He's fine now you're breathing on your own. The drug the Falgarans gave you works on the psychic centers and since he has a lot of power, the drug hit him pretty hard. You didn't get it so much because... well, we still don't know. That's part of why of Mellora is so cranky. That and finding out the bastard was tied into your mind and we didn't know about it. Doesn't really matter, though."

She shook her head to recover her train of thought but did not allow Dani the opportunity to ask any questions even if she had been able to.

"Lateef was recovering about the time we got here, but he's spent so much energy fretting, he wore himself out. Mellora caught him by surprise and knocked him out before he could object."

Dani slowly turned her head, relieved when she finally caught sight of long, black hair framing a pale face. His eyelids were bruised with exhaustion. She watched until she was certain he was breathing, but the warm touch of his hand on her arm was all she needed to know he was okay.

"He should wake up in a couple of hours. Probably about the time you crash again. This healing stuff is exhausting."

Dani's agreement was mental more than physical. She felt about as energetic as a wet noodle and her mouth was dry as dust.

The arrival of Amman and Taltos with glasses of a murky liquid interrupted her attempt at a question. Dani was very happy to see them alive and well. No one else should have to pay for her sins. Taltos had one arm in a sling, but it didn't seem to slow him down at all. Rissa gracefully rose from the bed with a sigh as Amman handed her a glass before pushing past her to help Dani raise her head enough to sip through a straw.

Dani hesitated, remembering the last drink she had been given. Things still seemed a bit confused, but this drink was cool and refreshing. She managed to swallow half the contents of the glass. She released the straw and relaxed, smiling at the Hatti matriarch.

"Thank you." Her voice was hoarse and weak. "How are you?"

"I am unharmed," Amman said. "I felt no need to display my courage by baiting the bull, unlike some people." Her angry eyes shot over to Taltos who merely regarded her calmly. "This one had to show his bravery by taunting the rebels until they could be subdued. Such foolishness to think they could take over the ship. Many generations will pass before such behavior will be contemplated again. And I will not even begin to comment on your own completely irrational behavior. At least you allowed the healers to work on you."

Taltos shrugged his uninjured shoulder. "My injuries are mild and a good reminder to always remain alert."

"I didn't know you were coming." Dani interrupted the argument. She was stronger by the minute, but still not up to running a marathon. Or holding a long conversation, for that matter.

"We became aware of a problem, so we came." She saw a much longer story in his haunted eyes.

"Tales of the futile rebellion will wait until you have rested." Amman appraised her condition with a critical eye. "It appears the Beryllian healer was speaking the truth." She shot Rissa a quick look at the girl's strangled laughter.

Rissa swiftly buried her nose in her glass, but Dani felt her continued amusement.

"Amman has been making sure everyone is well fed," Rissa said, with a strange emphasis on everyone. "I've never seen anyone boss Mellora around like this before. It's been a real treat."

"Amman is an excellent Chef," Taltos agreed warmly, causing a blush to appear on the stern woman's face. She glared, but he merely beamed at her and Dani had the feeling she would be seeing much more of Taltos in the future, if Amman decided to remain here on Earth.

"Finish your drink," the Hatti woman told Dani, helping her to drain the rest of her glass. "Then you must rest until you finish healing. You are to worry about nothing. I am in control." She patted the human's hand gently, and Dani felt the warm affection buried beneath the gruff, alien exterior. "You will recover and give up the ridiculous belief you are responsible for all bad things that happen."

The pair left, and Dani's muscles relaxed. Everyone was safe and the danger gone. She could rest. "Can't believe I want to sleep again."

"Not so surprising," Rissa said. "Healing is hard work. Some more sleep won't hurt you."

"But I wanted to see Lateef."

"My brother's not going anywhere." Rissa reassured her. "And everyone else is fine. That little dog of yours herded the kids out of trouble before anyone else realized what was coming. Most guests were out of sight when the Falgarans crashed the party. The sheriff managed to get hit with a ricochet, but he's back on the job. Anna had a black eye and a slight concussion, but that was the worst thing to happen."

Dani drifted, reassured by the summary. Then Lateef stirred and pulled her into a tight hug.

"I'm glad you're awake," he murmured in her ear. "You've got to stop scaring me."

"You scared me first. You didn't move when that monster hit you."

"Didn't feel it," he replied. He leaned up on his arm to look down at her with a goofy expression.

"I'm out of here," Rissa said. "You guys are going to get mushy and I don't want to see it. Don't piss off Mellora, okay, little brother? She'll blame me."

They ignored her, gazing into each other's eyes until they heard the door click shut.

"I nearly went crazy when I couldn't find you." He searched her face as he sent healing energy through her body.

"I heard you calling." She could hear the irritation in her tone and tried to cover it. He could never know how much she hadn't wanted to come back.

"I'm glad you did." He kissed her gently and she responded, though a numbness grew in her heart.

"What's wrong?" He pulled back and searched her face anxiously.

"Nothing," she tried to deny. "I'm glad you're okay." She tried to pull him closer to distract him with more kisses, but he resisted.

"There's something wrong."

He tried to slip through her mental shields, but she strengthened them, surprised it worked.

"You feel guilty, Dani. Why?"

She turned her head away from him, unable to respond.

"Dani, there's no reason for you to feel guilty about being alive." He gently tugged her head to face him. "You have done nothing wrong."

She stared over his shoulder, the numbness spreading through her chest. Her emotions were frozen. The time had come to finally admit her evil nature. Amman was almost right. She was the cause of so many bad things. Lateef deserved to know the truth, though he would leave her. The Hatti and all of the other people who had found a home with her, too. Even Anna and Charlie would know she didn't deserve their love. But she had to come clean. She couldn't bear to keep the secret anymore. Everything would have been so much easier if she could have ignored Lateef's plea.

"Dani?" Lateef's gentle touch and quiet question broke the dam.

"I killed Caitlin and Carl. I was supposed to be alone in my car." The words tumbled in an avalanche from her mouth before she could stop them. "It's my fault they died. It should have been me."

"The accident was not your fault." Lateef stroked her hair, pulling his legs up to sit beside her.

"We were arguing when the crash happened. The last thing my baby heard from me was angry words at her father, not how much I loved her." Fat tears slowly slipped down her cheeks. She closed her eyes, unable to face the condemnation she knew was on his face.

"They know you loved them," he said firmly. She blocked his efforts to share his emotions with her.

"I don't deserve love," she denied. "I tried to take it anyway, but I was wrong. I don't deserve any of this. Otherwise these horrible things wouldn't keep happening to people I care about. You should've let me go, Lateef. Everyone I love dies."

A noise at the door caused Dani to try to swallow her tears. Once again, she tried to stuff all the hurt and guilt down deep inside, ready to present a blank façade to the world as she waited for it all to end. She felt bad about the pain she knew she was causing Lateef, but that was so much better than being responsible for his death. She surreptitiously swiped the tears away.

Anna sat down on the edge of the bed. Her expression was stern, but her brown eyes gleamed with compassion.

"We won't let you do this again, Dani." She rested a hand on the younger woman's shoulder and captured her gaze. "I know you're up here trying to make yourself believe you brought those evil creatures here and that it was your fault Charlie and Lateef were hurt." A slight smile tugged at her mouth as Dani gaped.

"But you're wrong. Those Falgaran things have hated everyone not them for far longer than you've been alive, and they'll still be molesting people long after you're not even a memory to your great-great grandchildren. Charlie is the man he is because he's willing to stand up for what he believes is right, even when that means putting his life in danger. He wouldn't thank you for trying to take credit for his actions."

"But I..."

"That is what you are trying to do," Anna spoke over her feeble protests. "We all have free will and you cannot take responsibility for what someone else does. I thought you finally understood after you faced down Weatherly. It is well past time for you to give up your ridiculous attempt to blame yourself for Carl's death."

"That was my fault!" Dani cried, stung out of her numbness.

Anna shook her head. "I worked with Carl when you were getting this place started," she said. "I know what he was like and there's no way you could force that man to be anywhere he didn't choose to be."

Dani shook her head slowly, resisting the love coming from her. "I made him go to the trade show with me."

"That man only went because he didn't trust you to be out from under his control. That trip was the first time you stood up to him and you yanked his chain good and hard." Anna said. "Don't get me wrong. He loved you as much as he could. But if he was driving in a blizzard it was because he wanted to. You tried to talk him into stopping before the weather got too bad, didn't you?"

Anna's kind expression pinned Dani to the bed and she stammered, trying to deny the truth she was hearing.

"I saw your nightmares, Danielle," Lateef said softly. "They called to me and that's why I found you." His hand ran gently up and down her arm. "I know you did try to wait for the storm to end before driving home. I knew you felt responsible for the accident, but I never realized how much guilt you had repressed."

"Easy for you to say." She tried to pull away. To escape their concern. "You weren't there, you weren't covered in..."

Lateef gathered her into his arms and cradled her head against his shoulder. Then he forced his way through her defenses to pull her into a memory of the horrible event. *'The Falgaran was feeding off your pain, Dani. He manipulated your memory and grew strong on your emotions.'* Lateef cushioned her mind as the scene replayed in the way events had truly happened.

Dani thought he'd just go home once he read her note. It hadn't been easy to sneak away while he was loading the SUV, but they'd walked to a nearby hotel. She and Caitlin could fly home once the weather cleared. But barely an hour after she settled into a hotel room, he'd banged on her door, practically dragging them into the car. She wanted to avoid Raton Pass during a winter storm, but Carl was determined to get home.

And then he'd ignored her until their child slept.

"This needs to stop, Danielle. I've been patient, but it's time for you to stop trying to sabotage my career."

She blinked, stunned at the absurdity of his accusation. "How could I mess up your career?"

His fingers tightened on the steering wheel and his breath hissed out. "You're always undermining me. None of the other wives work outside the home. They support their husbands."

Dani's stomach clenched as if hit in the gut. She had been clear before accepting his marriage proposal that she would not rely on Carl's salary. She'd seen too many friends suddenly thrown back into the workforce by divorce, disease or accident to be comfortable relying on only one income. Her business allowed her the freedom to raise their child, be available for Carl's work events and to ensure that they'd survive if something happened to Carl. They'd agreed on everything. Until Carl's father had interfered.

"I do support you. You kept telling me we couldn't afford for me to stop working when Caitlin was born."

Carl shook his head and shot her a glare. "That was before my last promotion. Now I need you available to run our social life, not drag us off to trade shows for your hobby."

Dani resisted the urge to scream. It was her business, not a hobby. She drew in a deep breath to calm her anger. She wouldn't win a fight with him in this mood. Snow swirled across the windshield, obscuring the world outside the warm car. The tires screamed as Carl took a sharp turn too fast. They were near the mountain pass between New Mexico and Colorado and the weather was deteriorating.

"You didn't have to come with me." She kept her voice steady. "I thought you had a business meeting this weekend, so I planned the trip without you. The same way I do most weekends."

Carl snarled. She didn't recognize the face of the man she'd married. This creature was a stranger, and he hated her.

"That's the thing, Danielle. We're supposed to be partners, not a couple who does their own separate thing. It's time for you to hold up your part of our marriage. I tolerated your little catering business because it made you happy. But now that my career is steady, it's time for you to grow up. I'll take over my father's seat when he moves to the Senate, and I need you behind me."

Dani's breath caught in her chest. He had been one of the biggest supporters of her catering business. She'd overheard him bragging about her to his friends on more than one occasion. And now he was certain about winning two elections that hadn't even happened yet? That didn't sound good.

"I've always supported you, Carl. You know that."

He glared at her as he flipped the wipers and headlights to high at the same time. The highway curved sharply. The car went dark as the electrical system failed.

Dani screamed as Carl tried to make the turn, but it was like trying to move a mountain with a rope. The car flew off the side of the mountain then hit and rolled down the steep slope. Air bags exploded and the sound of metal scraping and crumpling followed her into the darkness.

"That can't be right," Dani protested as she slowly came back to the present. "Carl wasn't…"

"I'm pretty sure that's exactly what happened," Charlie said. His eyes were glazed and the look he sent Anna carried a trace of panic, but his voice was confident. "The accident was due to a short in the wiring that killed the engine at the worst possible time. I checked with some friends of mine in the New Mexico Patrol and there was a report filed of a man forcing a woman and child into a car. The case was dropped when they found out about the accident, so I never mentioned it to you. If I'd known you were letting yourself die by inches because you thought you were responsible..." He clenched his jaw, fighting his own internal struggle against guilt.

Anna quickly moved to her husband, pulling him into a hug. "It isn't your fault, either, Charlie White Bear. This foolishness needs to stop. Neither of you are responsible for every bad thing that happens in the world."

Dani could feel Lateef's fear of rejection as his arms tightened around her. "I'm sorry," he murmured. "I shouldn't have thrown you into the memory. I should've given you time to recover before hitting you with something else. I just never imagined the Falgarans would have enough psychic powers to warp your memories. I should have realized your guilt was too deep to be normal."

Heavy footsteps in the hallway gave her a chance to breathe as Amman stopped the visitors.

"I brought Dani some cookies. The first I made myself." Pride filled Mandy's voice as her volume rose to overcome Amman's hissed objection. "Everyone loves cookies. I used the most popular recipe on the Gourmet Foodie website. They had a video and everything."

Silence greeted the outburst and Anna and Charlie exchanged wide-eyed glances with Dani.

"We better get out there and help Amman ease onto the information highway." Anna darted to the door. "With any luck we can throw up some roadblocks for a bit."

Dani and Lateef watched as the door slammed shut on a rising babble of sound.

"You have some very good friends, Dani. I'm not sure I'd be brave enough to deal with a riled-up Hatti chef." He pulled her close and kissed the top of her head, projecting a calm belied by the pounding of his heart.

Dani took a deep breath, exploring the edges of the old pain in her mind. She was shocked to realize she had known the truth all along, but had ruthlessly suppressed the memory, accepting the imaginary, perfect life that had never existed. She tilted her head to meet Lateef's anxious face.

"I love you, Lateef." Her eyes shone with a happiness no longer tainted by any shadow of guilt. "And I intend to spend the rest of my life proving it to you."

His lips found hers and he poured all of his own love and relief and happiness into her, both of them forgetting their surroundings as they celebrated being alive and together.

To be continued...

Continue the journey with book two in the Beryllian Alliance ***Storm Clouds at Sunset.***

Excerpt from *Storm Clouds at Sunset*

Chapter 1 — The Dress

Danielle "Dani" Hamilton twirled in front of the full-length mirror. The beautiful white lace and satin dress swirled around her legs like a flock of white swans, slowly settling to the floor as she stopped.

"It's beautiful, Anna." Tears stung her eyes as she looked at her reflection.

"No point in letting it stay hidden in the closet." Anna White Bear's face flamed red, and she turned her head away.

"Thank you." Dani turned and embraced the older woman in a hug. "I still can't believe how much you and Charlie have done for me. I'm not sure I would have survived losing my family without you."

"Oh, nonsense." Anna returned the embrace before pulling away to grab a tissue and dab at her eyes. "You are a strong woman, Dani. You'd never let someone as petty as your father-in-law hold you down for long, even if he was the powerful politician he imagines himself to be. All we did was give you the space to get your feet back under you."

Dani nodded but knew in her heart Anna was wrong. She had almost given into the black hole of despair before Anna and Sheriff Charlie had whisked her out of the hospital after the accident that had taken her husband and child. And they'd stayed with her until she'd found Lateef and brought a clan of aliens to the small mountain town of Folly Springs they all called home.

"Besides." Anna dabbed at her nose and blinked her eyes rapidly. "You know Charlie and I were never blessed with children. You're the daughter of my heart the Great Ones finally gave me."

Dani turned to look out the window for a moment as she worked to get her emotions under control. Her parents had died when she was too young to remember them. After a long list of foster homes, Anna and Charlie had taken on a parental role, even though she hadn't met them until she was in her mid-twenties when she'd arrived in the small town with her husband and child to build a fancy home to entertain his clients. Then she'd lost both in an unfortunate car accident long before she'd met Lateef and the incredible alien Hatti clan.

"Sometimes family is more than blood." She turned back to Anna. "I can't tell you how much you and Charlie have meant to me."

Anna tossed her long, black braid over her shoulder. "I know, child. And we feel the same. I'm so glad you finally found the happiness you deserve."

Dani grinned. "I don't deserve someone as wonderful as Lateef, but I'm glad he fell into my life."

"Literally fell from the sky." Anna laughed. She walked around Dani, making sure the dress was a perfect fit.

Dani nodded. "It still feels like a dream. Finding Lateef, and then meeting the Hatti warriors searching for him and stopping a war. That's crazy, isn't it?"

Anna clucked her tongue. "Who are we to question the spirits? Maybe your meeting was pre-ordained."

Dani laughed. "I hate to think it was all going to happen no matter what. I want to believe I had choices."

Anna rested a hand on her arm and captured her gaze.

"We all have choices, daughter-of-my-heart. You could have walked away at any point. You chose bravery in helping your life mate and the strangers who became your people. I am so very proud to call you family."

Dani swallowed the lump in her throat, determined not to cry. She wasn't anything special, no matter what Anna said. Heat flooded her cheeks. She'd been praying to die before Lateef had fallen into her life. She'd never do anything to make that happen, but she hated the fact that she hadn't fought very hard to hold on to life.

"I'm so very blessed to have such wonderful people in my life." Her gaze shifted to the mirror and she once again studied the beautiful dress.

Anna hugged her from behind. "One day, you'll understand how important you are. Until then, heart-daughter, Charlie and I will keep reminding you of your value. As will Lateef and his family and all the other people in your life."

"Okay!" Dani held her hands up in surrender. "My friends are incredible. I have trouble with the idea that I'm anything special. I'm not arguing with you, but I feel normal."

Anna squeezed her again and stepped back to check the length of the hem. "I can live with that. As long as you don't start feeling like you don't deserve to live again."

Dani snorted. "I won't. I can't let Lateef down, ever."

"Good." Anna nodded decisively. "Glad we have that sorted out." She unzipped the wedding dress and turned around as Dani slipped out of it and back into her normal tee shirt and jeans.

"Thank you, Anna." Dani said. "Knowing you and Charlie were taking care of Abby and the farm was the only thing keeping me sane while I was stuck in the Healer Hall on Beryl. Healer Mellora is a wonderful person, but all I wanted to do was come home." The Alliance healers were all very good and professional, but Beryl was a long way from home.

Anna patted her back. "I understand." Her voice was thick with unshed tears. "I was about ready to make the aliens give us a ride to Lateef's planet when Amarantha came back to let us know what was happening with you. I'm glad your man had the brains to send her back here while you were in such danger."

Dani wasn't sure what to say. Amarantha deserved all the credit. She was a soldier for the Beryllian Alliance who tolerated no nonsense. She'd known that Lateef was preoccupied with keeping her alive and didn't think of updating her Earth friends. Amarantha had taken the responsibility of informing her Terran friends of her progress in recovering from the poisoned bolt meant for the leader of the Hatti clan all on her own. Dani could never thank her for the simple kindness.

"It's all good, Dani," Anna said. "I know we had some terrifying moments, but the entire experience brought the Hatti clan to Folly Springs. And now we know we're not alone in the universe."

Dani nodded.

"And you found the love that brought you back to life." Anna squeezed her tight. "There is nothing in the world to top that."

Dani broke into a huge grin she couldn't contain. All of the events over the last year had brought her to the peak of happiness. She couldn't complain about any of it. She wouldn't even change anything in her recent past. Including her encounter with the evil Falgaran who'd drained her energy and tried to kill her. It had all made her stronger.

"Lateef is pretty awesome, isn't he?"

Anna nodded. "He is. Not as sure about his brother, but every family has that stick-in-the-mud-butthead."

Dani's breath caught in her lungs. "I hope he's the exception. I adore Rissa, but I haven't met his other sister. Could she be like Johfrit?"

Anna snorted. "I seriously doubt it. People like Johfrit are special. Even good parents occasionally throw off a loser. Lateef is a keeper. And Rissa is great, too. No family is perfect."

Dani laughed. "Thank you. I needed the confidence boost."

Anna squeezed her again. "Life is good. And you deserve happiness. Don't let anything from your past make you forget that."

Dani returned the embrace. "I try. My inner critic is loud and obnoxious, but you make it settle down. Thank you."

"Have you decided on your wedding dish?" Anna put the dress on a hanger and covered it with a garment bag to keep it safe.

"Which one?" Dani collapsed onto the well-padded chair by the tall window in her bedroom. Even with all the new buildings on her land, she still lived in the original house, which the Hatti had remodeled while she was in the Healer Hall. And she had no complaints about the changes. Other than wishing she had thought of some of the improvements.

She and Lateef would move to the master bedroom after their ceremony. She'd gotten a sneak peek the other day. The room was a haven that could pass muster at any high-end resort. And the bathroom was to die-for. Not only would she have a shower with body jets which had the magical ability to loosen every stiff muscle in her body, but the supply of hot water never ended.

She'd always planned the house to be independent of an energy grid, and the original solar power was more than adequate for her needs, except after several cloudy days in a row. But the Hatti had upgraded the power system to something similar to what they used on their ship. They never had to worry about hot water, refrigeration, or a power source.

"What do you mean? I thought you only had to do one dish to prove your worth to the Clan." Anna hung the dress in the closet and placed her hands on her hips as she stared at Dani.

"Fortunately, Madam Amman is in charge of most of the courses." She shook her head in admiration. "Seven courses for the guests, which includes all the clan members on planet, and she's upset we don't have any other clanships close enough to invite." Dani took a deep breath and willed her heart to beat slower. She didn't want to disturb Lateef since he was working a shift at the Healer Hall on Beryl, and he noticed every time she seemed nervous or worried. It was a potential downside of the psychic bond they now shared.

"I need to prepare one clan dish to show I can follow directions, and one signature dish to prove I can cook on my own. And only for about a thousand people. Most of the clan will remain on the *Alalakh* since we don't really have enough room here. Amman gave me permission to tweak the clan dish a little to suit our local ingredients, but it's easy. For my dish, I'm making a pastry-filled chocolate sculpture of the valley, complete with mousse-filled goats and sheep. I wanted to do dinosaurs, but Amman thought the goats would be better." She grinned at Anna. "More modern, anyway. Apparently, the clan left Earth before cacao beans were widely known, so anything chocolate is exotic."

"Wow." Anna sat in the matching chair. "Hard to believe they don't have chocolate."

Dani nodded. "The clan chefs have been absolutely gaga over chocolate. The master botanist acquired seeds and saplings and even imported midges to pollinate the cacao trees on the ship and here. That's what they're working on in the smallest greenhouse."

"I wondered what all the activity was about. Seemed like a lot of commotion last month." Anna grinned. "I can't say I'd be upset at having our own candy factory."

"I don't think it will go that far," Dani said. "But who knows with this crew? I didn't expect my toiletry business to expand like it has. If you'd asked me what my life would be like in the future a year ago, this wouldn't even have been a guess."

Dani took a deep breath and stared out the window. There were a few more buildings visible around the main house, but most of the growth was underground or highly camouflaged. Most of the new gardens were hydroponic, which made sense since the alien clan had spent most of their time on board the enormous space ship. Only a few of the Hatti lived on Earth with her. Most of them remained on the Clanship *Alalakh* and continued the trading circuit they'd developed over the years.

"At least I don't have to bake or decorate the cake. The process is full of clan symbolism I can't even begin to understand. But bring a wheelbarrow to the wedding party. Everyone will be too full to walk afterwards."

Anna laughed. "There will be dancing. We'll burn off all those calories."

"Good point. Maybe we should make sure there are a couple of dance rounds between the courses?"

"I'm sure Amman has everything figured out. This can't be the first wedding ceremony she's overseen."

Dani shivered. "I don't think so, but it seems like such a big deal. Even the tweens are excited."

"Every kid loves a party." Anna patted her knee. "And the entire town loves those Hatti kids. They are always so cheerful and helpful. Even Fran hired a team to help her out."

"No," Dani breathed. "Does she realize they come from...far away?" Dani couldn't help trying to hide the true origin of the Hatti tweens.

"Yep. That young scamp, Lokar, saw Fran fighting with a raccoon one evening. Scared it off and came back the next day with a way to keep her trash can sealed. She actually gave him a candy bar in return."

It was Dani's turn to gasp in amazement. Fran was the meanest person in Folly Springs. Not nasty evil, but she was cranky and anti-social and didn't want to accept help from anyone because it made her feel incompetent.

Anna nodded. "Now Lokar and a couple of his friends are doing odd jobs for her and making sure she has some good meals. She actually showed up at the last town hall sober."

Dani struggled to close her mouth. She'd known the alien Hatti kids had made a good impression on the town, but hadn't expected that to include Fran, the woman who hated everything and everyone.

"I keep saying you did a good thing when you brought the Hatti home. The whole town got a boost. It might not last forever, but all the local artisans and food-related vendors are doing good. The Hatti bought almost the entire batch of honey from the local hives."

"I've heard the honey is a big trade product. And our spring water has some special property that makes baked goods different. They were bragging about selling a ton of water after giving out samples on the last trip."

Anna snorted. "Millie at the bakery has always told me that. New York might have the best bagels because of their water source, but Folly Springs water is good for everything. And no one knows why. Amman told me the clan's chemists had analyzed the water, but couldn't find the reason why it's so special."

"I'm betting on love, and some kind of cosmic link to... something." Dani laughed. "I don't know why we need an explanation for everything."

Anna nodded in agreement. "I guess it's human nature."

Dani's smile faltered. "Have you watched the news lately?"

Anna snorted. "I gave up on TV news years ago when they started spending half the show talking about their personal lives and reality shows like anyone cared."

"I know." Dani shuddered. "But I have to admit something feels weird lately. They spend hours on things I know didn't happen, and a few minutes on things that did happen, but they spin to make it look bad, even when it wasn't."

Anna rose to her feet. "No point in worrying about the craziness of the outside world. I'm glad we are more self-sufficient than ever with the Hatti here. Don't have to worry about being cut off from civilization when you have space ships."

Danni grinned. "So true. We're set if there's a nuclear apocalypse. Not as sure about the next winter blizzard."

"Nothing can stop winter storms." Anna brushed the garment bag, flicking off invisible motes of dust. "Now your dress is ready, you can't lose any weight. So make sure you eat, but not too much."

"Not much chance of that being a problem. Healer Mellora and Matriarch Amman agree I am in the most appropriate weight range and will ensure I remain there. Fortunately, it isn't a problem since the food is so great."

"And always tastes better when someone else cooks."

"At least I don't have any more medicine to drink. And the coffee station now has more than very mild decaf options."

Anna laughed. "I'm not sure how you survived that phase of your recovery."

"It wasn't easy." Dani shuddered. "But Lateef smuggled some of the good stuff a few times when Amman was busy with her sweetie-pie, Taltos."

Dani resisted the urge to reach out to her love. She'd promised the Hatti Matriarch to do her best to follow Hatti custom and not see or talk to her groom for the week before the wedding, except for approved, supervised events. She wondered if it was merely an excuse to keep her busy all day. But there had been no restrictions about psychic connections.

"I bet she knew."

Dani's smile faded. "You're probably right. She gave me extra potions after every time I had real coffee. I can't believe she doesn't read minds."

"It's the Hatti kids. They are the best spy network in the universe. They see everything. I'm not sure how we're going to have any surprises at Christmas."

"I have to get through the wedding before I can think about a big holiday. Are you sure it's too late to elope to Vegas?"

Anna patted her shoulder. "You can do whatever you want, sweetie. You and Lateef could even head off to that beach resort his sister keeps talking about. But it would be a shame not to wear the dress."

"It is a beautiful dress. And I know Amman would be disappointed. Besides, most of the food is already prepped, and it would be a shame to waste anything."

"That's the spirit. Do you need help with anything?"

Dani shook her head. "I don't do much in my business beyond talking to a few customers and puttering around trying new recipes. Speaking of which, I have a batch of soap I need to unmold."

She threw her arms around the older woman. "Thank you so much for letting me use your beautiful dress, Anna. And for everything else, too. I don't know what I'd do without you."

You can continue reading Storm Clouds at Sunset on Amazon.
Did you like the book? If so, please leave a review on Amazon, GoodReads or BookBub
You can find me online at my website: https://katherinematzen.com/;
Facebook: https://www.facebook.com/KatherineMatzenWriter
Loving the universe? Go to my website and join my newsletter to get free stories, news about new books, fun science tidbits and a series of short stories about an alien scholar living on Earth who is studying people. Along the way he's given the task of protecting alien geese sent to live on Terra to protect them from a genocide on their native planet.

Acknowledgements

There are so many people I need to thank. Val and Zac from Scarlet Tie Elite who did an incredible job of editing. Any mistakes left over are mine. And thank you Zoey at ZDesign for the beautiful cover.

To Linda, Grace, Jodi, Mary, Cheryl, Lesli, Sue, Sandra and Jane – thank you all so much for reading, cheerleading, hand-holding as well as the occasional well-timed threats. They were all needed. All the members of Heart of Denver and Colorado Romance Writers who are so generous with their time and expertise. You've all made this possible.

And finally thanks to my family for all of their help and patience with my random questions, requests for advice and absent-mindedness when caught in the middle of a story. And all of the "are you done yet" comments. Your belief in me pushed me to finish. Love you all!

About the Author

Katherine Matzen is the author of the Beryllian Alliance series and after twenty plus years of research, works in a clinical histology lab by day.

She writes science fiction with romantic elements including a strong dose of optimism, and hope. No matter how dark the journey gets, everything will work out the way it's supposed to. She lives in Colorado with her husband, teenagers, huskies, goldfish, tropical fish, guinea pigs, and hermit crabs, as well as an assortment of very hardy plants.

She's always wanted to meet some nice aliens and maybe stow away on their ship for a vacation. She'll pass on the bad guys out to destroy the universe, thank you very much.

Also By

At Night's End – Book 1 of the Beryllian Alliance

Alliance Master Healer Lateef D'Oro narrowly escaped the Hatti Clanship, but will he die alone on this primitive planet?
Lateef had anticipated a peaceful state dinner on a Hatti Clanship, renowned throughout the galaxy for their eternal "Search for the Most Perfect Ingredient". He would enjoy some exquisite food, advocate for joining the Alliance battle against the oppressive Falgaran Empire and then return to his Healer Hall on Beryl.
Instead, a total misunderstanding leaves him injured and fleeing in an escape pod, desperately hoping that the nearby blue-green planet will provide shelter and a way to call for help.
Young widow Danielle 'Dani' Hamilton stumbles upon a wounded stranger near her isolated mountain home. He is utterly unprepared for the terrain, there's something undeniably otherworldly about him, and she can't shake the belief that she can sometimes hear his thoughts.
Against her better judgment she offers him sanctuary, just until he can find a ride back home. She knows all to well what it means to be injured, abandoned, and alone.
Lateef feels an inexplicable connection to Dani, believing she is the woman he had been searching for, but never hoped to find.
Just as she starts to believe they can have a future, Lateef's past intrudes in the form of a squad of fierce Hatti warriors determined to make him pay for his insult.
Can Dani find a way to save the man she is growing to love, and maybe keep Earth out of an interstellar war they are not prepared to fight?

At Night's End is the first book in the Beryllian Alliance series. It is a stand-alone story, but the adventures continue. All roads lead to Folly Springs, CO where Terrans and aliens coexist.

Storm Clouds at Sunset – Book 2 of the Beryllian Alliance

Danielle's first wedding attempt was interrupted by an alien invasion.

Danielle "Dani" Hamilton is finally recovered from the injuries she sustained during the Falgaran attack on her home in Folly Springs, Colorado. Now she's ready to enjoy the fairy-tale wedding her human and alien Hatti Kanesh Clan friends have planned. Her bride courses for the seven course feast are nearly complete. Her dress is perfect. Even her canine companion is ready to play her role in the event.

Master Healer Lateef D'Oro long believed he would spend his life alone in the Healer Hall. Until he met Danielle on a planet far from his native Beryl. For him, it was love at first sight but he had to convince her they were fated to be together. Now, nothing is going to stop him from claiming his bride. Not his family, not his Falgaran enemies, and definitely not the lack of a matched pair of albino jangxing. He's okay with never seeing the giant, feathered lion-like creatures the Hatti use as bloodhounds ever again. But he'll do anything for his beloved Danielle.

But when the Kanesh Clanship returns to Earth, the jangxing aren't the only thing they bring home.

Storm Clouds at Sunset is the second book in the Beryllian Alliance series. It is a stand-alone story, but is better when read after *At Night's End*. All roads lead to Folly Springs, CO where Terrans and aliens coexist.

The adventure continues with *Shadows of the Sun – Book 3 of the Beryllian Alliance.*

Shadows of the Sun – Book 3 of the Beryllian Alliance

Sabra Narvi knows exactly which planet she's from. And this snow-filled nightmare of a place isn't it.

While protecting the terminally ill Secretary of Defense at his Wyoming family ranch, Medic Evan Stone and his team are trapped by an unexpected blizzard. As the storm strengthens, Evan finds a woman wandering in the snow who is dressed for a summer day and has no memory of how she got there. And the things she does remember make no sense.

Sabra Narvi had an eidetic memory. But now she doesn't know where she is, how she got there, or if she can trust the scant memories that haunt her brain. She's a diplomat and a skilled fighter, but has no training in First Contact procedures. And the men who saved her from freezing to death have no idea their planet is on the verge of being invaded by the alien Falgarans.

Evan tries to deny his growing attraction to the woman who claims to be a healer, even though she drives him crazy with her insane statements.

Sabra lost all chances at love when her family died, but who would know she broke taboo on an alien planet?

When she finds signs of an alien invasion can Sabra convince Evan she isn't delusional? Or will the Falgarans succeed in taking over Earth?

Shadows of the Sun is the third book in the Beryllian Alliance series. It is a stand-alone story, but is better when read after *At Night's End* and *Storm Clouds at Sunset*. All roads lead to Folly Springs, CO where Terrans and aliens coexist.

Can Sabra convince them that their mutual enemy is on their doorstep?